Corrupt and Ensnare

Also by the Author

PUBLISH AND PERISH

Corrupt and Ensnare

by Francis M. Nevins, Jr.

toExcel
San Jose New York Lincoln Shanghai

Corrupt and Ensnare

All Rights Reserved. Copyright © 1978, 2000 by Francis M. Nevins Jr.

No part of this book may be reproduced or transmitted in any form or by any means, graphic, electronic, or mechanical, including photocopying, recording, taping, or by any information storage or retrieval system, without the permission in writing from the publisher.

This edition published by toExcel Press, an imprint of iUniverse.com, Inc.

For information address:
iUniverse.com, Inc.
620 North 48th Street
Suite 201
Lincoln, NE 68504-3467
www.iuniverse.com

ISBN: 1-58348-998-3

For William Witney

Corrupt and Ensnare

ONE

It wasn't a night for hospital visits. Soft wet flakes sifted past the sodium-vapor streetlamps, covering the mounds of hard dirty snow from the past week's accumulation. Loren backed the VW into a space at the edge of the city park, across the boulevard from Stoner Memorial. He locked the car and half ran across the all but deserted street, through the powdery orange glow of the lights. Falling snow stung the back of his neck. Recorded music over a loudspeaker sounded faintly from the depths of the park. Loren recognized the tune: "God Rest Ye Merry Gentlemen." The tan-brick hospital complex stood bathed in saffron light behind the transparent curtain of snow. He mounted the stone steps and an electric eye slid back twin glass doors.

A tall young nurse with shell-rimmed glasses sat inside an octagonal information post. Loren slapped snow off his gloves as he approached her. "Professor Mensing," he said, "to see Justice Richmond."

The nurse rotated a Wheeldex file mechanically and stopped at a card. "Oh, yes, Professor," she said gravely. "Room thirty-thirteen; that's on the third floor. The judge's wife and daughter went back up a few minutes ago. They said you'd be coming." She pointed at the tiled corridor to her left. "The elevators are that way." Loren thanked her, trudged down the white hallway, pressed a buzzer. A huge antiseptic whitewalled cage lifted him two flights. He found the closed oak door of 3013 and twisted the knob softly.

It was a small private room. Bed, bedside table, three chairs. Walls painted dull green. No private bath, no television, none of the amenities. It was the room they took you to when they decided they could do nothing more and that another patient could make better use of the space you were filling in the intensive-care unit. The place where you were to say good-bye to your loved ones and die.

The man lying under the bedcovers looked less like a man than a pale empty shell, ancient and drained. The two swollen-eyed women sitting on one side of the bed looked up as Loren entered, releasing the old man's hands so that he could grasp them. The fingers felt cold as the snow.

"Merry Christmas," the dying man whispered as his hand stirred loosely in Loren's embrace.

"And to you, Ben," Loren muttered without thinking. He functioned poorly in hospitals. The disinfectant smell, the ugly labored breathing sounds behind curtains, the maimed people trudging or wheeling themselves through the halls, the sense of death in the air—everything reminded him too vividly that the house of concepts in which he lived and worked and hid himself was a paper fortress and that he owed the worms his own death. He looked down at what was left of the man who for a while had been more of a father to him than his real father and he remembered how Ben Richmond had been at the peak of his powers—sturdy bodied, mind like chrome steel, with a voice that could roll out over a courtroom like a thunderclap one moment and could be as gentle as a small child's an instant later. Loren looked into the judge's almost vacant eyes and his own eyes moistened. He pressed Richmond's hand more tightly, as if to hold off the end a few seconds longer.

"Thanks for ... coming." The voice was so weak Loren could scarcely make out the words.

"I wish I could do the last few years over again," Loren said. "Spend more time with you. Try to tell you how much I—"

The judge cut him off, thrashed about in the bed, trying to lift himself, to raise his mouth to Loren's ear. He gasped and fell back, and Loren bent over him. "What is it, Ben? What's the matter?"

"Tape." Richmond formed the word with his mouth. "Listen ... tape ... just ... you. ..." The words trailed off into nothingness and the judge's eyes went empty. Iris Richmond gave a little cry and threw her arms about her husband and pressed her lips against his and whispered, "Oh, Ben, I love you so much, so very much." Tears fell down her cheeks onto the judge's cold face. Jeanette ran blindly into the hallway calling, "Nurse! Nurse!" in a high tight voice.

At 12:03 A.M. the doctor pronounced Justice Richmond dead. From somewhere in the distance Loren heard the muffled peal of church bells.

It was almost nine and a half years since Loren had returned from law school in the East and taken the state bar and gone to work in his father's firm. But even before the examination results were announced and he was fully licensed to practice law, he knew that he did not want to spend his life in this profession. The incessant pressure to bring in business, the technically legal but distasteful trickery, the obsession with property rights, the competitive ethos, created a world which he found repugnant in direct proportion to his growing certainty that he was incompetent to work in it. Yet he knew his father expected him to stay with the firm and eventually to become a partner, to put down roots in the legal community of the city. Loren was programmed to be a lawyer, and he dreaded to let his father know how much he had grown to hate the life to which Stephen Mensing had dedicated both of them. It was agony to come to work every morning, not just because he couldn't stand the job but because he lived every day with the fear that his division against himself would lead him sometime to do or to fail to do something crucial and that his father's firm would suffer the consequences. He had no one to share his agony. He took to drinking too much and too often.

And then Ben Richmond's mother died, and a door opened.

The old woman's will had left half her substantial estate to various charities and the rest to her son, who had been appointed a judge in the state court of appeals five years before. Judge Richmond had retained the firm of Mensing & Nalbin to settle the estate and Loren's father had assigned him to prepare the federal and state tax returns. "The experience will be good for you," Stephen Mensing had said. And so night after night Loren had sweated over the paperwork, sometimes literally banging his head against the wall in desperation, until finally the worst was over and he slipped the returns into his neat little attaché case and cabbed to the courthouse to get the judge's signature where it was needed.

In Richmond's chambers he had sat stiff and tense in a high-backed leather chair to the right of the judge's glistening desk. Richmond was tall, lean, with cobalt-blue eyes behind thick reading glasses, and hair graying at the sideburns. He looked strong as a redwood, and just as unbending. He finished scanning the tax returns and placed them in the exact center of the immaculately polished surface of the desk and leaned back in his black leather executive swivel chair and tapped a ballpoint pen against his thumbnail. He could have been posing for a portrait of a Wise Judge Pondering; it struck Loren as too theatrical. Then he broke the pose, tossed the pen onto the sheaf of papers and took off his glasses and looked into Loren's eyes with a hypnotic gaze that for a moment made Loren want to run.

"You are about as miserable in that firm as if you were in a Siberian salt mine," the judge had said.

Loren's eyes widened and he hunted frantically for something to say in reply. Instinct told him not to deny it; if it was so obvious Richmond had seen it, pretending he was happy in his work would do no good anyway. "Is it that transparent?" he asked, and tried to cover a nervous little laugh.

"I have an instinct about people in traps," the judge said. "Perhaps I could help. Suppose we talk it over tonight at the Boatmen's Bar."

For two hours that evening they sipped scotch in the nautical ambience of the Boatmen's and discussed Loren's situation. Within the first half hour together in the brown leather booth Loren had told the judge things about himself that he had never dreamed of telling his father. He talked of how he had loved the intellectual challenge of law school but had become disgusted at how the system translated theory into practice. He even mentioned his ambivalence about his father and his distrust of his own competence.

"You're twenty-four years old already," Richmond had said. "Every day you wait is going to make it harder when the break finally comes. And it will come someday, believe me."

Loren grinned halfheartedly, like a gambler resigned to making the most of a poor hand. "But, Judge, all I'm qualified to do is use my law degree. How can I support myself if I don't practice?"

"I need a clerk," the judge said. "Someone who can do research in the library for me eight to ten hours a day, draft some opinions, sit around a table with me and help me clarify my thinking when I have to decide a tough one. There's pressure, but not like in an office. And you'll have some time to help find yourself. Quite frankly, I made a few phone calls about you this afternoon and from what I learned I'm satisfied you'd be good in the position."

Loren resigned from his father's firm the next morning.

Before he had completed a month as Richmond's clerk, Loren knew that he had made the right choice. For the first time since law school he could wake up in the morning and shower and shave and dress and make his breakfast of orange juice and coffee and a chunk of hot French cheese bread in a spirit of looking forward to the day's work instead of dreading it. He would walk the twelve downtown blocks, dense with office buildings and coffeeshops and parking lots, that separated his cramped studio apartment in a riverfront highrise from the courthouse across Broadway from the city government complex. He would ride the elevator to the eighth floor, where the Court of Appeals had its chambers, and unlock the door to the judges' law library at the end of the paneled corridor, and across the glossy surface of one of the long mahogany tables that dotted the room he would spread the briefs and memoranda and the volumes of the state judicial reports that dealt with the case he was working on. A little before nine, when Loren was surrounded by his notes and jottings on the case, Richmond would poke his head in the doorway and invite Loren into his chambers for a conference, and for half an hour or an hour or as long as current business required, the two of them would sit on the judge's overstuffed couch and sip coffee out of stoneware mugs and talk law. Richmond was gently critical of a good deal of Loren's early work for him but it took only a few weeks for Loren to get the feel of what the judge expected. Within three months he was enough in tune with Richmond's thinking to be able to draft opinions for the judge on almost any legal issue that might confront the court, and more often than not Richmond would make only minor editorial changes. Richmond was brilliant at drawing intricate distinctions to avoid applying higher court precedents that he felt would work injustice in the matter before him, and Loren soon became proficient not only at making such distinctions himself but at discovering or inventing distinctions that Richmond had overlooked and persuading him that they were sound.

The Richmond home was an elegant showplace built in 1906 at the foot of Boxwood Drive, in an affluent suburb west of the city. The corners of the high ceilings were decorated with frescoes of cherubs and roses. Opulent chandeliers and mantel-topped fireplaces and full-length pier glasses graced most of the rooms. Loren was welcomed into the house as a frequent guest. Iris Richmond, slender and gracious and perpetually aflutter, as though a thousand lovely little knickknacks were constantly smashing into fragments around her, took him under her wing as if Loren were the son she had never borne. With her outrageously selective memory for exact visual and verbal details of incidents that had occurred months or years ago, she was a never-failing source of amazement and delight. And Jeanette, who was dark and softly curved and enticing at sixteen, developed a fondness for Loren which was not at all that of a sister for an older brother and which Loren neither sought nor encouraged but had no idea in the world how to deal with. Only her subsequent passion for the right halfback on the local university's football team relieved Loren of an involvement that had begun to embarrass him. Throughout the difficult weeks Richmond prudently refrained from mentioning the matter.

On a storm-soaked summer morning in the fifteenth month of his clerkship Loren hung up his raincoat and umbrella in the law library closet and strode to the shelves built into the north wall to take down a volume of the annotated rules of civil procedure. Richmond stepped into the book-lined room from the corridor leading to the judges' chambers, the perennial stoneware coffee mug in his hand.

"Got a few minutes?" He motioned Loren to follow him back to chambers, where they took their usual places on the couch and Richmond poured Loren a steaming cup from the percolator on the table. "How does the name Professor Mensing sound to you?" he asked.

Loren had not thought of his father for weeks. He stared at the judge, uncomprehending. "Some law school wants Pop to teach?"

"Not your father," Richmond said. "You."

Loren almost spilled the coffee into his lap.

Richmond went on. "When I was in law school, my best friend, the guy I roomed with, was Conor Dunphy. He used to practice criminal law but a couple of years ago he became the associate dean at City University Law School. Right now they're hurting very badly for new faculty. Ken Cole had that heart attack last month, and Dick Patterson just got a Fulbright to spend a year at the University of Iran. I think you'd make a damn good law teacher, Loren, and I want to phone Conor and tell him so, but I had to check with you first to see if you'd be interested. With your academic background and my recommendation, I think the job's pretty much yours for the asking."

Loren felt a rush of almost unearthly lightheadedness. In law school he had looked on the best of his own professors as almost godlike in their wisdom, in the skill with which they explained the law, the mastery with which they could direct the intellectual energies of classes of more than a hundred students. They fielded whatever questions might be asked, framing their own questions and making use of whatever answers the students gave, right or wrong or indifferent, to carry the analysis further. At times Loren had dreamed of being that kind of Socratic questioner someday.

"You want to get rid of me that bad, huh?" he said to the judge, and lay back on the couch and laughed uncontrollably.

He went out to the law school that afternoon and spent an hour talking with Eli York, the fierce and white-haired dean. Their conversation seemed to begin nowhere and end nowhere, like a random doodle on scratch paper. Then Loren spent an hour and a half with Associate Dean Dunphy, a big hearty Irishman with wild thatches of reddish-gray eyebrows above his bifocals, who kept a bottle of Tullamore Dew in the lower left drawer of his desk like a private eye in a 1940s movie. An interview with the full faculty was arranged for the following week.

By the end of the month Loren had been offered a position as assistant professor of law, which it took him less than ten seconds to accept. He continued with his work at the court until Richmond had hired a replacement clerk he felt comfortable with; then he called Dean Dunphy's office and read off the titles of the casebooks he wanted the law-school bookstore to order for his first semester's courses and spent his last day at his old job cleaning out his desk in the courthouse library. That night Richmond treated him to dinner at Poe's, one of the most lavish restaurants in the city, and they sipped scotch as they had in the Boatmen's Bar and laughed and reminisced and tied up whatever loose ends remained in Loren's work. In the restaurant parking lot they shook hands for the last time, and Richmond threw his arms around his young clerk and embraced him like a father. And after a ten-day vacation cruise in the Virgin Islands with a petite and passionate young blonde who would shortly be returning for her senior year at Yale, Loren reported to Conor Dunphy's cluttered office in the fading brickwork wreck that was the administration building of City University Law School.

"You'd have to be a blind man to miss it," the associate dean thundered heartily as he tossed Loren a key. "Third floor, right above the law library, second from the end. Ken Cole's name's still on the door but his widow cleared away Ken's personal things last week, poor girl. I hope you stay with us a long time." Dunphy gave Loren a brisk clap on the shoulder. "And when you have a few minutes free, come down and visit with a poor devil of an administrator and share a drop of Dew with me. I'm editing a criminal procedure casebook and could use a bright young partner. This book will revolutionize the field, young Mensing, and you can be in on the ground floor."

"Sounds interesting," Loren said without committing himself. "What approach are you taking?"

"The Supreme Court, bless its collective soul—not to mention all the lower federal courts—has been cranking out decisions for four or five years now, applying constitutional rights to more and more corners of the criminal justice system. More power to them, says Dunphy! But how are the law schools going to find time to teach all these brave new concepts? I'll tell you how. They're going to take the traditional crim-law curriculum and split it into one course on substantive concepts and a second on straight procedure, stressing constitutional aspects. My casebook, or rather our casebook if you want to join the team, will be the first one on pure procedure, which means for a while at least it stands a fair chance of being the only book a school can use once it decides to bifurcate crim-law. And"—he grinned slyly at the prospect—"at the rate the courts are grinding out new decisions in the field, we'll need to do annual supplements of current developments as far ahead as the mind can foresee, with nice piles of the glorious green stuff that makes the world go round for you *and* for me. And by the way, if there are any faculty committees you don't want to serve on, let me know and I'll see that you avoid them."

"Doesn't the dean have anything to say about that?" Loren queried innocently.

Conor Dunphy looked around his office as if suspecting an eavesdropper, then lowered his Irish tenor to a conspiratorial wheeze. "Eli York," he said solemnly, "has been the dean of this institution since the memory of man runneth not to the contrary. Respect him, defer to him, think of him as you would think of General Patton if you were a second lieutenant on his staff. But don't forget that he has long ago passed the usual age of retirement, and don't be surprised if now and again he acts, well, just a wee bit erratic."

"Thanks for the tip," Loren said. "See you after I've moved in." And he walked down the echoing corridor to the rear stairway that led to the law library and above that to the faculty offices, wondering what he had let himself in for.

Loren, like most beginning law professors, was given a light teaching load his first year, but before many weeks had passed he found himself thrust into a life radically different from anything he had experienced before. Frantic preparations for each class. Hopeless attempts to anticipate and prepare answers for any conceivable student question on the cases assigned for the day. Interruptions, invariably timed to take place at Loren's busiest hours, when a student would knock on his office door with a problem or a complaint or just to pass the time. Wrangles with Dean York over certain rather unenthusiastic comments Loren had made in class about the foreign and domestic policies of the United States. Endless committee meetings and endless faculty meetings. (Loren discovered that law professors had an uncanny ability to debate for hours what an ordinary person could resolve in five minutes flat.) Working on law-review articles which had not the least connection with his ability as a teacher but which he had to grind out if he hoped to receive promotion and tenure. Preparing final examinations. Grading final examinations. Long bitter encounters with students who had received D's and demanded C's, or who had been awarded B-pluses and insisted stringently that they had earned A's. Skimming the advance sheets that reported Federal court decisions, carefully reading every case on criminal procedure involving constitutional claims, conferring twice a week with Dunphy over what materials should and should not go in the casebook. Every few weeks he would resolve to call Judge Richmond when he could snatch a few spare moments, but he never seemed to find the time. Days, weeks, months, the semester itself, passed in a blur as if he were living on a rollercoaster.

On a Thursday morning late in the spring term of his first year, Loren sat in Dunphy's office with the working copy of the embryonic Dunphy & Mensing casebook on the desk between them. "Damn it, I want those cases in there!" Loren insisted. "Ex parte *Starr* and all the other outrageous decisions I dug out. Students have to get a sensitivity to the infinite capacity of the legal system to dispense with basic decency and fairness, and it's part of our job to give it to them."

"Well, maybe we could squeeze some of your material into Chapter Seven," Dunphy conceded wryly, "if we knock out those radical hypotheticals you posed at the end of the police perjury section."

There was a hesitant tapping on Dunphy's door and Ellie, Dean York's secretary, stood nervously in the doorway. "Has either of you seen the dean?" she said.

Loren shook his head no. "Not since nine or so," Dunphy replied. "Wasn't he supposed to meet with Judge Mills here at eleven?" He threw a glance at the electric clock on the file cabinet, which read 11:14.

"The judge has been waiting for twenty minutes," Ellie said, "and he's getting impatient. Dean Dunphy, *would* you please help us try to locate Dean York?"

Conor Dunphy sprang to his feet. This kind of problem had arisen before, Loren knew; all too many times before. Dunphy had become an expert at sniffing out where his superior might have wandered on any given occasion. "Loren, we'll have to continue pounding each other's heads against the wall another time. I have an illegal search of the building to make. If you're not doing anything, could I draft you to try the other usual spots?"

"No trouble." Loren pushed himself out of the visitor's chair and headed out of the law-school building and across the fragrant green meadow to the center of the campus. He checked the main library and found no dean. He tried the school bookstore and found no dean. He half ran along the cindered pathway that connected the bookstore and the venerable old mansion that had been turned into the faculty club.

The cool dim hallway of the club building led to the faculty dining room and three high-ceilinged lounges furnished with easy chairs and divans and tables stacked with current issues of popular and scholarly magazines. None of the downstairs rooms had the dean in it. Loren mounted the grandly sweeping staircase two steps at a time and tried the lounges on the second floor.

In the smallest and most remote room on that level he found York, lying prone on the floor, not breathing, not moving. Loren bent over him, took his pulse, listened for a heartbeat, then ran out the door and downstairs for help.

By the end of the afternoon Eli York was in the coronary-care unit of Universal Hospital and Conor Dunphy was acting dean of the law school.

And the semesters and the years rolled past. The administration launched a nationwide search for a successor to York and eventually returned to home base and offered the permanent position of dean of the law school to Dunphy. Loren's father had a heart seizure during the negotiation of a corporate merger and died instantly, leaving no will, so that thanks to the laws of intestacy Loren became a moderately wealthy man all but overnight. Within two years of its publication the Dunphy & Mensing casebook had been adopted by three dozen law schools. Loren's festering sense of outrage at the America of the late sixties and early seventies came to a boil and propelled him into deeper involvement in the marches, the demonstrations, the protests, the massive, quixotic lawsuits on behalf of the government's victims. He was denied tenure twice.

The university rule was that any professor failing to be granted tenure three times was discharged at the end of the academic year of his third attempt. During the weeks when Loren's third application for promotion and tenure was before the appropriate committee, he spent most of his off-duty hours in his office, wrestling with his thoughts. He knew that the committee was stacked with "America: love it or leave it" types, and expected to find himself canned in short order. He had thought for months about beating them to the punch, resigning from the faculty and working full time and without pay as a lawyer for the peace movement. On a certain Friday afternoon late in the spring he sat slumped over his desk, scanning the latest *U.S. Law Week* listlessly, half listening to the Mendelssohn Symphony Number Five, the "Reformation," over the university's FM station on his tiny radio. He came close to making up his mind to go downstairs for a heart-to-heart talk with Dunphy about his future.

The phone rang. He let it blare three times while he lowered the volume on the radio to a whisper; then he lifted the receiver. "Mensing."

"And a glorious afternoon it is, Loren. Just wanted to make sure you were in. May I run up for a minute?"

Dunphy's tone told Loren that something had happened, but whatever it was, the dean would not want to break the news impersonally over the phone. "Sure, Conor," he said quietly, "I'll be waiting."

He hung up, adjusted the radio volume again, and irrationally began to straighten the office clutter, picking student seminar papers and advance sheets and junk mail off the windowsill and the seats of the chairs, removing a pile of law reviews from the segment of an old gray sectional sofa he had bought at a secondhand store for ten dollars, rummaging in his desk for a cloth to dust with. When the knock sounded five minutes later and Dunphy walked in, the office was more orderly than it had been in months. The dean closed the door and dropped onto the sectional and set his attaché case flat on the faded shag rug. Loren swiveled around to face him, awaiting the verdict.

"I have sad news for you," Dunphy said solemnly, and sat back, savoring the pregnant pause like a ham actor. "The damn fools decided to keep you. Welcome to the ranks of the tenured!" And he beamed and bounced up from his seat and clasped Loren's hand between his own, and then, as if ashamed of displaying his emotions, he sat down again and snapped his attaché case open. Nestled inside were two squat glasses and a half-full bottle of Tullamore Dew. "No ice, but what the hell, it's a cool day." With due ceremony he poured two generous drinks and they touched glasses.

By 4:30 the bottle was dead, and Dunphy squinted at its emptiness against the light and sprawled back against the sectional's single arm. "I'll tell you, Loren," he said, "I had the devil's own time fighting for you in that rank and tenure committee. Your views on the war and the other evils of the system are distinctly unwelcome in certain quarters. I don't always see eye to eye with you myself, and I've never made any bones about admitting it; but damn it, that sly old frog was right about defending to the death somebody else's right to express different ideas."

"You might not have gotten tenure here yourself, spouting the views of a godless degenerate like Voltaire in Middle America," Loren said. "I ... don't know quite how to tell you this, Conor. You put yourself on the line for me, and I owe you. I hope we spend a lot of years here together so I can begin to pay you back."

"Ah, but we won't." Dunphy laid his glass on Loren's desk. "You see, this little celebration isn't just for you. It's for the two of us." He indulged himself in another pregnant pause, then cleared his throat as if in prelude to an important announcement. "You knew that the governor had two vacancies to fill on the supreme court?"

Loren nodded slowly. "I haven't stopped following the state news just because most of my crusades are federal. The advisory committee's been screening names since Chief Justice Edwards died." Then the significance of what the dean had said penetrated the Irish mist, and Loren blinked in amazement behind his glasses. "Conor, do I understand that—?"

"You are now looking at the noble countenance of the next chief justice." Dunphy made a comic monster face. "I was at the top of the advisory committee's list. The governor had me on the phone for an hour this afternoon. He'll make the official announcement at a press conference tomorrow morning."

Loren stumbled over to the sectional and threw his arms around the dean in a burst of joy. "Congratulations! Bravo! Wow!" he shouted stupidly. "My God, what a crazy day this has turned into for both of us. So I guess you'll be packing your bags and moving to Capital City?"

"Not just myself, either, Loren. You forgot to ask me who the governor picked to fill that other opening on the court."

"All right, Mr. Bones," Loren said. "Who did—no, strike that—*whom* did Thornton pick to fill the other opening on the court?"

"My best friend from law school," Dunphy told him. "Ben Richmond."

"Oh, God," Loren muttered. "And I haven't even said hello to him in ages. This is just fantastic news, Conor, and I've got to call him right away before court closes and wish him my best." He lurched off the sectional and across to the phone, kicking over the empty bottle of Tullamore Dew as he went, while Dunphy beamed indulgently and sprawled back in his corner.

That night Loren hosted a dinner at Poe's in honor of his own good fortune and that of the two new supreme court justices. In a cool dim booth curtained in blue they feasted on caesar salad tossed at their table, filet mignon and lobster tails, champagne, an obscenely rich Black Forest cake, and coffee with Grand Marnier. Dunphy and Richmond produced twenty-dollar bills and bribed the five-piece orchestra to play music from the big-band era, the slow sentimental danceable tunes they had grown up with. Richmond and Iris rose from the table and moved in a stately waltz across the gleaming floor. Mischievously sensuous at twenty, Jeanette Richmond in a backless white evening gown reached out for Loren's hand, motioning that she wanted to dance. "You don't need your glasses," she said, and Loren obediently set them on the tablecloth for Dunphy to watch over. As they glided about the open floor amid other dancing couples, she molded her body tight against him, letting him feel her warmth and enjoy the loveliness of her breasts. "Oh, Loren, I don't think I've ever been so high, just so high I want to fly around the room and kiss everyone I see and tell them I'm so happy, not just for Daddy and Mother and Conor and you but for the whole beautiful world."

"I know." Loren held her close and smelled the fragrance of her long dark hair. "I know. It's all I can do to keep from busting out myself."

Jeanette pressed even closer against him. "Let's bust out together," she whispered into his ear. "Later, after the party. After we drive Conor home." Across the dimly lit room the dean beamed like a drunken angel and poured liqueur into his coffee. "I'll tell Mother I want to spread the news among a few girl friends. I know the way to your place. If you want me?"

"There are some invitations even a law professor can't refuse," he said.

A month later Loren made the hundred-thirty-mile drive upstate to the capital for the swearing in of the two new justices. The governor administered the oath of office to Dunphy and Richmond in the vast high-ceilinged courtroom on the fourth floor of the State House building where the justices heard oral arguments; afterward coffee and creamy petits fours were served from tables covered with snowy cloths and set up in the corridor outside the courtroom. The mob of judges, lawyers, state functionaries, media people, friends, relatives and strangers surged around the two men of the hour. Loren squeezed his way into the center of the throng just long enough to shake the justices' hands and give them his best wishes.

"And how do you like your new house?" he asked Iris Richmond.

"It's a lovely old place." Iris kept her arm entwined in her husband's as if afraid the crowd would carry him away. The fine lines and wrinkles of early middle age had crept into her patrician face since the last time Loren had seen her. "Not quite as large as the one we had before, but I've fixed up a suite for Ben so that his bedroom and study are right next to each other. We'll have to invite you up for dinner once things settle down a bit."

"I've got an apartment in town now," Jeanette told him. In a bright-orange knit skirt and jacket over a scoop-necked brown top, and with her hair falling softly below her shoulders, she seemed to Loren the loveliest woman in the building. "And a job with the Bureau of Community Affairs Uncle Norm got for me. You've met him, haven't you, Loren?"

"My brother, Norman Abelson," her mother explained, and tried to point through the mass of bodies toward one of the refreshment tables. "There he is, standing next to Justice Lutz. The tall well-built bald man in the gray suit. He's the deputy administrator of the Department of Institutions and Agencies. I'm sure I've mentioned him a hundred times."

"Oh, yes, of course," murmured Loren, who had never seen the man before.

"Loren!" Chief Justice Dunphy called out. "Come on over here a second. . . . What's this I hear about your taking leave from the law school and going to work for the police?"

"Not really leave." Loren had to shout to make himself heard over the babble of legal and political small talk that surrounded them. "A sort of shared-time arrangement. Comes of getting a liberal mayor in November's election, I guess. Bill Sturm's always been concerned about abuse of police power, and a few weeks ago he called up and asked if I'd be interested in a part-time appointment as deputy legal adviser to the commissioner's office. I'm supposed to root out illegal practices by persuading the brass they're counterproductive. It may turn out to be a waste of time but I said I'd give it a whirl. As if I didn't have enough complications in my life already."

The complications multiplied as Loren's involvement with the police deepened. Over the next year, almost in spite of himself and by means he was never sure he understood, he was credited with having helped the department solve a number of bizarre crimes, including a few murders, and developed a kind of underground reputation as the man to call in when a situation seemed too crazy for normal procedure to be of much use. Before too many months had passed he found himself the object of a strange amalgam of attitudes on the part of the police, even of Sergeant Hough, who had worked with him on several cases. They had nothing but contempt for his social philosophy and for the minor restrictions on their power that he had bulldozed the commissioner into imposing, but they couldn't help but respect him for his detective abilities. Sometimes he thought that this astuteness and his connection with the mayor were all that saved him from being framed on some charge, beaten to raw meat in some station-house back room, and railroaded into prison by a friendly judge. At least three officers had subtly threatened to do just that. After a year Loren resigned in frustration and disgust and returned to law school to concentrate on battles he stood a chance to win.

And as the early seventies turned into the middle seventies, and the hideous war had ended as it deserved to end and the White House pigsty had been cleansed as it needed to be cleansed, Loren began to tire. There seemed to be fewer issues of good against evil these days, and the social problems were not as clear-cut as they had appeared a few years before. He was uncertain whether it was society or he, and a lot of burned-out rebels like him, that had changed. The campus grew quiet; the students were cool, better groomed, self-seeking and uncommitted, worried about jobs and their own futures. Loren no longer felt guilty about his inherited money, and was only vaguely uncomfortable about his lack of guilt. He sensed his life winding down into a cycle of mechanical academic ruts. Except for Christmas cards, and a get-well note to Dunphy after he'd heard that the chief justice had lost a foot in some grotesque auto accident, he fell out of touch with his old friends on the state's high court. When he was promoted to full professor, he didn't bother to celebrate. His fortieth birthday was still years off, but getting uncomfortably close.

The call from Jeanette that he received in his apartment that snowy December evening stunned him like a blow in the face. "He hasn't got long, Loren. He wants to see you badly."

"Stomach cancer," Loren repeated grimly. "And he's known for a year or more and didn't tell you or your mother till last month?"

"He just kept working," Jeanette said, and he could hear the grief in her voice. "Like a demon. We thought he was pushing himself too hard but we never suspected, or at least I didn't, and I don't think Mother or Uncle Norm did."

"And it's been so long since I've seen him or even talked to him," Loren said. "God, I feel putrid inside. ... You say he's in Stoner Memorial, the intensive-care unit?"

"Since Tuesday," Jeanette told him. "We tried to call you at the law school but they said you were out of town and wouldn't be back till tonight."

"Tell me how to go after I get off the Interstate." Loren reached for the pad and pencil beside the telephone on the coffee table. "I'm leaving right away."

TWO

Forty-eight hours before Christmas, on a bone-chilling morning of leaden-gray skies and sifting snow, Justice Richmond was buried. Loren had stayed in the capital to help Dunphy and Norman Abelson with the funeral arrangements and to serve as one of the pallbearers. A line of black limousines, headlights ablaze, crunched in stately procession through the snow-packed city streets from the funeral home to Eternal Rest Cemetery. A shivering clergyman stood under a hastily erected canopy and read words over the grave, and a forklift device lowered the polished casket into the hungry earth. Loren and a ghost-faced Jeanette stood on either side of Iris Richmond, their arms tight around her, supporting her, trying to shield her from the bite of the wind. Her eyes were raw with grief and she sobbed quietly against Loren's snow-crusted overcoat.

At the other end of the knot of mourners the six surviving justices of the court stood wind-whipped and erect. Chief Justice Dunphy took a few hesitant steps toward the lip of the grave as if to look down and say a last farewell to his old friend. He moved slowly, planting his thick heavy cane into the treacherous ground before venturing each step. His eyes were hooded with a bitterness Loren had not seen there before these last few days.

It was the accident, Loren thought. In the downstairs lounge of the funeral home, the first night of Richmond's wake, he had seen the chief justice sitting in a wine-colored armchair in the far corner, playing with an unlit pipe, the knobby cane propped at an angle against the paneled wall. Loren had crossed the lounge and dropped onto a hassock nearby Dunphy. Conor looked older and more tired than Loren had ever seen him during their years together at the law school.

"Just your usual garden variety auto negligence case," he had said, trying to treat the loss of his foot lightly and failing so miserably Loren almost winced. "And the hell of it is that I hadn't drunk a drop that evening, except two bloody marys. It was a Sunday, around nine I guess, pitch dark, downtown was pretty much deserted, and I was just leaving the bar and jaywalking across Broadway to the parking lot when this state police car comes tearing out of nowhere at seventy miles an hour without even its siren on and roars by within a couple of inches of my face. Have you ever been stepped on by an elephant, Loren?"

"Not to my recollection," Loren said.

"Well, I've been stepped on by a police cruiser," Dunphy said, "and it smarts. Where my right foot had been looked like a basket of crushed strawberries. And mind you, I was still standing upright somehow, as if my brain hadn't gotten the message yet. Well, they rushed me to the hospital and the doctors had to cut off the whole foot and a chunk of the ankle and give me a plastic contraption I still haven't learned to walk on properly. It didn't cost me a cent. The state gives us complete insurance coverage, and I even got them to pay for the cost of Sean Patrick here." He clutched the lethal-looking cane in his powerful hand. "This is an authentic shillelagh from the old country, I'll have ye know. Made in 1824 by Seamus O'Fearna of Dublin, the finest woodcraftsman of his generation. Just what I've always wanted to have." Loren didn't know whether or not to believe Dunphy's account of the cane's history; it was the kind of blarney Conor had a talent for improvising at a moment's notice. The chief justice squeezed his eyes tight shut for a moment, as if to hide something. "But I didn't want it like this," he whispered hoarsely. "Oh, Christ, not like this." There was the sound of squeaky-shoed feet descending the staircase into the lounge, and Dunphy sniffed hastily and straightened in his high-backed chair. "Ah, Jonathan, I could tell you were coming a mile off. Come on over here and meet a young friend of mine. Professor Mensing, Justice Lutz...."

After the funeral there was a quiet luncheon at the Richmond house for Loren, the family, the justices, Norman Abelson and his wife and a few friends. Loren picked absently at the cold turkey and potato salad on his plate, remembering that on the day Ben Richmond had been sworn in, Iris had promised to have him up for dinner sometime and it had never happened. Late that afternoon he drove back home on the Interstate, keeping the VW at a safe forty miles per hour as it slid through the softly falling snow, the auto heater turning the interior into an oven. He thought about Richmond's last moments, that night in the hospital, when he had thrashed about in bed, forcing his dying body to sit up, straining to whisper those last desperate words in Loren's ear. "Tape," he had croaked, so softly it was almost as if he had said nothing. "Listen ... tape ... just ... you."

Loren wondered, not for the first time, what the words could have meant. He had debated whether he should ask Iris or Jeanette if either of them knew anything about a tape, but it was the wrong time for questions. Let the grief subside first, let their life return to some kind of normal pattern. There would be time enough in the weeks and months ahead. But would the judge have wanted him to ask the other members of the family? "Just ... you," he had said, as if perhaps the tape involved some private secret.

Loren put the puzzle out of his mind and concentrated on the road. He noticed that the gas gauge was low, remembered the Benneco station just off the next exit and hoped it was open. The VW's tires slithered through the sea of slush.

And then another semester began, and as new problems fought for his attention, Richmond's dying words receded from his mind. Late in the spring a large cardboard box arrived at the law school for Loren, postmarked CAPITAL CITY. An envelope bearing the letterhead of a Capital City law firm was attached to the upper side of the box with strapping tape. Loren lugged the box up to his office, set it on the floor, and used a paper knife from his desk to cut the letter free.

Dear Professor Mensing:

Enclosed please find one (1) calf-bound set of the 1833 edition of *Commentaries on the Constitution of the United States,* in three (3) volumes, by The Honorable Joseph Story, Justice of the United States Supreme Court. These books come from the personal library of the late Justice Ben Richmond of our own high bench and were specifically bequeathed to you in the will of Justice Richmond dated June 14 of last year. We trust that you will be happy with this memento from the distinguished jurist.

Very truly yours,
LATIMER, MARTIN & GASH
Sidney J. Latimer

Loren attacked the industrial tape that secured the bulky carton. Piled firmly inside the box were three heavy volumes bound in rich calf, each wrapped for protection in a swatch of clean white cloth. Loren arranged the books on his desk, sat in his swivel chair and rubbed the luxurious bindings with an almost sensual delight. He opened a volume at random and read a few pages and remembered that Story's three volumes had occupied the top shelf in Richmond's chambers when he had been an appellate judge and Loren had been his clerk. He must have eyed them fondly even then, and the shrewd and gentle judge had remembered. Loren took down some legal texts from the top shelf of one of his own bookcases and reverently installed the Story volumes in their place. When he had cleared away the remains of the box and the tape scraps, he sat down at his desk again and placed a long-distance call to Capital City, to tell Iris how much he appreciated Ben's gift and to find out how she was feeling.

He thought of asking if the judge had ever mentioned a tape recording to her, but the fear that the matter might be a completely private one kept him from raising the question. The meaning of those cryptic words of Richmond's had begun to nag at him again, like the ache of an old wound. Someday, he thought, he'd mention the matter to Dunphy and see if the chief justice could shed any light. Someday.

When he finished grading the spring semester examinations, and made his ritual appearances at the university graduation exercises and the weekend round of student parties that followed, he felt drained and purposeless and alone. He wanted to go away somewhere but knew that he would feel more isolated than ever if he went off to a strange place by himself, and there was no one he felt like asking to go with him who he thought would be free and willing. He spent a week staying in his high-rise apartment like a hermit, systematically listening to his classical music albums, fussing with minor maintenance chores he had never been able to get the building's handyman to attend to, reading a few best-sellers desultorily, feeling at loose ends and sorry for himself. When he had worked the melancholy out of his system he went back to the office for the first time in ten days and read his accumulated mail. Then he crawled under a scratched old conference table in the corner and exhumed a thick fiberboard carton and tore the tape from its edges. Inside the carton were the research materials and the seven unfinished chapters of one of his major scholarly projects, a legal history of the Third Reich. He hadn't touched the project in more than a year. He rummaged through the papers and reread a chapter he had begun to draft three years earlier, and made up his mind that since he had no summer classes to teach he would spend the hot months working on the history again.

The law school was all but deserted after graduation. A few professors stayed around the campus, as did the law review candidates and some recent graduates who were cramming for the bar examination. The summer session wouldn't start for another three weeks. Loren carved out a new daily routine. He slept as late as he wanted, and made himself pork roll and a cheese omelet for breakfast or stopped at a quick-service restaurant on the way to school when he felt too lazy to cook. He would whirl the VW down the circular ramp that led to the depths of the university's underground parking facility, and maneuver into the tiny slot on the fourth level stenciled MENSING, and stroll through the long underground tunnel that connected the garage with the basement level of the new law library. From there he would take the self-service elevator to his office on the fourth level and sort through the notes and rough drafts in his files, selecting the materials to be worked on that day. He would pack what he needed in his gray Samsonite attaché case and lock the office and take the elevator down to BB, the subbasement level, where most of the foreign legal materials were kept. And there he would enclose himself in one of the cell-like study carrels, and read and think and scrawl on pads of yellow paper, sometimes all day, sometimes just for a few hours. Once in a while he could hear through the thick ceiling the muffled scrape of footsteps or the blur of voices from overhead. It was rare that anyone came down to the subbasement between semesters. The few who did moved so quietly he didn't hear them.

That Tuesday the work was going well. He was revising the chapter on a curious phenomenon of Hitler's Germany, the secret statute, the law whose existence was unknown and unknowable to the people but whose violation was punishable by imprisonment, conscription, forced labor, torture or death. He had hunted for parallels in recent American legal developments, and found them with little trouble. He read and wrote through the day in the cool dark carrel, oblivious of time.

In a corner of his consciousness he noted the hum of the elevator descending, the snap of its door sliding back. He wondered idly if it could be one of the maintenance crew, come to dust the shelves. He listened for the sound of footsteps echoing on the concrete floor and heard none. He thought nothing of it and bent over the legal pad on the carrel table and kept writing.

Until a prickling at the back of his neck told him to turn around.

He almost didn't do it. He had been alone in empty, cavernous places before. He had experienced sudden feelings of insecurity, an urge to run, and had known they were irrational and had resisted. He resisted again. He was in the law library of a major urban university, and he was a grown man, built like a bear, able to take care of himself if he had to. He was alone. He must have imagined the elevator noises, or else the cage had stopped on the floor above.

He thought he heard a quiet cough behind him, the shuffle of feet. *Someone was watching him.* He whirled out of his chair. He half ran into the nearest aisle, sighted down between the ranks of gray steel shelves to the elevator at the far end of the corridor. Nothing. He laughed at himself and turned back toward the carrel.

Two men stood in front of him.

Loren felt a stab of cold fear.

There was nothing to be afraid of. They didn't look like street muggers. They wore shirts and ties and summer-weight business suits and their neatly polished shoes glistened under the recessed lights. There was a vaguely Latin look about them: visiting South American lawyers, perhaps. One was tall and slender with eyes slightly hooded and a trim tiny mustache and a look of cool self-possession, as if he would refuse to sweat even on the hottest day. The other was shorter, chunky but sturdy of build, with a receding hairline and a rumpled suit jacket. They stared levelly at Loren, as if they were laboratory scientists and he was the experimental animal. No one moved. No one breathed.

"Professor Mensing?" The slender one finally broke the silence. His voice was velvet smooth, evoking soft lights and seduction.

Loren said nothing. He wrestled with a wild impulse to run down the aisle in the opposite direction.

"You are Professor Loren Mensing, sir, is that not so?" the slender one said. "The two young women on the main floor said that you were working in the subbasement."

"I'm—I'm Mensing." It came out half a stammer and half a wheeze. Loren felt panic and disgust with himself for being panicky. Nothing was wrong here. Nothing.

"My name is Moraga," the other said. "This is Mr. Rojas." Moraga reached tapered fingers into the breast pocket of his jacket and extracted a tooled leather card case, hinged at one side. He flipped back the lid and displayed an identification card. Printed in dignified-looking type at the head of the card was UNITED STATES OF AMERICA and beneath it CENTRAL INTELLIGENCE AGENCY.

"Would you mind coming with us, sir?" Moraga said politely.

Loren was a veteran of the peace movement. He had learned that encountering a CIA operative was like running into a cottonmouth in a swamp. But his irrational fear was gone now that the enemy had shape and identity. "Would *you* mind telling me where you'd like to take me," he demanded, "and why?"

"We would mind very much, sir," Rojas replied. His voice was hoarse, deep, froglike. Loren stored its sound in his memory. "Just come along with us, okay?"

"You characters must be out of your skulls." Loren raised his voice, hoping against hope that someone would hear them. "I am not going to budge an inch unless you give me a damn good reason. Now come on, what the hell is this all about? Or do you want me to call a security guard?"

Moraga and Rojas exchanged sharp glances. Rojas dug into his jacket. A small polished revolver materialized as if by magic in his hand. He trained the pistol on Loren's middle. Loren backed away a step.

"This is not a request, sir," Moraga said politely. "And please don't think too harshly of us. We're simply following instructions."

Rojas edged closer, held the revolver two inches from Loren's middle. "Over to the elevator," he croaked. They marched single file past the twin rows of tall musty lawbooks to the green door at the end of the aisle. Moraga pressed the second joint of his finger against the plastic circle set in the wall. The button glowed and a motorized hum descended the shaft, snapping off when the cage dropped into place and the green door slid back. Moraga's eyes darted about warily, like the eyes of an animal sensing a predator. Rojas' breath was an unhealthy rasp. Loren heard no other sound.

"In you go, Professor," Moraga said, too loudly. "And press the button for B. We're not going far, just to the underground lot." The cage door clanked shut and the motor hum rose with them, then shut off. The door opened and they motioned Loren out. Rojas walked beside him, Moraga five steps ahead like a scout. A heavy fire door gave onto the tunnel to the parking lot. They strode down the walkway briskly, in silence.

From the far end of the long tube Loren heard the echo of approaching footsteps. His heart pounded wildly. His brain raced. The sweat of fear drenched him. *Let it be security guards coming this way.*

"You'll keep our business private, sir, I hope," Moraga said politely, and chewed his lip. Their shadows flowed along the whitewashed tunnel walls. The steps from the other end boomed loudly and the people they belonged to came into sight, small at first, growing in size as their steps grew in sound.

They were two young men, in sloppy shirts and jeans, talking animatedly of baseball. Loren had never seen either one of them before. The groups passed without contact and the young men's steps receded behind Loren.

"Speed it up, Professor," Moraga muttered. He stayed a few paces ahead, arrived at the door to the parking garage, opened it by pressing his forearms against the steel bar. "After you," he said. They passed through the door and Moraga let it clang shut behind them.

"Bottom level?" Rojas asked.

"Affirmative." Moraga pointed to a flight of concrete steps leading deeper into the earth. "Take him down those and prepare him; I'll get the wheels." He pivoted smartly, like a soldier on parade and marched across the dark empty garage. Rojas motioned Loren to precede him down the steps to the lowest level. "Watch you don't trip," he said. "You'd think a school would spend some of our tax money for decent lighting in this damn place." They reached the foot of the stairs. Loren thought about running. He thought about trying to take the gun away from Rojas. He kept walking.

Between semesters the lowest level of the underground garage was as empty as a graveyard at midnight. None of the few people who came to the university between semesters wanted to wrestle his car all the way down the spiral auto ramp and then back up again to the street level when he left. Bright bulbs in triple clusters like electric fruit threw long shadows across the concrete floor as they walked. Loren felt dank and clammy and helpless.

"Okay, Professor," Rojas said. "Lie down. Right there. On your gut or on your ass—I couldn't care less." He pointed with the pistol barrel to one of the empty slots, its borders marked in faded yellow paint. "Your legs sticking out into the aisle, the rest of you in the slot like you'd park your car."

Loren knew then. Every muscle in his body and every bead of sweat that ran down him told him the truth. These CIA agents were going to kill him. He would be a twitching pile of dead meat in a few moments. His body refused to move. He stood there, frozen.

"Lie down, God damn you!" Rojas shoved him with his foot. Loren sprawled onto the cold dank floor. Somewhere he heard the hollow drip of water in a pipe. He concentrated on the sound, clung to it as if it were a life raft. Rojas kicked him with the toe of his shoe, made him stretch his legs out into the aisle, raise his arms over his head.

Loren couldn't hear the dripping anymore. A motor gunned into life on one of the upper levels, killing the sound, roaring nearer, down the ramp at the other end.

"That's him," Rojas said. "Now, if you'll just lie still, Professor, it won't be all that bad."

Loren began to twitch uncontrollably. His mouth was bone dry. It was agony to speak. "What"—his voice sounded like the rattle of a dying animal—"what are you going to do to me?"

"Well, Professor, Mr. Moraga is going to train the car on you like you were a target on the firing range." Loren made himself turn his head to face the distant ramp. The car was reversing, running forward a few feet, reversing again. Getting into position. "Then he's going to put on the gas and fly down this lane." Rojas traced a swift line with the pistol across Loren's ankles. "It doesn't really hurt as much as you think it will if you try to relax and put it out of your mind."

Loren imagined the bones of his legs crunching into fine

powder under those wheels. He saw himself trapped in a wheelchair for the rest of his life. Vomit rose in his throat. He gagged, coughed. Helpless now, no way to make a break from flat on his back. He would have given anything—ten, twenty years of his life—if he could relive the last few minutes and try to escape back in the tunnel or on the stairs.

"Why are you doing this?" He forced the words out through the vomit on his lips.

Rojas shrugged quizzically. "It's a job." The sound of the car grew louder. Loren turned his head toward the car again. "It's easier if you don't watch," Rojas said paternally. "And, look, uh, don't worry about, you know, losing too much, like not being able to make it with women when you're healed up." An auto horn honked once, short, crisp. "He's ready," Rojas said, and started to move out of the way.

A door boomed somewhere in the garage. Running steps echoed—two, three sets of steps. Loud, furious, urgent. "Loren!" A falsetto screech tore through the air. Rojas whirled about, pistol raised, searching for the sound.

Loren snaked his left foot behind Rojas' heel, kicked at the knee savagely. Rojas hit the concrete with a grunt. Loren sprang up, stamped on Rojas' hand as if it were a poisonous insect, ground it into the floor. Rojas shrieked, let go the gun. The car roared down the lane toward them. Loren kicked the gun across the garage and began to run, frantically. Rojas stumbled to the car. The car shuddered to a halt; the passenger door flew open. A tall man in uniform leaped to the bottom of the concrete steps. "Halt!" he roared. The car rocketed forward to the ramp at the far end of the level, raced up the spiral, tires screaming.

Loren clutched a concrete pillar for support. The red-bearded young man in a university security guard's uniform ran up to him, halted a few steps away, holstered his pistol.

"You okay, Professor?"

"Yeah," Loren panted. "If I ever see those goddamn pigs again, I'll tear their hearts out."

"Get the make or license number?"

"Just a dark blue sedan," Loren said. "Late model. They were going to run over my legs, cripple me." He began to shudder uncontrollably, his body rocking against the damp pillar. The guard whipped a walkie-talkie from his leather belt, spoke into it low and urgently. Loren heard the word "doctor." He sank into a sitting position on the floor, knees drawn against his chest.

Steps raced toward him and a young woman in jeans and a man's white shirt slid down beside him, landing like a baserunner stealing second. "Oh, Loren, did they hurt you?"

"Not bad," Loren mumbled. Gael Irwin wiped his face and mouth.

With her high childish voice, her perky clown face and tangled mop of dark curls, her lovely body and impossible causes and her total lack of awe before anyone and anything on the planet, Gael had always been a very special student for him. He looked at her and drank her in and wanted to crush her against him just out of the sheer joy of still being alive.

"You got here," he said brokenly. "And the guard. How did you?"

She seemed to understand what he meant. "Loren, Adjoa and I were in the library working on that project for Legal Aid and two men walked in who looked like contract killers in a *Godfather* movie and stopped us and asked where they could find you. After I told them, they started to leave, and I saw a gun under the short one's jacket. I told Adjoa to get a cop fast, but she had to run halfway across the campus before she found a security guard and then the two of them started hunting for me and I was trying to leave a trail of dropped lawbooks for them and follow you. Loren, what have you done to make the Mafia want to take you for a ride?"

"Not Mafia," he said. "CIA."

"Jesus!" Gael screeched. "We're back in the sixties again!"

A high keening sound stabbed through the garage and a blue and white sedan with city police emblems on the doors twisted down the ramp, with siren screaming, and slid to a halt twenty feet from Loren. Two uniformed men raced out with revolvers drawn and scanned the vast empty area. A tall young black woman with an Afro and the red-bearded security guard converged on Loren from opposite directions.

Loren struggled to his feet. His legs were like putty, refused to support him. He sank back to a squat against the pillar and told the officers what had happened. They took down his story dutifully and exchanged polite skeptical glances when Loren reported the CIA credentials the hit men had shown. The younger officer went back to the patrol car and used his radio to request a plainclothes team and the lab truck.

An hour later it was all over. The uniformed men were gone; the detective team was gone; the evidence technicians had collected what they could find, which was nothing, and departed in the square white lab truck. Only Loren and Gael and the black girl were left in the garage. The two women helped him to his feet. He was shaky, but he could stand now. He took a few steps experimentally, tottering like a small child. The image flashed into his mind of Conor Dunphy trying to learn how to walk on an artificial foot.

"Gael," he said, "is your car around here somewhere?"

"I drove us in today, Professor," Adjoa said. "My car's on the upper level."

She had been at the law school only since spring semester, a transfer student from the East. She had not attended Loren's classes but Gael had brought her in to see him four months ago and asked for his help when the university registrar refused to process the new student's records under her self-chosen name, which was Ghanaian and meant female born on Monday.

"Would you mind dropping me off in front of the library?" he asked. "I . . . don't think my legs want to walk much yet."

When the ancient Honda braked at the main door of the library, Loren turned to Gael, squeezed her shoulders gratefully. "Thanks again," he said. "I owe you one. Both of you."

He wobbled to the door and went inside and followed the corridor around the circumference of the building, walking clumsily. His watch read 4:36 as he stabbed the UP button. It seemed weeks ago that he had taken the elevator from his office to the subbasement. As the cage lifted him, he remembered that his attaché case and the day's research were still sitting in that underground study carrel, but he was reluctant to go down there alone to retrieve them. At the third floor he left the elevator and crossed the hall to the faculty secretaries' office. All but two of the desks were empty, their typewriters shrouded for the day. He checked his mail slot, which was piled with papers and buff-colored message slips.

"Professor Mensing, what mischief have you been up to?" Rose, the senior secretary, took in his disheveled appearance with equal measures of amusement and disapproval. She had been with the law school longer than the oldest faculty member, and she delighted in the prerogatives of seniority. "You've been getting urgent messages from the capital all day. We've tried your office, the dean's office, your apartment.... You get right over here and sit down and call Chief Justice Dunphy. Don't stop to read your mail. This is an emergency! Here, I'll dial for you." Her fingers poked the buttons as Loren approached her stunningly uncluttered desk and sat in her leather-padded chair. When she had the connection, she put the phone to his ear and retreated to the stationery cabinets, out of hearing range.

"Conor?" Loren said.

"Loren, where in God's name have you been all day?" The chief justice's voice was tight with anxiety.

"You wouldn't believe me if I told you," Loren said. "A couple of goons tried to turn me into a cripple.... No, no. I'm all right, just a little shaky. Tell you more about it later. What's all this about an emergency?"

Dunphy answered with another question. "Are you free tonight? Can you get up here right away, this evening? We're having a special meeting of the justices and I think we're going to need you."

"Conor, I'm not really up to that long a drive tonight. Could you give me some idea what the meeting's about?"

"No," Dunphy said. "But it's urgent, vital. It's state business, and it involves people you and I both care about very deeply. If you don't want to drive, take a plane. Transstate runs flights up here every hour on the half hour and the court will pick up the tab. And, oh, yes, are you teaching summer school this year, or do you have any other firm plans for the next few weeks?"

"Just working on a book. You know, that Third Reich thing I began when you were still dean. Why?"

"Pack a bag then," Dunphy said. "We may ask you to stay awhile. And I think you'll want to stay when you hear why. Now, what flight do you think you'll make?"

Loren made quick calculations in his head. Clean up his desk here, retrieve his papers from the subbasement, drive home, pack, grab a bite to eat, drive to the airport. "Eight-thirty's about the earliest I can take off, Conor."

"Then ye'll be landing at nine-fifteen. A limousine will be waiting to pick you up. If you don't make that flight, call me collect at my private number at the court." Loren tore a sheet from Rose's calendar pad and scrawled the unlisted number Dunphy gave him. "Thanks for obliging us this way, Loren. I hate to be so mysterious about what's happening but— Well, more about that when you get here."

"See you tonight," Loren said. He hung up, stood, waved thanks to Rose, crossed to the mail slots. His legs felt firm again. He looked through the mail, threw the pile of phone slips and all but one envelope into the wastebasket and went out to the elevators.

THREE

Through the plane window the dark brown hills and scattered white pinpoints gave way to a panorama of fixed and moving lights, thousands of microdots of brightness that grew in size and brilliance as the Transstate commuter flight swooped to the airfield. Loren unsnapped his seat belt, lifted his two-suiter from the carry-on luggage bin and strode briskly down the steel steps to the tarmac. The cool night air lifted his somber mood. He entered the terminal and paused to study the knot of men and women and cranky children who milled about the arrival lounge, waiting to greet deplaning passengers. A tall powerful-looking bald man in a tailored leisure suit separated from the crowd, surged forward purposefully. "Mensing, right?" Loren nodded. "Norman Abelson, Department of Institutions and Agencies. I'm Iris Richmond's brother. You remember—we met during poor Ben's wake."

"Oh, of course." The hand Loren held out was crushed in the other's grip. "I'm sorry I didn't recognize you, but this has been a hellish day for me."

"Likewise up here," Abelson said. His voice was so deep it seemed to be coming from a cavern. "Come on. I've got a state limo waiting in the VIP parking area. I'll take your bag." He scooped up the heavy suitcase as if it were a handful of balloons and marched along the airport corridor and past the security checkpoint at a pace Loren had to jog to keep up with. The man must be a physical-fitness nut, Loren thought. They came out of the terminal into the breeze-scented night and stopped at a long sleek car parked against the curb, its chauffeur smoking patiently, oblivious of the chaos of taxis and airport buses and private cars disgorging travelers. Abelson entered by the rear door, leaned forward to give terse instructions to the driver, then beckoned Loren in. The car hummed into quiet life and glided smoothly out of the bedlam around the airport. The driver turned into the ramp to Capital Expressway West.

Loren jerked forward in his seat. "I thought downtown was east of the airport. Aren't we supposed to be going to a meeting of the justices?"

"Not in chambers," Abelson said. "Out at Ben's house." His eyes were grave and brooding; his bald head glistened in the dark. The limousine's headlights sprayed the highway. Loren thought of demanding to know what was going on but something told him it would be a waste of time. He leaned back in his corner and watched the wooded ridges glide past the windows.

The limousine turned off the highway, wound among two-lane blacktop roads through the hills. Lights from isolated houses glowed dimly in the thickening night. The chauffeur turned left into a private lane and drove up a steep hill. The massive stone house stood at the end of the drive. Abelson climbed out of the car, took Loren's two-suiter from the trunk, carried it to the front door and pressed the bell. Light flamed in the vestibule; someone approached; the door opened. "Loren." Iris Richmond held out a frail and withered hand. "It's good of you to come."

She seemed to have aged ten years in the six months since the judge's death. Her patrician face looked defeated, her figure shrunken. Her hand seemed to shudder in his grasp. Behind her look of welcome the pale blue eyes were bright with a kind of horror.

Abelson set the suitcase down in the cloakroom off the vestibule and Loren deposited his attaché case alongside it and followed Iris to the huge front room. Nothing about the room had changed since Loren's last look at it, the afternoon of the funeral: high white ceiling; walls painted doeskin; landscapes in wood frames blending with the soft colors; parquet floor, walnut stained, dotted with bright-patterned area rugs; clusters of couches and easy chairs and tables and floor lamps. Jeanette rose from a hassock and kissed Loren on the cheek. She wore a tan sweater and slacks and a mint-green vest decorated with gold frogs and chains. Her eyes were raw and swollen.

Six men and a middle-aged black woman sat on facing couches at the far end of the room. A wheeled cart beside the white marble fireplace held an assortment of bottles: whiskies, mixers, wines. Bowls of crackers and plates heaped with sliced cheese and cold ham and dips and a gleaming stainless-steel coffee urn cluttered the end tables that framed the couches. The buzz of conversation died as Loren and Abelson and the Richmond women strode into the group. On the glass-topped coffee table between the couches a magenta shoebox stood. None of the group touched it; none had placed cups or glasses or saucers on the table; but their eyes couldn't leave it alone.

Conor Dunphy shifted his thick walking stick to his left hand and stuck out his right. "Pardon me for not rising; this couch is just too soft. Professor Loren Mensing, you've met most of my colleagues before, I'm sure. But just for the record: Justice Lutz, Justice Berendzen, Justice Goldner, Justice Colasanto, Justice Lawless—don't laugh—and the most recent member of the court, Justice Hale." Loren nodded, shook hands, murmured amenities. Then he turned, and sank into a barrel chair. Jeanette poured him coffee and with a tiny smile set the cup on the arm of his chair.

"The court," Dunphy said, "is aware of your reputation, Loren, as a sort of detective without portfolio. We've asked you to join us because we can't think of a better way to handle this . . . awful mess that's been dropped into our laps." He swiveled his head to indicate Iris, who sat rigid and tense on the couch beside him. "Mrs. Richmond can best tell you what's happened."

Loren had noticed that even while Dunphy was speaking, the other justices and the Richmonds kept darting glances at the magenta shoebox on the table, as if they were birds hypnotized by a snake, and then turning their eyes away in revulsion. Iris reached out for a water tumbler, and ice tinkled as she raised the glass shakily to her mouth.

"I found the box before breakfast this morning," she said, licking her lips. "I was sorting through Ben's clothes. There's a charity drive this week and I was asked if there was anything I could contribute. You've been upstairs, Loren, haven't you?"

"No, but I remember you said something—I think it was the day Ben was sworn in—about making a suite of rooms upstairs into a combined bedroom and study for him."

"That's where it was—wedged behind his suitcases on the upper shelf of his bedroom closet. I'd never seen it before and couldn't figure out why it was there, so I took it down and put it on the bed and opened it. I think my heart skipped a beat when I looked inside; for a second I was afraid I was having a seizure. Norman always goes early to his office. I called him at once and asked what I should do. He canceled his morning appointments and drove out and we talked it over and called Justice Dunphy and told him the whole story."

"Luckily we haven't scheduled oral arguments this week," Justice Goldner put in. He was the oldest member of the court, lean, soft-voiced, with wispy white hair and a mustache. The word in judicial circles was that he would retire at the end of the current court term. "We held a quick meeting and Conor proposed that we call you in, Professor, to be ... well, to be a sort of detective for the court. To conduct your own investigation outside of official channels and report to us on the origins of this box and what action the court should take. Will you do that for us?"

Loren leaned forward, his own gaze fixed on the box. "No one's told me yet what's in it," he said. "I'm afraid I can guess."

"You don't have to guess. Gentlemen, if I may." Justice Aldona Berendzen, the only black female appellate judge in the Midwest, drew a pair of dainty white gloves from her purse, delicately raised the lid of the box by two of its corners and set it down on the coffee table, its underside facing up. Loren bent on one knee beside the table. The inner surface of the shoebox lid was creamy white, with one word printed in ornate gold script: RADISSON.

Piles of crisp green paper filled the interior of the shoe box. Twenties, fifties, one stack of hundreds. Loren leaned over the box, almost unwilling to believe his eyes.

"You'd better not touch, Professor," Abelson said. "My prints and Iris's are on the box and the bills already. We counted very carefully. The total is forty-nine thousand dollars, exactly. I've made a list of the serial numbers." He drew several folded sheets of paper from his breast pocket and handed them to Loren. "There are several consecutive runs of numbers, if that means anything."

The crisp green bills glistened evilly in the lamplight, like snakeskin.

"Loren." The voice of Conor Dunphy broke Loren's concentration. "You know as well as we do that that amount of money, hidden away in Ben's closet so carefully, suggests one thing and one thing only."

"Bribe," Loren said.

Iris flinched at the word as if she had been slapped. Her brother, who had been leaning against the mantel, came forward and put an arm around her shoulders.

"Sometime before he died Ben took a bribe to decide the way he did on one of the cases before the court. Is that what you're suggesting?" Loren said.

"My God, Loren, *I'm* not!" Dunphy protested. "Ben was my best friend for thirty years; I knew that man as well as I know myself, and I'd stake my other foot and both my hands he'd never do that. And he was your mentor, too. I remember—oh, nine years ago—when he called me at the law school. This was right after Ken Cole had died and we had a faculty slot we needed to fill in a hurry, and Ben called and said he had this bright young clerk with an incredible legal mind and that he'd hate like hell to lose you but he thought you'd make a first-rate teacher."

Loren stared emptily at the neat stacks of bills. He had no illusions about public officials and had long ago reached the conclusion that the kind of person who is appointed to office is the kind of person who more likely than not will abuse his power sooner or later, often or rarely. But Loren had always made exceptions for the people he knew and trusted: Mayor Sturm, back home; Sergeant Hough; Dunphy; Ben Richmond. Loren couldn't believe the obvious meaning of that shoebox. He didn't want to believe it, but he was desperately afraid that if he investigated the matter for the court, he might in time be forced to believe it. And yet if it wasn't true, if there was another explanation, Loren wanted to be the one to find it. He owed the judge that and so much more.

"I don't know," he said. "Maybe the police ought to handle it; they can be more objective."

Jeanette Richmond went down on one knee beside Loren. "I need you, Loren," she said softly. "We all need you. Please don't say no to us. Please?"

"There must be an innocent explanation." Her mother's

voice was a broken whisper. "Loren, I'll give you anything, anything in the world, if you find it. You can't know what I'm going through. You can't know what it's like to live with someone, and love him for half a lifetime, and suddenly lose him, and then find something like this that threatens to turn the whole life you shared into a wreck and a lie." Abelson slung a protective arm about her shaking shoulders as she dabbed a handkerchief at eyes that looked fragile as blue glass.

"Please," Jeanette said again, in a hoarse and frenzied whisper that conjured up incongruous memories in Loren—memories of that feverish night after the dinner party at Poe's, when she had tapped on the door of his riverfront apartment long after midnight, and they had made love until dawn, tenderly and savagely, in violent explosions of need and longing. The others in the lavish front room waited for his answer, silent now, intent. Loren felt as if a chain saw were tearing him apart. He wished he had never come to this meeting.

"Sure," he said quietly, and let out a long breath. "If you want me, I'll do it."

"Thank you, Loren," Conor Dunphy said, and leaned back with a sigh of contentment. "We'll work out a per diem arrangement, of course, to compensate you for your time." The other justices and Iris and Abelson murmured words of gratitude in unison, and Loren sprang to his feet and paced to the mantel and studied the relieved faces of his ten clients.

"If"—the word came out a quack, and he cleared his throat—"if it turns out to be as bad as we suspect, I will not tolerate a cover-up. Understood?"

The justices bent their heads together and consulted buzzily. Dunphy's flamboyant boom broke through their undertones. "Understood," he answered proudly. "This court is not going to repeat the mistakes of certain other public institutions."

"Good enough," Loren said. "Now, Iris, this may be rough on you. I have to ask you some questions about the arrangements here when Ben was alive."

The judge's widow raised her head to Loren's and held it high. "I'm ready," she said simply.

"Who had access to Ben's rooms besides you and Ben himself?"

She thought for perhaps ten seconds before she answered. "Well, no one, really. There's only one entrance to the suite; in the old days it used to be a sitting room and boudoir, I suppose. Ben used the outer room as his bedroom and the inner as a study. He kept the door locked whenever he wasn't inside because he did a lot of work evenings in the study and at times he had things there—drafts of opinions, confidential memoranda that had to be kept secure. The suite has been locked since he died, except for cleaning, of course."

"Who actually did the cleaning? The luncheon we had here after Ben's funeral was catered, but I seem to recall a maid taking our coats and overshoes as we came in." He thought back, tried to capture the image of that gray and snow-laden noon. "A black girl, I think she was. Very pretty, with sort of a button nose."

"Angella." Iris put the accent on the second syllable. "Angella Carmer, her name was. She was our maid then, and she did the cleaning, too."

"Is she available tonight? I'll need to talk with her."

"She quit to get married last month," Iris said. "But she lives in the city, or at least she did when she worked here. I don't know if she and her husband stayed or not. I'll give you her address later."

"Then she didn't live in?"

"Oh, no. With the cost of this house and all, we couldn't afford a live-in maid. She drove out three days a week to do the heavy cleaning, and on special occasions, when we were having a lot of dinner guests, things of that sort."

"How long was she working for you?"

Iris cupped her chin in her hands and lowered her eyes. "Let me think. It was, yes, a year ago last March that we hired her." That couldn't have been very long after Ben first learned that he had cancer, Loren thought. "So she was here about fourteen months in all. A lovely girl, hardworking and ambitious and helpful. I liked her very much."

"Jeanette, how did you feel about Ms. Carmer? The same as your mother did?"

"I barely ever saw her," the judge's daughter replied. "I haven't lived here for three years, you know. I have my own apartment in town. Angella was always very nice and pleasant the few times I did speak to her. Why are you so interested in her?"

"Isn't it obvious? From what you've told me, Iris, she's the only person besides you and Ben himself who had the opportunity to put that shoebox in the bedroom closet."

"Oh, that's impossible!" Iris protested indignantly. "I let her in every day she came to work and all she ever brought to the house with her was a tiny purse. You'd need something large to hold that shoebox—a shopping bag or a small suitcase."

"There wasn't a single day you can remember when she brought a package of any sort into the house?"

"Not one," she replied. "When Angella began working here she told me very frankly that a few years ago a cousin of hers had unjustly been accused of stealing things from the house where she was the cook. Angella had always been extremely careful ever since that incident not to give even the appearance of dishonest intentions. That's why she wouldn't bring any shopping bags in with her when she came to work."

"How about Christmas presents?" Loren asked. "Could she have smuggled the shoebox in, wrapped up like a gift?"

"I think I'd remember something like that," Iris insisted.

"But you didn't actually watch over her when she'd clean the judge's suite?"

"Of course not." She swung her Dresden-shepherdess head vigorously from side to side. "Why in the world would I do that?"

"Did Ben ever complain that papers or anything else were missing from his study? Or did you ever notice anything missing from any part of the house during the time Angella worked here?"

"Never," she said, then paused to think back, and repeated, "No, not once."

Loren whirled to Chief Justice Dunphy. "Conor, did Ben ever complain to you about anything missing from the house? Or to any of you on the court?"

"Not to me," Dunphy said. The other justices murmured agreement, except for Justice Hale. "I wasn't on the court yet," he said in a high, mousy falsetto.

"All right," Loren concluded. "For now it looks as if Ms. Carmer couldn't be responsible for the box. But I'll take her address and talk to her later anyway. Now, who else had opportunity to get the box into Ben's rooms? You spoke of sometimes having a lot of dinner guests, Iris. Did you and Ben entertain often?"

"Very little, really. This house is *such* a long way from the suburbs, where everyone else seems to live. Norm, I suppose you and Blanche were our most frequent guests, wouldn't you say?"

Abelson relaxed from the strange tensed position in which he had been sitting, and Loren suddenly realized that throughout the questioning the man had been doing isometric exercises. "About once every six weeks, on an average," he told Loren carefully, "my wife and I would come out for the evening. Most of the time it would be just the four of us, or occasionally another couple or two would be invited also. Lawyers, professional people, mainly."

"Did you ever stay for the night? Bring suitcases with you?"

"We'd have no reason to," Abelson said. "Our place is only twenty minutes east of here. And besides, as Iris told you, Ben kept the door to the suite locked whenever he wasn't in there."

"We'd have other members of the court occasionally," Iris continued. "And the governor came once, I think. But I'm certain none of our guests ever brought anything into the house large enough to hold that shoebox." Her eyes swerved again toward the box as if it generated an evil magnetism. "Why, it wouldn't even fit into a large attaché case."

"In all the time you've been living here you've never put up a single guest overnight?" Loren asked incredulously.

"I've stayed over a few times," Jeanette Richmond volunteered. "Mainly when Dad was out of town, to keep Mother company. It can get pretty lonely out here when you're by yourself. I'd generally bring an overnight case when I came. I suppose it's big enough to hold that box, but not with my nightie and slippers and toilet things crammed in, too."

"How about visitors since Ben's death? You must have had a lot of people who dropped by to pay condolence calls."

"Oh, there were dozens," Iris acknowledged. "But no one carried anything that could have held a shoebox—except boxes of flowers, perhaps. But when anyone brought flowers he'd take them out of the box right away to show them to me and we'd put them in a vase then and there. No, I don't think anyone could have brought the box in that way. But there was one strange thing. . . ." Her voice trailed off into a vague silence.

"Even if you think it can't possibly help," Loren urged, "tell me."

"It was . . . in March, I think. About three or four months after the burial. A man from Ajax Exterminators in a van with a dead insect painted on the side knocked at the front door. He said Ben had called their firm late in November and ordered an inspection of the house for termite damage and the order had gotten misfiled and no one had come. The man was so apologetic it embarrassed me. And then I told him Ben had passed away in December and *he* got embarrassed and said that under the circumstances he'd see to it there wouldn't be any charge for his services. Well, he went through all the rooms on this floor, tapping and doing whatever these exterminators do, and then he took his toolbox and spraying equipment down to the basement to check down there. When he came up he said everything was safe and sound. He hadn't seen a sign of a single termite. A week or so later the company sent me a bill marked 'canceled.' Wait a minute—I think it's in one of those drawers." She scurried across the room to an ornate secretary-desk against the wall and leafed through pigeonholes full of loose papers. Finally, with a little sound of triumph, she yanked a sheet from the pile and brought it back to Loren. The letterhead of the bill read AJAX EXTERMINATORS, INC. and gave a city address he didn't recognize. Beneath the rubber-stamped cancellation of the charges was a brief hand-printed note:

Sorry about mixup. If you see any signs of termites in the future, please appraise me and I will reinspect.

C. ADESE
Inspector

"Peculiar," Loren said. "Do you know of your own knowledge that Ben *had* called an exterminator?"

"He didn't do it in my presence, no. But—" She turned to Dunphy, who was polishing the head of his cane with his palm. "You remember, don't you, Conor, that time you and Norm and Blanche and Ben and I had dinner at the little Lebanese place in town and you and Ben were talking about some case where a man sued because he bought a house that turned out to be infested with termites, and that made Ben worry about the possibility of termites in our house and he said he was thinking about having someone come out and look things over?"

"That's right," Abelson cut in. "Saleem's. That was the name of the restaurant. This must have been last fall, I suppose. September, maybe October. My wife could probably give you the exact date if you need it, Professor, and a complete rundown on what everyone was wearing, too. Blanche is like Iris; she has that kind of a memory for little things."

"He could have called the exterminators from his chambers," Dunphy pointed out. "Most of us take care of routine items of business from our offices when nothing urgent is happening on the court."

"Did this exterminator go upstairs to inspect the judge's suite?" Loren demanded. So far, the big question of the night, he thought.

"He never went upstairs at all," Iris answered firmly. "I was sitting right there on that divan by the door, the gray one with all the pillows, and I could see the stairway every minute and he never used it. And"—she anticipated his next question—"there is no back stairway."

"He didn't go upstairs even to use the bathroom?"

"He used the one on this floor," Iris said.

"Another dead end," Norman Abelson said, and he drained the last of his coffee and took a conspicuous glance at his watch. "Gentlemen, it's late, and I have a miserable day at the office tomorrow. If I'm not needed any longer, I think I'll head for home." He jackknifed up from the soft low couch, bent to grasp his sister's hand, shook hands with Loren. "I can let myself out," he announced, and marched briskly to the foyer.

"Before you go," Loren called after him, "one more question."

The administrator whirled and faced Loren, waiting.

Loren pointed at the lid of the magenta shoebox. "What is 'Radisson'?" he asked. He looked around the circle of faces. "Can anyone here tell me?"

"I can," Jeanette Richmond said. "It's an exclusive women's shoe store in the city that opened about a year ago. The corner of Twelfth and King. An excitable little Frenchman named Albert Radisson owns it."

"You've shopped there? Do you own a shoebox like this one?"

"Not that color," she told him. "But I've bought two pairs there, I think, since the place opened. And, Mother, you bought me a pair of slippers for my last birthday that came from there, didn't you?"

"Yes. Yes." The answer seemed to terrify Iris as she stammered it, and she took another gulp of water from her tumbler.

"Have you ever bought shoes there for yourself?" Loren asked the widow.

"No!" she shrieked. Then, more calmly, "There's a very nice shop in the Spruceknoll Mall, about ten miles from here. I've bought all my shoes there since we moved to Capital City."

The justices were shifting restlessly in their seats, finishing their whiskey or wine or coffee, checking watches. Justice Goldner cracked his knuckles; Justice Berendzen played with her white gloves. Loren sensed that it was time to call it a night. "Let's wrap it up for now," he proposed. "But I want all you men to do one thing before we meet again—call it a homework assignment." Justice Colasanto fought to suppress another of his giggles. "Check with your wives tonight and find out if any of them have bought shoes from this Radisson. If they have, see if any of the boxes they came in is missing. Report to Conor in the morning; and Conor, I'll call your chambers to get the results. Jeanette, if any of your shoeboxes are missing, you call Conor, too."

The justices rose and the hum of their conversation drifted

across the large front room as they moved toward the foyer, shaking hands again with Loren as they passed him, some leaving at once, a few waiting to use the bathroom. Dunphy stayed behind until he had placed the shoebox in a brown paper bag. Then he lurched to his feet and trailed behind his colleagues, leaning heavily on his shillelagh, the bag nestled protectively under one arm.

"Jon Lutz drove me out here," he told Loren, "and is dropping me off at the State House so I can lock this damned shoebox in the court's safe, and then he's driving me home. Like a lift into town with us? My secretary made a reservation for you at the Belvedere Inn downtown and you'll want to rent a car in the morning." He shifted his weight to his good foot, put down the paper bag and drew a cracked cowhide wallet from a hip pocket, removing a plastic rectangle from one of the wallet's compartments. "You can use this credit card to charge your expenses to the court." He pressed the card into Loren's hand.

"I'll be with you in a minute," Loren said. "Iris, before I go, would you mind giving me a quick look at Ben's suite? I want to see exactly where you found the shoebox."

Iris and Jeanette led him up the carpeted staircase to the second floor. The key shook in Iris' hand as she unlocked the door to the place where her husband had worked and slept. Loren spent five minutes exploring the rooms, feeling among the suitcases neatly arranged on the shelf of the walk-in closet, sensing the women's eyes watching him from behind as he rummaged.

And found nothing.

With his back still turned to them, he thought of the bizarre words Judge Richmond had fought to whisper in his ear in the moments before his death. Now was the time. There just might be a connection. He faced them, stepped out of the closet, shut the door. "Iris," he said, very carefully, "you didn't happen to find anything else hidden in there, did you? A letter, a record, maybe a tape of some sort?"

A look of puzzlement and anxiety held the widow's exhausted face. Loren would have sworn her emotions were completely genuine, that she was hiding nothing and had no idea what he was talking about. "No, Loren," she said. "Just the box."

"God," Jeanette said, "wasn't that enough?"

They locked the suite behind them and descended. Loren found his two-suiter and attaché case set outside the foyer closet and Justice Lutz waiting patiently on an antique wooden chair near the front door. He exchanged farewells and quick kisses with the women and hefted his luggage and followed the justice into the thick warm night. Ragged clouds raced across the star-sprinkled black sky. Cricket chirps sounded in the tall grass.

With Lutz behind the wheel and Dunphy and Loren riding in silence in the backseat, the paper bag between them, the Fleetwood sped east on the Expressway with a blithe disregard for the fifty-five-mile-per-hour limit. At 12:25 A.M. Loren said goodnight and stumbled wearily out under the portico of the Belvedere Inn. He dragged his suitcase into the empty lobby and registered under the indifferent gaze of the night clerk, a tired heavyset woman. The elevator shot him to the fourteenth floor. Inside his room he double-locked the door, set the chain, braced a plastic-covered armchair against the knob. Then he threw off his clothes and scrubbed himself under the hottest shower he could stand, letting the roaring water redden his body, relax and unwind his nerves, so he could forget the shoebox and the encounter in the subbasement of the law library for a few hours and get some sleep. He toweled himself dry and lifted his two-suiter onto the luggage rack and unzipped it and pulled out of it a sport jacket and two pairs of slacks. Something fell out of the suitcase and onto his bare foot. He bent over to pick the object up. It was a small white cassette, and through its tiny plastic window he could see a stretch of tape.

Loren paused, then went to the phone and dialed the desk clerk. Apparently the hotel didn't have a cassette recorder. It would have to wait until morning. Almost relieved, he turned to bed.

He tossed fitfully through what was left of the night. As first light crept through the heavy drapes, he fell into a frenzied half doze that was worse than no sleep at all. He dreamed that he was stretched out paralyzed on a highway, his back and arms on the gravel shoulder, his legs extended into the road, and that hundreds of automobiles roared over his legs, one after the other, an endless parade of autos, Fords and Chryslers and Lincolns and Hondas and Cadillacs and Buicks and Volkswagens, all systematically pounding his lower body into a bloody pulp.

FOUR

By seven he was awake but as exhausted as if he hadn't slept for a week. His muscles felt stiff and cramped. A numbing fog dulled his thinking. The bedclothes were a frenzy of twists and tangles. He stumbled to his feet, showered again—this time with ice-cold water—shaved and dressed, then went to the hotel restaurant off the lobby and fueled himself with tomato juice and French toast and roast beef hash and eggs. After a fourth cup of black coffee he paid his check and walked to the front desk where he picked up a complimentary map of the city and asked the clerk for directions to the nearest budget car-rental office. He walked five blocks through auto-choked downtown streets, rented a Volkswagen, inquired how to reach the nearest audio store. At Elston's Soundarama he bought a battery-powered Japanese cassette player and, yawning lustily, fought inbound traffic back to the Belvedere. In his room he hung the cardboard Do Not Disturb tag on the outer doorknob and double-locked the door and took the cassette from his pocket and inserted it in the player. He lowered himself into the stiff armchair, put his feet on the bed, pressed the PLAY switch. Listening was not going to be easy, not if this tape was what he thought and feared it was.

The tape wound through the player heads, but for a minute there was only silence. Then a little static—sudden, crackling. And then the voice came on. A deep familiar voice, but speaking low, as if afraid someone might be listening.

"*Testing, testing,*" it said.

Loren could not mistake the voice. It was Richmond's. There was another half minute of silence before the voice returned, stronger now but hurried, running words together, as the judge never had when Loren had known him.

"*I'm dead now, Loren. If you're listening to this, it means I've been dead for a year. I am making this recording in my chambers. It is eleven-twenty P.M.; the date is April tenth. I've been thinking all evening how to go about this. Loren, I have to tell you some things no one else knows. Please don't be hurt by what I'm going to say.*

"*Last month my doctor told me that I have inoperable cancer.*"

His voice did not lose a fraction of its strength or dignity as he said it.

"*In all likelihood this is the year I'll die. I have decided to tell nobody but one person, and to continue my work on the court until I reach the point where my illness may affect my judgment. But meanwhile I have to get my life in order. Loren, I need your help.*

"*I'm going to put it bluntly; there's no time to waste words. Iris and I have not been together—we haven't been lovers—for nearly twelve years now. She developed what I can only call a refined disgust with the physical side of a relationship. I've done some reading about this condition and found it isn't unheard of for women in their mid-thirties. There was nothing I could do about it. She wouldn't even discuss it with* me. *She didn't want a divorce, she didn't want to have to raise Jeanette alone, and I didn't have the heart or the guts or whatever you want to call it to divorce her."*

So that explains the separate bedrooms, Loren thought.

"Eventually we worked out a kind of tacit understanding. We'd continue our lives as normally as possible, and as far as other women were concerned, I would be ... I guess you could say ... a free agent. Iris knew I would be extremely careful, and I was. The proof of how careful is that unless you are a hell of a better actor than I think you are, this is all a ghastly shock to you. I won't go into details, Loren. Not now, not ever."

No wonder he had such empathy for people caught in traps, Loren thought.

"Most of the women were casuals. Some were in impossible marital situations as I was. I never even hinted to any of them what I'm telling you straight out now. By being very selective and very cautious, I avoided even a hint of scandal all the time I was on the court of appeals.

"When I was named to the supreme court and moved here, I knew I'd have to redouble my care. The suffering that my family would endure, and the other justices, and the people who entrusted this responsibility to me, the tortures they would go through if any of this should ever leak—when I thought about that, I was ready to give up the physical side of my life if it meant jeopardizing so much. And then, Loren, it happened.

"I won't tell you her name or anything about her, not now. But about eight months after I came on the court I met a woman. It was almost as if a miracle had happened. She was everything I ever wanted and needed. She wasn't a teeny-bopper or anything; she was a grown, experienced woman, poised, sophisticated, liberated, loving, understanding.... It was magic, Loren. I don't know if it's ever happened to you that way. I hope it has."

Loren thought of Lucy, of how he had loved her, and

thrown her away, and how he had loved her again years later and lost her again. It was all he could do to keep from shutting off the tape and tossing it into the trash. But he had made a commitment. He had to know what Richmond would say about the forty-nine thousand dollars.

"*We were lovers within twelve hours of the time we met. It wasn't just physical desire, Loren; it was everything. We each had our separate lives and neither of us intruded into the other's world, but we built a world of our own, just for us, as often as we could see each other; we—oh, Christ, I can't go on with this. . . .*"

Loren's nerves tautened at the sudden silence. Was that the end? Had he or someone else erased whatever came later? He studied the sweep second hand of his watch. Ten seconds, fifteen, twenty. . . . Richmond's voice faded in again, strong as ever. Loren released a long-held breath.

"*She is the only person I've ever told about my . . . domestic situation, until now, when I'm telling you. I loved her so much I had to tell her. She accepted it. It changed nothing between us. Then, about a year after we'd met, one night she cried in my arms and told me something she had been keeping from me but couldn't any longer. In the first few months she had been careless. She'd gotten pregnant.*"

Another pause; two, three, four, five, six seconds.

"*She knew we couldn't have the child. She had gone away and had an abortion.*"

Pause, two, three, four.

"*She said she'd done it for the sake of both our separate lives and our life together. And she hadn't told me, because she didn't want me to feel guilty. . . . And tomorrow evening I have to see her and tell her I'm dying. Making this tape is like flaying myself alive, Loren, but tomorrow's going to be worse.*

"*I can't say any more. Just this: I have to make sure she knows how much I cared. Obviously I can't leave her anything in my will. In the time I have left I am going to liquidate certain securities I own, turn them into however much cash I can obtain without making waves. Somehow I'm going to arrange for that money to reach you after I'm gone. This money will be yours, Loren, in trust to convey it to her. To my woman. I'll have to arrange for you to know her identity after I'm gone, too. Loren, I know I can't compel you to do this for me, but please, remember the night at the Boatmen's Bar when I asked you to come to work for me, and that rainy morning I called you into my chambers and told you about the faculty opening at the law school that I had recommended you for, and please, Loren, do this for me. Good-bye, and thank you."*

The player made a sharp clicking sound and silence flooded the room again. On the chance that there might be more at a later part of the reel, Loren kept the machine running. The high whine of a vacuum cleaner sounded from the corridor. After seven minutes of silence from the tape he no longer expected anything but didn't dare turn it off prematurely. He sat in the stiff green chair and thought about what he had heard, and what he hadn't.

Who was the woman, and how could he find her? Was the recording genuine? Was that in fact the voice of Ben Richmond, speaking of his own volition? Loren would have wagered his career that it was. The precisely detailed references to the time the judge had hired Loren as his clerk and to the time he had worked behind the scenes to secure him a faculty position proved the authenticity of the tape more surely than a dozen witnesses.

Had Richmond actually obtained the money he expected to raise? Unanswerable. But Loren could make a reasoned guess. The forty-nine thousand dollars in the Radisson shoebox might very well be the funds for the nameless woman, raised legitimately but in secrecy. If Loren could somehow trace those bills and tie them to property transactions in Richmond's last months, the circumstantial evidence that the judge had taken a bribe would vanish like morning dew. He would have to get hold of a private detective who could be trusted, retain him to trace the money without explaining why. Then, if the hunch proved out, he would have to tell Dunphy, but perhaps no one else would need to know and the money could still be transferred as Richmond had wanted.

The cassette player gave another click. Loren saw that the tape had been played through. He reversed the cassette in the machine and pressed the PLAY button again. The opposite side of the tape began its silent journey through the player heads.

Of course, there was another possible explanation for the money. Suppose Richmond had found he couldn't raise the amount he needed without leaving too broad a trail. Might he not in desperation have solicited an under-the-counter cash payment to guarantee a favorable vote in some pending case? Another unanswerable. Loren felt a sick emptiness in the pit of his stomach.

Then there was a further puzzle: Who had slipped the cassette into his luggage, and why? The possibilities fell within a tight circle. The only time his two-suiter had been out of his control, from the time Norman Abelson had carried it to the limousine until Loren had unpacked it in this room, had been the period when it had been stowed away in the foyer closet of the Richmond house. The case hadn't been locked, and anyone at the meeting—Iris, Jeanette, Abelson, one of the justices—could have ducked into that closet and slipped the tape into the two-suiter within fifteen seconds. And there had been enough confused milling about when the meeting had broken up that almost anyone in the group could have done it while Loren had been upstairs with the women, inspecting the judge's bedroom closet.

And a final question: Where was the balance of Richmond's communication to Loren? How had he arranged for

Loren to discover the whereabouts of the money and the identity of its intended recipient? Or had that part of the plan gone haywire?

The ruby button glowed in the base of the telephone and a harsh ringing scattered Loren's thoughts. He stretched in his chair and grabbed the receiver. "Hello."

"Top of a lovely morning, young Sherlock!" It was the lilting brogue of Chief Justice Dunphy. "Just wanted to report that all the men justices checked with their ladies on your shoe question. Mrs. Lawless and Mrs. Goldner are the only ones who've bought footwear from the elegant Monsieur Radisson, and neither of them found a shoebox missing. And Jeanette says none of hers is gone either."

"Okay, Conor, thanks," Loren muttered absently.

"I detect a note of distraction in the voice. Did you go barhopping after we dropped you this morning?"

For a moment he considered telling Dunphy about the tape at once; then he decided to keep his mouth shut until he had more facts. "Just worn out," he said. "I never sleep well the first night in a strange bed. . . . Thanks again for calling. I'll be in touch." The chair's cushion hissed as he stood to replace the receiver in its cradle. He perched on the unmade bed and resumed his thinking.

There was no way of knowing whether Richmond had worked out a satisfactory plan to give Loren the rest of the needed information. But if he didn't want to throw up his hands and abandon that part of the puzzle, he had to assume for now that there had been such a plan. Somewhere outside this hotel room there was a message from a dead man, waiting for Loren to find it. Where? Loren thought back to the time between April 10 of last year, when Richmond had sat in his darkened chambers and made the tape, and the raw December evening when Jeanette had called from Stoner Memorial Hospital and told Loren that her father was on the edge of death. Had he had any letters or phone calls from the judge in those months, any contact at all that might have contained a clue? He tortured his memory and couldn't recall a single letter or conversation. Well, if not before Richmond's death, then how about afterward? No, he had received nothing after the judge's death, nothing except the set of Story's *Commentaries on the Constitution* the judge had left him in his will.

Lawbooks. Will. That was it! That had to be the answer.

He snatched the phone, dialed eight for long distance and a number back home that he knew by heart. After two rings a chirpy female voice came on at the other end. "The Hooft Agency. May I help *you?*"

"Marc Hooft, please.... This is Loren Mensing.... No, that's *M* as in 'mnemonic,' *E* as in 'eiderdown.'" Ms. Chirp giggled wildly into the mouthpiece as she did whenever Loren played that game with her, and said she'd see if Mr. Hooft was free.

The voice on the line after a series of harsh clicks was the musical burble of Marcus Jaan Hooft. "*And* how may I serve the distinguished legal scholar this morning?"

"Hi, Marc. I'm up in Capital City today, and you may serve me by going down to the law school right now and breaking into my office."

"What violent behavior for a mild June day!" The voice of the oversized private detective remained unruffled. "May I use a skeleton key, or do I have to kick the door in? And what do I do when I'm inside?"

"The first thing you do is search for a folder labeled 'Richmond, Ben.' It's probably in the second drawer from the bottom in the file cabinet up against the window. When you've found it, call me from my office." He read off the digits typed on the center of his dial. "And before you go, one more thing. I'm going to need a Capital City detective, a good reliable person who doesn't mind working in the dark. Got any suggestions?"

Hooft's singsong hum drifted over the wire as he thought. "Tremaine Investigations," he pronounced finally. "I don't have the number handy, but they're listed. Tremaine is a tough and competent an operative as, um, as you'll desire. May I ask what unholy brew you are fermenting?"

"Later," Loren said. "Much later. Call me as soon as you find that folder, Marc. And my expenses are covered on this one, so bill me what the job's worth.... Thanks much." He hung up, dug the phone directory out of the bottom bureau drawer, found TREMAINE INVESTIGATIONS, dialed nine for a local line and then the number.

"Good morning, Tremaine's." Judging by her voice, the woman on the other end might have been a TV pitchperson. Bright, cheery, eager to sell the world. Not quite what Loren expected from a detective agency.

"I'd like to make an appointment to see Mr. Tremaine today, if possible," he said. "My name is Mensing."

"Well, you can't see Mr. Tremaine," the woman told him zestfully. "He doesn't exist. I am the Tremaine of the business, Mr. Mensing."

Stupid, stupid, Loren berated himself. Assuming that a private operator recommended as tough and competent had to be a man. Hooft had set him up for this. In fact he had even dropped a subtle hint with that comment about Tremaine being as competent as Loren would desire. He wondered how attractive this woman really was.

"I'd be delighted to have the appointment with you, then," he said, "and tell you in person that I'm sorry. That is, if you don't mind a client who's still tainted with sexism."

"If I did, I'd starve," she told him. "Eleven-thirty this morning?"

Loren's watch read 10:23; he could give Hooft till eleven to call back and still make it. "Looks good. See you then, Ms. Tremaine. And thanks."

With thirty-five minutes to occupy before he left for the appointment, he hauled the sticky armchair in front of the portable color TV and turned on the set. Twisting the channel selector, he discovered that the city was served by four stations. Two were running game shows, one a cartoon-frolics festival and the fourth an old Charlie Chan movie. He settled back to enjoy the proverb-spouting Chinese who made detective work look so damned easy.

At 10:49, by his watch, the phone shrilled. Loren snapped off the set in the middle of a Confucian aphorism and caught the call on the second ring. "Marc?"

"Speaking. From your office and with file in hand. What do I do now?"

"Look through it for a letter from a Capital City law firm. I forget the name, but it's dated a couple of months ago and talks about some lawbooks Judge Richmond left me in his will."

"Momentito." Loren heard the crackle of paper behind the Hooft hum. "Found it."

"When does the letter say Richmond executed his will?"

"Hum *hm*, hum *hm* ... dated June fourteenth last year," the detective said.

Which confirmed what Loren had dimly remembered: that the execution of the will postdated the making of the tape. "All right," he said. "Now look up at the top shelf of the bookcase that faces my desk. Do you see a three-volume set of books with calfskin binding? ... Fine. Take them down to your office and search them for some kind of communication. ... No, I don't know what kind. Maybe a letter, maybe one of those new miniature tape cassettes stuck into the spine, or it could just be that some printed words are dotted or pricked with a needle to make a code message. It could be anything. If you find it, keep calling me here till you get me in."

"How roughly may I treat the books?" Hooft asked. "They look to be rather rare."

"Rare and valuable. Treat them as gently as you can. And by the way, Marc, I've got a date with your macho colleague Tremaine. You didn't really think I'd miss that blatant hint of yours about her being a woman?"

He depressed the phone button long enough to get a dial tone, then drew a scrap of paper from his wallet and dialed a number he had scrawled the afternoon before: the private line of Chief Justice Dunphy.

"Good morning again, Conor. Things are moving. Didn't you say last night that you were going to stop at court after you dropped me off and put the Radisson shoebox in the court safe?"

"Yes, and that's just what I did."

"I have an eleven-thirty appointment," Loren went on, "and I want to take the box with me. Without the money, of course. If I come by in, say, fifteen minutes, can you have it ready for me?"

"Can and will," Dunphy promised. "I trust you won't drop it down a convenient sewer."

"You know me better. Thanks, Conor. See you soon."

FIVE

It was the first time he had heard of a private eye who kept an office in a shopping center.
Loren drove along the pavement that fronted Midwood Mall. The macadam field to his right held parking slots for more than a thousand cars, but seven out of ten spaces stood vacant in the bright June morning. On his left, the supermarket and two discount stores and the cafeteria and the cheese shop and the movie house and several specialty stores waited for hordes of customers who never came. Some plutocrats had sunk millions into building a suburban-style shopping center carved out of what had been five square blocks at the edge of the black ghetto until the bulldozers had leveled the neighborhood to rubble. The hundreds of empty spaces in the parking lot showed that the idea had been a disaster.
Loren parked the rented VW, picked up the shoebox in its protective paper bag, locked the car and followed a side pathway through the heart of the mall, past a record shop

and a plant store and a sewing center and a soft ice cream emporium. Thirty-seven Midwood Mall was the last building in the row. He turned the shining brass knob and stepped in. A rush of chill air greeted him.

Chairs and low tables were arranged along one pine-paneled wall, and a government-gray steel desk took up the center of the reception room. Loren could hardly make out the furniture for the greenery that choked every spare inch of space: in pots, in windowboxes, in wall brackets, in terraria, hanging from hooks in macramé slings. Giant plants, dwarf plants and all sizes in between. Phoenix palms and zebra plants, calamundin and angel princess and goldenrain trees, krimson queen, African violets, Boston ferns and the lowly begonia, all neatly labeled as in a store or a public garden.

A woman rose from a kneeling position between two mismatched armchairs as Loren entered. There was a long-spouted watering can in her left hand. She was tall, slender, fine boned, and her blue-gray eyes were alight with laughter. She wore her long pale-blond hair in a ponytail. Her office attire was a thin beige shirt and blue jeans, with nothing beneath the shirt. Loren guessed her age at twenty-eight.

"Hi," she said. "I'm Val Tremaine, and it's eleven-thirty, so you must be Loren Mensing. You know, it wasn't till after you'd hung up that I recognized your name. My God, you're practically a celebrity!" She held out a strong but delicate hand. "Just let me finish nursing my babies and we can go into my office and chat."

There was something so disarmingly natural about her that even before he had said a word he was glad he had come here. She finished her circuit of the reception room, watering plants, smoothing their leaves, talking to some of them, ignoring Loren completely until the job was done. Then she set the can under a table piled with out-of-date business magazines and beckoned him to follow her.

The first piece of furniture in the inner office that caught

Loren's eye was a corner worktable that had obviously once been a door, lying on its side and supported by two low file cabinets. The walnut desk was bare except for several small plant pots along its edges, and another group of plants was arranged in a row on top of the supply cupboard. Loren and Val dropped into the room's two armchairs. "Brown-bagging lunch today?" Val shot a glance at the paper sack in Loren's lap.

"That's no lunch," Loren said. "It's your job. The first part of it, anyway. But maybe I'd better tell you a little bit more. You may want to kick me out when you hear how little."

"I used to go with a man who was a cop downstate while you were legal adviser to the commissioner," Val replied. "He told me a few stories about cases you got involved in. If you're on one of those again and can pay a reasonable price, I'll be glad to work with you."

"Even if you have to do things without knowing why?"

She leaned forward, her bright eyes serious now. "Mr. Mensing, a woman private detective doesn't have the world beating on her door, offering jobs. I don't like to work in the dark, but if you say there are reasons, I'll accept that—for now, anyway. So where do we start?"

Gingerly Loren slid the magenta shoebox out of the paper bag and onto his chair arm. "Don't touch," he warned. "I want you to dust this for fingerprints. Inside, outside, all surfaces. Then I want you to trace whatever you can about its history. It came from an exclusive shoe store in the city, run by a Frenchman named Albert Radisson. I'll have more jobs for you later." He reached into his breast pocket for his checkbook. "And a retainer now, of course. How soon can you get started?"

She rose and took a fresh yellow legal pad from her desk and slid it under the shoebox. "I started when you walked in. If you'll give me five minutes, I'll dust this right away." He leaned back and watched her clear a space at the corner table and set the box down. She rummaged in the supply cupboard for a brown leather kit and sat on an old kitchen stool in front of the workbench and spread magnetic black powder on the shoebox lid with a camel's-hair brush. She seemed to know exactly what she was doing. While she worked, Loren made a mental list of people whose prints might legitimately be found. There was Iris Richmond, who had first discovered the box; and her brother, Norman Abelson, who had counted the money with her; and Loren himself, if he'd been careless handling the box either the night before or this morning. He would have to call the court again and ask if Conor had handled the box.

"Nothing but smudges," Val Tremaine called from the workbench after five minutes of dusting and brushing. "And not a whole lot of them, either. Come on over; take a look." Loren crossed the office and stood behind her, looking down at the powder-speckled box. Val began to replace the implements of her fingerprinting kit as she talked. "So it's on to Radisson's, right? But, you know, I don't think a shoe store is likely to be able to tell who bought the shoes that came in any particular box."

"Neither do I," Loren admitted. "Someone has to check it out anyway, and I've got other business this afternoon. When you finish at Radisson's, lock the box where it's safe and call me at the Belvedere Inn, room fourteen-nineteen. I should be in this evening."

"Is there time to grab a sandwich before I go? I never eat breakfast, and I'm starved."

After his own hearty brunch the idea of another meal left Loren profoundly disinterested. But he wanted to know this young woman better, and convinced himself that he could at least nibble at a salad. "My treat," he said. "Name the place."

They dawdled over their plates in the cafeteria on the main avenue of the mall, and Loren asked casually how she had got into the detective business. "Inherited it," she said, sipping iced tea. "My husband started the agency six years ago, right after we got married. Just a little business:

bodyguard service and some industrial-security work—nothing fancy. I did the bookkeeping and helped out when Chris needed an extra person in the field. We were growing very nicely for a year or so, then—well, Chris died."

Christopher Tremaine. Loren remembered the name now, and the story in the papers five years ago. "He was murdered, wasn't he? One of those unfancy cases turned out to be connected with political graft and somebody got afraid he'd learn too much?"

"We were on a surveillance together." Her voice was a low monotone, all emotion screened out. "It was a clammy, drizzly night, and we were sitting in the car together. I had to go find a pay phone and call the office on another matter. When I got back, I found him slumped in the driver's seat with his hands clenched over his middle, trying to keep his insides from spilling out. They'd shot him four times with a silenced forty-five and he died on the operating table. No one was ever arrested for it. That's how I inherited the business."

"I'm sorry," Loren said. "I shouldn't have asked."

"It was a long time ago, and I'm over it," she said. "For a year after it happened I'd wake up in the night screaming like a banshee. I knew it was only pure dumb luck that I wasn't in the car and shot with Chris. Eventually I recovered enough to reopen the business, but before I did I went down to the police firing range and practiced and practiced till I was better than half the cops in the city. I still visit the range once a week. Then, later, I located a runaway daughter for a Japanese immigrant who runs a dojo and took my fee in martial arts lessons. Every morning, as soon as I'm up, I do twenty minutes of belly dancing and twenty of karate exercises. No one's going to catch me off guard the way they caught Chris."

Loren lifted his water glass in a sort of tribute. "You're remarkable, Val. Aggressive, competent, fragile, and you love those plants as if they were your children. I'm delighted Marc Hooft recommended you. So would I."

She took the last bite of her roast beef on rye and the last swallow of her iced tea. "Which means you think I have a fantastic body and don't know how to say it inoffensively." She laughed. "Your eyes say it for you. Okay, now that you've torn the scabs off my sores, tell me about yourself. Married, living with someone, celibate, gay?"

"None of the above." He plunged his fork into the remnants of his salad and tried to hide his embarrassment. "Sort of alone. There was a woman I cared for very much but I lost her. Twice. The second time was final." He told her a little about Lucy, who had died because she had walked up a staircase at the wrong moment.

"Oh, Loren, forgive me." Her hand reached under the table for his. "This seems to be the day for opening old wounds, doesn't it? Uh, look, I'd better hit the road for Radisson's, I guess." She rose awkwardly to her feet and Loren stood a second later.

"I'll call you after dinner, right? Thanks for the sandwich," she said.

He pushed the revolving door for her and they left the cafeteria and headed for their cars, not even saying good-bye when they separated in the sunbaked parking lot. An observer would have taken them for total strangers.

Loren kept the VW at fifty-five, heading east on the Donovan Parkway, exited at the Fenton Boulevard ramp, took Fenton along a three-mile stretch of factories and polluted air. Just beyond the smokestacks the state university campus began, and he swerved among narrow streets until he found a parking lot that was open to visitors. He locked the VW and hiked six blocks north to the red-brick fortress of the law school. The building was all but deserted, like his own school downstate: a few students and faculty secretaries wandered aimlessly through the high-ceilinged halls. Loren bought several pads of legal paper in the tiny bookstore and followed the main corridor to the swinging oak doors at the far end that gave on to the law library. Orienting himself with a diagram on a bulletin board just inside the doors, he climbed narrow stairs to the mezzanine and settled into a deep alcove. Behind and on both sides of him were high steel shelves that held the volumes of the official state reports of appellate court decisions. Loren thumbed through the numbered reports until he had located the first book to contain decisions in which Ben Richmond had taken part, four and a half years ago. Systematically he took down one volume after another, working his way forward, skimming every decision the court had handed down during Richmond's time on the bench.

The justices decided perhaps a hundred cases a year, so that Richmond had voted in nearly four hundred decisions. Which cases would have been most likely to lead to an offer of a forty-nine-thousand-dollar bribe in return for his vote? The only way Loren could answer that question was to read the court's decisions, eliminate those that seemed improbable and hope not too many remained. He began with two assumptions that were reasonable, but not, he knew, airtight. One: only a case in which far more than forty-nine thousand was at stake would lead to a bribe in that amount. That eliminated almost all of the court's criminal rulings; the vast majority of defendants were indigents, represented by public defenders, and couldn't have raised that kind of money if their lives depended on it. It also eliminated many of the cases interpreting state statutes or procedural rules, and a lot of the negligence cases, in which, win or lose, an insurance company footed the bill and passed on the cost to the consumer. Two: assuming that a bribe had been offered to Richmond and to him alone, the case must have been a close one, with Richmond likely to have the swing vote.

Loren read, skimmed syllabus paragraphs, took notes, eliminated, read more. In the relevant four-year period he found only a handful of high-stakes cases that had been decided by four-to-three or five-to-two votes. At 4:10 he went down to the main floor, asked the student attendant at the front desk where he might find the books on business history and law, snatched three fat volumes from the shelves housing the business materials, returned to the mezzanine.

He forced his bloodshot eyes to study more pages and scrawled more notes that he could barely decipher.

By 5:30 he was bone tired, fiercely hungry, his eyes so bleary he half believed he was going blind, and he was almost certain he had found the case he wanted.

In re Bennell's Will. July, 1976. The majority opinion had been delivered by Justice Richmond.

> The issue to be decided on this appeal concerns the premature termination of a testamentary trust established under the will of the distinguished industrialist Stanford Ives Bennell, who died a domiciliary of this state in 1919. The facts are complex, the legal issues close and difficult, the amount of money involved prodigious. After full consideration we hold that the termination of the trust, within the lifetime of one of the life beneficiaries named therein, is not permissible under the terms of the trust or the applicable law, and consequently we reverse the decision of the court of appeals to the contrary. . . .

Loren looked at the notes on the history of Benneco Industries that he had taken from the business books. All he could make out were dark scratch marks on a yellow surface, meaningless as ink smears. He laid his glasses on the table, rubbed his tortured eyes. A dazzling phantasmagoria of shapes swam and cavorted against inner darkness. With his head buried in his arms he rested his eyes and thought about what he had read on the life and times of Stanford Ives Bennell.

The founder of Benneco Industries had been a nineteenth-century robber baron in the grand style, a ruthless and expert player in the game of capitalism. Like his peers, he ruined competitors, manipulated markets, bought and sold politicians, hired goons to maim and kill union organizers. Unlike his peers, he diversified his holdings before it became accepted business practice. His companies held the oil rights to thousands of Texas and Oklahoma acres and to lucrative petroleum concessions in Venezuela. Brazilian coffee, tropical fruit, tin, rubber—there was hardly a Latin American export that a Benneco subsidiary did not control to one extent or another. To guarantee a steady supply of cheap native labor and the right to do business exactly as they pleased, Benneco and similar large corporations shoehorned friends of free enterprise into the seats of power in the Central and South American countries in which they operated. If a popular movement should arise that seemed to threaten the companies' profits, the friendly authorities would call out troops, fire into crowds, beat a few of the leaders to death, jail the rest and disperse the movement in short order. If radicals should gain footholds in the local government itself, Benneco had enough influence in Washington to demand that Marines be dispatched to crush the evil forces. That was the way things were done. By the time Stanford Ives Bennell died, of lobar pneumonia at the age of seventy-eight, his personal fortune amounted to more than seventeen million dollars. According to the most recently published of the business histories Loren had consulted, Benneco was still a power south of the U.S. border, at least in the dictatorships of the right. And when he thought back to certain newspaper columns he had read over the past few years, he remembered rumors of connections between the corporation and the CIA that set his teeth on edge. The Latin American and CIA elements just might explain why Moraga and Rojas had tried to cripple him yesterday afternoon.

He knew that his theory was far from irrefutable, but it was the most likely hypothesis available. All of the criteria were met by the Bennell case more completely than by any other. Even the date of the court's decision fit the pattern: July of the previous year, three months after Richmond had made that tape and spoken of secretly raising money. He couldn't be certain his theory was right but he knew it had to be tested.

Loren checked his watch. Through a blur of mist the hands seemed to read 5:52, eight minutes before the library's closing hour when school was not in session. He needed more time, had to refresh his basic knowledge of trust law and form an opinion as to whether the Bennell ruling squared with the general principles in that field. If it didn't, his theory would be much stronger. Then Loren remembered that he had read in a legal-education newsletter last year that Jerome J. Deckler had accepted an appointment at this law school. And Jerry was both a specialist in trusts and estates and an old compadre of Loren's.

It was worth taking a chance on. Jerry had always been the hard-driving type, the kind of person who never took a vacation, never knocked off early, had to be accomplishing something every minute or pay the penalty of feeling guilty. He was one of the few professors who was likely to be in his office at six o'clock on a beautiful summer evening. Loren gathered his papers, made a photocopy of the Bennell decision at a coin-operated machine, and pushed through the doors out of the library. The faculty directory in the entrance foyer gave him the number of Jerry's office. He took the stairs to the second floor and found two-thirty-eight and rapped on the gray door. "Come!" a fierce, familiar drawl called out, and Loren entered.

He almost didn't recognize the man. In the summer after their first year as professors Loren and Deckler had spent a frantic two weeks living on cheeseburgers and three hours' sleep a night while grinding out a tactical manual for lawyers representing conscientious objectors and draft resisters. In those days Jerry had been a vibrant, energetic maniac, with a rangy Gary Cooper build and a deep cowhand accent and long thick hair and beard and an insatiable lust to exhaust himself in the good fight. The man who sat at the desk surrounded by mountains of blue examination books was clean shaven, and only a few strands of hair were left across the center of his head. He wore a gray three-piece sharkskin suit with hand-knitted tie, and the Swiss gold watch on his wrist gleamed in the late sunlight. "Loren!" he thundered, and leaped up and squeezed his hand in the grip Loren remembered of old.

"Eight years," Loren said. "My God, that's a long time. And they seem to have turned you into a Wall Street groupie. All out of righteous causes?"

"Oh, years ago. The firebrand from Arizona's burned out. Been through two marriages, changed faculties twice, and I'm going to be forty in August. It's time for peace and stability. As Hegel, or whoever it was, said, 'Let pass in contemplation what occurs.' The sixties are dead, chum. There's nothing left worth crusading for. Why, do you realize how many contradictions there are just in the Bill of Rights? All those B-Western-movie good-guy-against-bad-guy fights are over. Now it's just the good guys fighting the good and the coyotes eating each other. Deal me out." His words came in a torrent. At least the old excitable motor-mouth delivery that drove students into hand-crippling frenzies of note-taking had survived the acid of the years.

"Jerry," Loren said, "I need your expertise for a few minutes. And I'm going to collapse if I don't get supper pretty soon, so let's talk over grub, okay?"

They sat in scooped-out orange plastic chairs at a table in a remote corner of the student-union cafeteria and concentrated at first on the food and small talk. The coffee was tepid and muddy, and Loren had eaten better mostaccioli in frozen TV dinners, but he was too hungry and preoccupied to care and he chewed his meal mechanically.

Over wedges of tolerable lemon pie he brought up the reason for his visit to Deckler. "Jerry, I've got a problem," he began, "and I can't tell you what it is. But I'd like you to give me a rundown on a case the supreme court decided in your area a year ago. *In re Bennell's Will.* Know it?"

"Lovely case," Deckler muttered through a forkful of pie,

and swallowed hastily. "Probably get printed in half the T & E casebooks over the next ten years. Lays out the policy considerations on premature trust termination better than anything I've seen lately."

"Go over the case for me. I want to make sure I understand the situation."

"You asked for it." Instantly Deckler was transformed into a professorial lecturer—precise, analytical, speaking in a rush of words and almost defying the listener to follow the line of argument. "Bennell's will directed that most of his estate—and this included several thousand shares of Benneco Industries, which he founded, so it was a huge estate—was to be transferred in trust to a foundation he created in that same will: the Bennell Foundation. It still exists, by the way; the headquarters is here in the city. The will named several trustees and set up procedures for replacing those who resigned or died during the life of the trust. Now the trustees were directed in the will to invest and reinvest the trust assets and use the proceeds to pay annuities in various specified amounts to each of . . . I think it was forty-three different members of the Bennell family, which was a pretty widespread one. Each of these forty-three annuitants was to receive this amount every year as long as he or she lived. When the last annuitant died, the trust was to terminate, and the will directed that at that time the trustees were to divide the property equally among eight remaindermen, all of them Bennells, of course, but different people from the forty-three annuitants. And if any of these eight lucky dogs should happen to be a dead dog at termination time, that one-eighth share was to be divided among his or her next of kin, as in intestacy. As fate would have it, all eight of the remaindermen died while some of the forty-three life annuitants were still kicking. Got all that so far? I haven't seen you take a single note."

"Photographic memory," Loren said. "Okay, what precipitated the lawsuit?"

"The last living annuitant," Deckler went on. "A guy in his eighties named S. Gordon Bennell, who lived in St. Louis, I think. This old bird signed some documents relinquishing his midget annuity to a descendant of one of the eight original remaindermen, and that descendant transferred what had been S. Gordon's share to the trustees of the Bennell Foundation. Well, obviously, these transfers had been set up so as to cause the trust to terminate and get the corpus distributed right then rather than wait till old S. Gordon hung it up. That's what started the suit. On the one side you had those descendants of the eight original remaindermen who'd share in the assets if the trust were terminated then and there. That group argued that you didn't have to wait till S. Gordon died to end the trust, that his signing away his rights amounted to the same thing. On the other side you had the children and grandchildren of the living descendants of the eight remaindermen who wouldn't get cent one if the trust terminated right then because their own living parents would bump them, but who just might wind up with shares through the intervening deaths of their own ancestors if the trust was left intact till S. Gordon's death."

Loren held up his hand like a traffic policeman. "Whoa, boy. That last sentence of yours lost me. Remember, I haven't studied property law since I was in school."

"Okay, let's call one of the eight dead original remaindermen B. He has three living children, X, Y and Z, and *they* each have two kids, X^1 and X^2, Y^1 and Y^2, Z^1 and Z^2. If the trust ends at that point, X, Y and Z each take one twenty-fourth of the total pot. Their kids would take nothing because there's a basic principle of intestacy law that a living parent bumps a child from an intestate share of an ancestor's estate. And remember, old Bennell specified that the descendants of dead remaindermen should take as in intestacy. *But* if the trust ends at a later point, and if, say, Mr. X dies before S. Gordon Bennell, then X^1 and X^2 split their parent's share and each takes one forty-eighth of the property.

"And so the X group and the X^1 and X^2 group fought it out. There were issues about whether S. Gordon's interest was properly conveyed to the trustees—who might or might not have legally accepted it—and issues about whether the trust instrument allowed termination in S. Gordon's lifetime. The district court said terminate, the court of appeals affirmed, and the supreme court reversed, four to three. Richmond wrote the opinion of the court. Dunphy and ... I think it was Lutz and Ms. Justice Berendzen dissented."

Loren forced himself to swallow the last of the coffee. "How good technically was the court's opinion? Was it sound, consistent? Anything, er, askew or off key about it?"

"That's a bizarre question if I ever heard one. Well, personally I think Dunphy's dissent is the better view. I don't believe in the dead hands controlling property from the grave, but I guess you'd call that a policy disagreement I have with the court. I could be a nitpicker and punch some technical holes in Richmond's reasoning, but by and large it's a good sound piece of judicial craftsmanship."

They pushed back their chairs and carried their loaded trays to the conveyor belt inside the hatchway that led to the dishwashing area. "So," Loren summed up, "the trust still exists and the Bennell Foundation still runs the show."

"Unless S. Gordon curled up and died recently," Deckler said as they pushed through the turnstile at the exit. "Okay, Loren, I've opened up for you. So how's about you doing the same? Why this sudden interest in a case that's been *res judicata* for a year?"

"The blue spruce in front of this building is the loveliest I've seen on any campus," Loren explained.

Deckler frowned. "If I didn't have a bar association meeting in half an hour," he said, "I wouldn't take that for an answer. Well, my Ferrari's over in lot G. Tell me what you're up to when you can, okay?"

"When and if," Loren stipulated, and they shook hands and separated. As Loren headed back to the visitors' lot he made a resolution that tomorrow, whatever else he did or did not accomplish, he would pay a visit to the headquarters of the Bennell Foundation.

Pale blue dusk was blanketing the skyline when Loren swung the car into the Belvedere Inn parking lot. There was nothing left to do till morning, and bone-numbing exhaustion held him in a vise. When he crossed the parking lot to the side entrance of the hotel he walked like a man in a straitjacket. He swore that he would fall straight into bed and sleep like a corpse for twelve hours minimum before he would think about or touch the damned case again.

At the front desk he asked if there were any messages in his box. The gray-haired woman clerk handed him six pink slips of paper. Loren almost cursed her aloud, but offered polite thanks and trudged blindly to the elevator. On the ride up he spread them in his palm like a poker hand. Two were from a Miss Tremaine, who had called at 6:15 and again at 7:00 P.M., leaving no message and no number for him to return the calls. The other four were from a Mr. Hooft, who had phoned every hour on the half hour from 4:30 on. Loren let himself into room one thousand four hundred and nineteen, locked himself in, shucked off his clothes and crawled into bed.

He was just drifting off into sweet oblivion when the harsh ring of the phone jolted him awake. He said some words he was glad there was no one to hear and groped blindly for the handset. "*Unkh*," he muttered into the mouthpiece.

"No, this is not your uncle," the familiar amused burble sang in his ear. "In the best Sherlock Holmes manner I deduce that I woke you."

"Sort of." Loren focused on his watch on the bedtable, which read precisely 8:30. "Should have known you'd call now. All the phone messages must mean you found something."

"Merely a sheet from a thin three-by-five scratch pad,

folded over and sealed around all the edges with strapping tape. There seems to be a key inside, and some writing, but I haven't tried to make it out. It was inserted in the spine of Volume Two, held in place with a few dabs of glue. It, ah, took a bit of doing to find and free the thing, and I'm afraid your precious books are going to need rebinding. Should I cut the tape and read you what's inside, or just mail it to you?"

Loren held a brief donnybrook with himself over the answer. If that paper contained a second message from Richmond, he wanted desperately to know what it said, but he was simply too exhausted to wrestle with any new problems tonight, and he didn't dare have the paper and the key entrusted to the tender mercies of the United States Postal Service or risk their lying exposed in his hotel mail slot for the hours between the time they would arrive and the time he would return to pick them up. "I know it's asking a lot," he said finally, "but I want you to send the thing up here tomorrow morning with an operative you can trust not to open it. Have this person drive or fly up and meet me in this room between nine and ten A.M. I'll hang around waiting till ten."

"It will cost you," Marcus Jaan Hooft trilled cheerily, "but, if that's how you want to play it.... Which somehow reminds me, I happened to be down at headquarters this afternoon on another matter and bumped into your old amigo Sergeant Hough. What's this I hear about two men with forged CIA credentials trying to unleg you yesterday?"

So the official line was that the credentials were forged. That meant either that Moraga and Rojas were private hit men and the police had a lead on them, or that they really were CIA and a cover-up was in the works. Loren knew that he could never hope to learn which was the case by making any more long-distance calls tonight. "Oh, just one of the routine incidents in a busy law teacher's day," he answered lightly. "You didn't tell Hough you were on a job for me or where I was staying?"

"Have I ever betrayed a client's confidence?" Hooft declaimed. "All right, I'll have Tommy Novo drive up first thing in the morning. May I be of further assistance?"

"Let you know later," Loren said.

"Then nighty-night and pleasant dreams," Hooft chimed, and broke the connection. Loren dialed the front desk and left word that any further callers should be asked to call again after eight the next morning, and, to make doubly sure, he set the phone in the bed-table drawer before he snapped off the lamp.

When he woke again, the window drapes were lightening from black to dirty gray. He stayed under the covers, listening to the hum of the air conditioner, wriggling his toes under the sheets, luxuriating in a slow languorous adjustment to the waking world. After a while he showered and shaved, straightened the room, switched on the TV and absorbed half an hour of national and local news. By eight he was ravenous. Visions of the sumptuous breakfast buffet downstairs danced before his eyes, but he was afraid to risk leaving the room because Novo and the second Richmond message might arrive at any time. He studied the room-service menu propped against the bureau mirror, winced at the tripled price of every item, then remembered his credit card and pulled the phone out of the drawer and called downstairs with an order for orange juice, the international omelet, toast with marmalade and a pot of coffee. Waiting for his breakfast, he fidgeted in front of the TV and wished he had thought to pick up some paperbacks to fill the empty time.

A light tapping shot him out of the chair and over to the door to let in the room-service boy.

Who wasn't a boy at all. A tall slender young woman with pale-blond hair in a ponytail and steel-blue eyes gleaming with delight wheeled in the service cart and made him a butlerlike bow. "Breakfast is served," she intoned. "I'm sorry, Loren, I couldn't resist coming up unannounced after I tried to call last night. And then when the kid with the tray stopped at your door, I paid for it and tipped him and told him I'd do the honors. He probably thinks we're lovers or something."

"I was dead on my feet last night, Val." Loren deposited the covered tray on the round table by the windows. "Sit down, grab a bite if you're hungry, we can share the silverware."

"I told you—I never eat in the morning." She perched on a corner of the bed and with a look of pleasure watched him eat, as if seeing someone else devour a hearty meal satisfied an appetite of her own. "Want my report now?"

Loren washed down a mouthful of eggs and melted cheese and chili relleño with the last of his juice. "Ready when you are," he said.

"Well, I told you I'd probably strike out, and I did. Albert Radisson is a darling little gray-haired Frenchman in his fifties who wears Nehru jackets and an ankh around his neck. He opened the shoe shop two years ago and does very well weez eet. There is no way he or anyone else can trace who bought the pair of shoes that box of yours originally held. He tried to date me three times in less than an hour and insisted that I take a complimentary pair of sandals when I finished interviewing him."

Loren debated asking whether she planned to go out with Radisson and decided that it was none of his business. "Where's the box now?"

"Locked up in my office desk," she said. "What's my next assignment, if any?" She swept her hand back through her silky hair.

Loren sipped coffee, thinking how he could use her help today, savoring her company but wanting her out of the hotel before Novo might pop his head in the door. "How are your contacts with the city newspapers?"

"Couldn't be better. My best girl friend is sports editor of the *Demagogue* . . . I mean the *Democrat*. Local joke. Want some tickets to a ballgame?"

"I want everything you can dig up for me on an institution here in the city that's called the Bennell Foundation. They run the estate of Stanford Ives Bennell, the guy who founded Benneco Industries."

"God," Val whispered, "the Bennell syndrome."

Loren tossed her a look of incomprehension. Not only had his research into the history of Benneco and the litigation over the old pirate's trust uncovered no such entity as a "Bennell syndrome": he wasn't even sure what precisely a syndrome was.

"You haven't heard of Bennell's disease, then?" Val asked.

"Well, I knew Stanford Ives Bennell had died of something," he said, "but I understood it was some kind of pneumonia."

She shook a playful finger at him, like a grammar-school teacher correcting a child who spelled cat with a *k*. "No, no, Bennell's disease is something that runs in that whole family. There was an article about it in the feature section of the Sunday paper a couple of years ago." Her voice grew serious and a little strained. "It scared me," she said.

Loren glanced at his watch: eight-forty-two. He didn't want Val and this Novo to see each other, but the disease sounded worth pursuing. He finished his coffee and shifted his chair around to face her directly. "Tell me what you remember," he said.

"All I can recall is that it's a very rare form of degenerative nerve disease that goes back to the first Bennell that settled in America, early in the eighteen hundreds. He had a mess of children and passed it on to them and they passed it to their kids and here we are. It's a genetic disease and there are supposed to be about three hundred descendants that have had it. No one realized what it was till recently. All through the generations the family thought it was congenital syphilis and kept it hushed up."

"What are the symptoms?" Loren asked.

"You lose your coordination and start to walk with a

stagger, like a drunk, and your speech gets slurry. That's the beginning of the end. Once you have those symptoms you've got a year, maybe a year and a half, to live. If you call watching your body break down living."

Loren fought to hold back a shudder. "God," he said. "What a birthday gift for your children. Makes you know there's a lovable old man watching over us from the sky. . . . But wait a minute. Stanford Ives Bennell didn't die of this disease, and there's an old Bennell in St. Louis who's over eighty and still healthy as a horse. How many people in the family get hit with it?"

"I don't know," she told him. "So much of the medical history over the generations has been hushed up by the family and the doctors that probably it's impossible to tell. One in two, one in three. But in every documented case the first symptoms struck before the person was thirty. I remember reading that."

No wonder certain members of the Bennell family might be desperate to take their share of the trust immediately rather than count the crawling days until S. Gordon Bennell would die. If he had happened to be born into that family, Loren wondered, and if he were still in the under-thirty danger zone, would he have offered Ben Richmond a bribe in order to secure a measure of comfort, and perhaps specialized medical care, for himself and other members of his family? Had Ben known anything about the disease? If he had known, compassionate man that he was, how could he have resisted voting to terminate the trust at once, letting those millions be spent on research to cure this hideous sickness? Or was he thinking primarily of the litigants on the other side, the younger ones, who would take nothing if the trust were distributed at once? Purely in human terms, which was the better decision? And might not Richmond's position be rationally defensible even if he had been paid to adopt it? Loren was suddenly very thankful that he was not a judge.

"Knock knock"—a soft female voice scattered his thoughts—"anyone home?"

"Got carried away, I guess." He shook himself like a drenched dog. "Imagine what it would be like to carry that damaged gene with you day after day, knowing that any morning you might wake up and start staggering on your way to the john and that once that happened you had a year or so of physical degeneration to look forward to and then you'd be dead. ... I almost said a thank-you that neither of us and no one I care for is a Bennell."

"So did I," she confessed, "and I don't like myself for it. Loren, something in your face tells me you want a lot more information about Bennell's disease."

"I think it may be relevant," he said slowly. "Yes, that's exactly what you'll do next. If you find that article you mentioned, copy it for me, and make copies of anything else that's been written on it. Check the State U Medical School library; there might be some specialized stuff in one of the journals. Plus, I want some general background on the Bennell family and the foundation, and last but not least, if you run across any hint of CIA involvement in Benneco Industries operations below the border, copy everything you find."

She sprang from the edge of the bed with a bound of eagerness. "I feel like I'm back in school and you've just assigned a term paper, Professor," she said, grinning. "Not the usual PI work, but I can cope. Anything else?"

"Would you happen to have a portable printing press in that supply cupboard of yours?" Loren asked. "The kind you can use to print up phony business cards?"

"No good eye would be without one," she said. "Need a new paper identity?"

"I think I might. Tell you what: On your way to the newspaper morgue, stop at the office and print me something that makes me a journalist." He thought for a moment.

"From *Businessways* magazine. And my name will be—oh, make it Jack Mackenzie."

Val nodded her head. "I've got someone office-sitting today, so you can drop by later and pick the cards up. Anything else?"

She seemed to want him to ask her for some additional item, and Loren screwed up his courage and decided to take a leap. "Oh, yes," he said casually. "Why don't you give me a number where I can reach you after hours? Uh ... just in case it becomes necessary."

"Thought you'd never ask." He sensed a provocative glimmer in her eyes as she dictated the number, but she might have been teasing, or he imagining. "That's my apartment in town," she explained. "It's a dump. I've got a house I built myself out in the sticks forty miles from here, but there's no phone, so I can't be reached when I'm there."

"I'd like to see the place sometime," Loren said. He had a sudden fantasy of lying in her bed in that isolated house, after a night of lovemaking, and watching as she did her morning belly-dancing exercises for him. He lowered the curtain on that scene instantly and hoped she hadn't guessed what he'd been thinking.

"Uh, look," she said carefully, "I'd better hit the road for the *Democrat* morgue before we both get sidetracked. This job should work out better than the disaster yesterday. Give me a ring tonight and I'll let you know." They said good-bye at the door and Loren watched her walk smoothly down the corridor. He felt a racing inside him, and ordered himself to be cool and skeptical and lawyerlike. His body ignored the instructions and his mind kept conjuring images of her. He paced to the bed and sat down and realized he was sitting precisely where she had sat and jumped to his feet and paced some more.

Novo, Novo, where the hell was Novo?

He dropped into the hated plastic armchair and flicked the TV on savagely and beat a tattoo against the Formica-topped table and forced himself to sit through kiddie cartoons and reruns of ancient situation comedies, until, at 9:42 the phone shrilled. He leaped up and caught it on the first ring. "Hello," he barked.

"*Good* morning, Herr Doktor!" The honeyed tones of Marc Hooft sang in his ear. "I have a disturbing message to convey to you from Tommy Novo."

"Okay, let's hear it," Loren said, bracing himself for the worst.

"Tommy had the misfortune of two simultaneous blowouts on the Interstate a little before eight. It seems that a farm pickup dropped a load of tenpenny nails on the rural stretch halfway between here and the capital and two of those nails wound up in Tommy's front tires. The nearest garage is in a village several miles from the spot and he wasn't able to get a tow truck till a short while ago. What would you like him to do?"

For a wild moment Loren considered driving south and picking up the Richmond message from Novo at the garage. Then, on second thought, he dropped the notion. He had other things to do in the city today, and desperately as he wanted to see that message, it could wait a few more hours. "When will Novo be on the road again?" he asked.

"Oh, an hour, maybe two, maybe three. You can't rush these hayseed mechanics, Tommy tells me."

"All right. Call him at the garage and tell him to keep coming. When he gets here, he's to check in at the Belvedere and wait. He is not to leave his room unless there's a fire. I'll contact him when I get back this afternoon." He thought of the two hit men who had almost crippled him. "And tell him to be damn careful if he sees any Latin-looking strangers. Thanks for the call, Marc. See you later."

When he had broken the connection, he scooped up the directory from the niche below the night table and found the address and phone number of the Bennell Foundation.

SIX

The house was a beautiful monster, a soot-blackened limestone castle set on a half acre of meticulously landscaped grounds at the end of one of the private streets off Duke Boulevard. Loren parked the VW and stood in the narrow roadway and marveled at the place. Stone steps led under a double archway supported by granite pillars. Gable roofs stabbed the sky, Romanesque sculptures decorated the elaborate facades, and half the front windows seemed to be stained glass, like the windows of a cathedral. The edge of what must once have been a coach house was visible through a screen of birch and elm. From somewhere behind the mansion Loren could hear the whine of a power mower.

He climbed the front steps, passed under the archway, pulled at the bell. A polished bronze plaque to the right of the oak door read THE BENNELL FOUNDATION in proud but not ostentatious capitals. The door inched open the length of a chain bolt and a wedge of female face peered out at him.

"I'm Jack Mackenzie." Loren smiled, salesmanlike, and handed a freshly printed card through the opening. "With

Businessways magazine. I've been assigned to do an article on the foundation. May I come in?"

"Journalists usually make appointments with people they want to interview," the woman told him. Loren sensed the undertone of suspicion in her voice. He had expected to hear it and had prepared for it in advance.

"Why, my office did that, ma'am. My editor in New York told me that I had an appointment at the foundation for this morning at eleven." He stole a glance at his watch and gave her a sheepish grin. "Sorry I'm a few minutes late; that crosstown traffic jam was murder.... Why, ma'am, you don't think a *business* magazine would have flown me all the way from New York without setting up an appointment first?" He allowed a look of befuddlement to invade his expression, as if she had seriously suggested that the moon was made of caviar.

"Well, I can assure you, Mr. Mackenzie, that no appointment was made." The woman unchained the bolt and threw the door open to the bright summer morning. "But as long as you've come all this way I suppose we can spare you a little time. I'm Lillian Bennell." She switched her half-smoked cigarette to her left hand and held out her right. Loren shook her hand with just the right smile of awkward thanks for her graciousness. She was below average height, somewhere in her fifties, her face lined like a well-used map, her hair dyed silver and cut mannishly short. Her body was still firm and attractive. An armada of silver bracelets clashed on her wrists. There seemed to be an immobility about her eyes, as if she had trained herself never to look to the left or right of her but only straight ahead.

"Boy, will there be a flap at the office over this screw-up," Loren muttered darkly. "Fire someone for sure.... I can't tell you how grateful I am for letting me talk to you, Ms. Bennell." He gawked at the gleaming mosaic floor of the entrance foyer, the profusion of paintings and tiny sculptured figures on shelves in the broad corridor, the sweeping oak staircase at the end of the hall with a minstrels' gallery at the landing. "This is the most gorgeous house I've seen in my life," he said.

"It's a nice place to work," the woman admitted, making swift nervous gestures with her cigarette. "It was built by my great grandfather's brother in 1889 at a cost of half a million dollars—that's 1889 dollars—and was two years in the making. Stanford Ives Bennell imported a sculptor and two woodcarvers from England, traveled all over Europe picking out different woods for the floor of each room. At one time twenty-three people lived here, and that included eight maids, a butler, a carriage driver and a live-in doctor for the family."

In view of the Bennells' medical problem, Loren could see the need for the doctor. "You sound as though you've given people the grand tour before," he commented.

"I have to," she said. "The place is a damn landmark, the best surviving example of Richardsonian Romanesque architecture in the United States. It's open to the public one morning a week and I take them through the display rooms. Come on along; I'm doing the pitch again tomorrow and I could use a rehearsal." She led him through room after high-ceilinged room, cluttered with period furniture and artwork. The library was filled with built-in bookshelves fronted with glass, presided over by a gold-framed wall portrait of a mustachioed ancient. "My great-granduncle," Lillian said. "Stanford Ives Bennell. A noble American and a noble man."

Mirrors decorated with ornate filigree; grandfather clocks, polished, and ticking loudly; a monumental Flemish breakfront from the seventeenth century; rich Oriental carpets on the waxed and gleaming floors—only the chattering of an electric typewriter somewhere in the distance broke the illusion that he had traveled centuries into the past.

Lillian Bennell ended the tour by stepping into a small office next to what had been the servants' dining hall. She sat behind the antique desk, lighted another cigarette from a hammered-silver table lighter, and looked expectantly at Loren, who dutifully dropped onto a mohair divan and plucked a spiral notepad out of his breast pocket.

"What my editor is looking for is a portrait of a private foundation in action. That's his way of putting it, not mine," he said with a slight laugh. "But that's my assignment, so here goes. How many people are actually involved in administering the Bennell trust?"

"There are five trustees including myself." She puffed spasmodically on her cigarette between sentences. "We're scattered all over the country, however, and meet only twice a year. I am the president of the board of trustees and the active head of the foundation. We employ a full-time lawyer, an accountant and an investment adviser, plus two secretaries—that's their typing you hear—and of course the domestic help. And then there's a young woman who is a graduate student in American history, doing her master's thesis on Stanford Ives Bennell and the golden age of capitalism. We gave her a little office in the basement and access to the Bennell family records, but she's been out with the flu for the last two days. Otherwise, she could fill you in on the family history like nobody else in the world."

Loren braced himself for a crucial question. "Would it be possible for me to interview the other professionals? It would add tremendous depth to my article."

Lillian Bennell pressed a switch on the interoffice speaker and ground her cigarette butt into an overflowing tray at the same time. Four minutes later her tiny office was bursting with people and she herself was darting around the room like a silver firefly, introducing everyone, pouring sherry from a Victorian sideboard, gesturing compulsively, bracelets clicking.

"Harlow Emmet, our accountant; Mr. Mackenzie, from *Businessways*." The balance-sheet man looked about fifty, with the windburned face of a sailor, a stocky body and a vanishing hairline. He had a way of clearing his throat before everything he said that grated on Loren's nerves. When he was not talking he would crack his knuckles loudly.

"And this is Roy Taylor, who handles legal matters for the

foundation." The lawyer's hair was brown flecked with gray, trimmed precisely. He was compact of build, with a delicate and almost feminine way of moving, and a voice that was a hoarse whisper. "Bullet in my throat when I was in the service," he explained as he gave Loren's hand a gentle shake. "Korea, 1950."

"Corinne Kirk, our investment counselor." The woman was slender and subtly tantalizing, with naturally wavy reddish-blond hair. She wore a tailored gray pantsuit and carried a briefcase-size bag under her arm and moved in a self-created aura of cool, poised competence.

Loren had prepared a battery of questions on the drive from the Belvedere Inn. What was the present amount of the trust corpus? How much in annual income did that corpus generate, and in what kinds of securities was it invested? What percentage of the income of the trust was spent on administrative expenses, the upkeep of the magnificent house, the salaries of the professional staff? What was done with the balance of the income? Was the last surviving annuitant, S. Gordon Bennell, still enjoying good health? Loren felt his way carefully, like a soldier advancing inch by inch through booby-trapped terrain, accumulating information in small fragments without risking any of the direct questions that might be met with tight-shut mouths and the statement that the interview was over. And after nearly an hour of undermining their resistance, he asked the questions that most concerned him: questions about the litigation to terminate the trust; questions about the last surviving annuitant, the man from St. Louis whose signing away of his rights under the trust had precipitated the termination suit. "Just who is this S. Gordon Bennell, anyway?" he inquired of the room at large.

"A dear old gentleman," Corinne Kirk replied. Her high musical voice reminded Loren of Japanese wind chimes. "He'll be eighty-five years old in November and I understand he still plays golf and squash once a week and works out for fifteen minutes a day on one of those rowing machines."

"An old fool," Lillian Bennell corrected acidly. "And senile, no doubt, despite all that exercise. There's no other explanation for the way he relinquished his interest and started all this furor. We were just extremely lucky that the supreme court reversed the lower courts' decisions about breaking up the trust. But the life of the foundation depends on his life, so we have been subsidizing a combined bodyguard and nursing service for him round the clock over the past several years."

Loren cleared his throat carefully. "Er, I take it you're all happy with the outcome of the litigation?"

"Oh, there's no question the court came to the right conclusion," Roy Taylor croaked softly.

"It's not my field," Corinne Kirk said. "But I like this foundation; I like my job very much and I'm glad we're staying in existence awhile longer." She raised her sherry glass to the light that filtered in through the stained-glass window, almost in a toast to victory.

"Silly suit," Harlow Emmet stated bluntly after clearing his throat. "Not economically justified. The group that wanted to break the trust should have run a cost-benefit analysis first."

"I've told you over and over, Harlow, it wasn't a group!" Lillian Bennell slammed her palm against the desk blotter. "It was that disgusting degenerate John Philip Wood. I know it was. He would do anything to tear down this foundation." Her long red-nailed fingers curled into talons. Loren sensed a piece of the puzzle he hadn't yet encountered, and decided to pursue it.

"Uh, that name's a new one on me, ma'am," he ventured politely. "Who is this John Philip Wood?" He turned his notepad to a fresh page and prepared to summarize her answer.

"John Philip Wood is the only son of Harold and Roberta Wood. His mother was one of the eight original remaindermen—or should I say 'remainderpersons'—in my great-granduncle's trust. She died fifteen years ago. John Philip Wood is a long-haired bearded filthy hippie, a communist, a degenerate, a draft dodger, a fugitive from justice, a radical journalist who was in five or six guerrilla wars in South America. He is everything this great country of ours stands *against*. He is a dangerous maniac and belongs in prison or an asylum, or in front of a firing squad. If I ever see him again I think I would shoot him on sight."

Loren wrote frantically and fought to keep a sympathetic look on his face. "Well, ma'am, uh, that's a pretty strong statement, and my editor doesn't like libel suits. But maybe we can express your, uh, point of view without running any risk, if you'd let me ask a few more questions about this man Wood. What makes him so eager to break up the trust, anyway?"

"His reason is very simple." Lillian swiveled her tan leather chair to face him and let her diamond-bright eyes burn into his. "A considerable block of Benneco Industries stock is in the trust corpus. Wood wants as many of those shares as he can get for his one-eighth interest, and he can use the balance of his interest to purchase more shares from the other distributees or on the open market. With control over enough stock he hopes to dictate certain policies to management and perhaps even to put himself on the board of directors."

"But for what purpose?" Loren insisted. "What can he gain?"

Lillian Bennell tapped the desk top with her nails, studying Loren in cautious silence as if deciding whether he was to be trusted. When she had made up her mind, she leaned back in the swivel chair, lighted another cigarette, crossed her legs. "Mr. Mackenzie, I'm sure you're familiar with the published news stories, the rumors, the innuendos about Benneco's operations in certain Central and South American republics that are friendly to the United States. That muckraker Frank Bolish has devoted several of his columns to the subject, and Jack Anderson, and I forget who else."

"I've heard of the stories," Loren admitted, "allegations

that Benneco's had a long history of letting the CIA use company facilities in friendly countries as cover for... I think the term is destabilizing operations in countries that aren't so friendly."

"This foundation has nothing to do with managing Benneco Industries," Lillian said. "But I believe those stories have some truth in them, and I am proud of the company if they do. That is what Comrade Wood is determined to sabotage. And there is enough Benneco stock in the trust so that he has a chance to succeed if the corpus is distributed. I believe that he would stop at nothing to break up the trust, not even at murder. Which is why this foundation is paying a private detective agency in St. Louis to guard Mr. S. Gordon Bennell twenty-four hours a day."

Harlow Emmet cleared his throat but said nothing. Roy Taylor shifted uneasily in the straight chair he had carried in from the rear hall. Corinne Kirk's face wore a look of embarrassment, as if she wanted to disassociate herself from her employer's opinions without giving offense. Loren felt a strong urge to cross-examine Lillian Bennell until she withered, but he restrained himself and struggled to preserve his dispassionate journalistic front.

"Uh, you indicated that you had met this Wood at least once, ma'am. Did he tell you at that time that this was his intention?"

"Oh, no! The party trains its agents better than that. I'm sure we met four years ago when the entire Bennell family had a conference about the disease, but I literally cannot remember a thing about him from that occasion. But about two years ago, shortly before the lawsuit was filed, he came to see me on the pretext of asking what position the foundation would take if S. Gordon Bennell should relinquish his annuity rights, whether we'd fight the termination of the trust. Well, his clothes and his appearance and his manner and the comments he dropped about America and the Third World gave away his true purpose. He disturbed me enough so that I retained the Kurtz Detective Agency to run a check on him, and that report is the source of what I've told you about his background."

"Do you know where he's living now?"

"Anywhere. Nowhere." Her hands made nervous gestures in the air. "The agency couldn't find a permanent address for him. He had been a college student in the late sixties, a leader in the so-called peace movement. His draft board reclassified him one-A and he never showed up for induction. Vanished into the underground. Apparently he spent some time in South America and perhaps in Cuba. Eventually he was amnestied, like all the other draft dodgers, and I don't believe there are any charges against him now, but he's an elusive man who seems to prefer living in the shadows."

"I wonder," Loren mused, "if my article would be more, uh, in depth if I tried to find him."

"I advise you not to bother," Lillian said. "But if you should encounter him, Mr. Mackenzie, watch yourself. He's a smooth-tongued spellbinder and can talk very glibly about oppression and torture by fascist juntas and the suffering millions of the Third World. He could convince you white is black if you were gullible."

"Oh, Lil, international intrigue has nothing to do with it!" Corinne Kirk broke into the conversation impatiently, and bent forward to touch Loren's arm with her forefinger. "Mr. Mackenzie, are you aware that every member of the Bennell family is subject, until they're over thirty, to a very rare genetic disease that science just doesn't know how to treat?"

"Uh, yes, I researched that a bit before I flew out here," Loren said, and hoped the investment counselor wouldn't question him further on the subject.

"A big share of the trust income goes to fight the Bennell syndrome," Corinne went on. "We've endowed chairs in genetic medicine in the three leading medical schools in the country, and we are underwriting experimental research at the National Genetics Foundation. Four years ago, when the doctors identified Bennell's disease, we financed a gathering of every member of the family we could trace, paid expenses for three hundred-odd people to go to a medical center in Los Angeles and get all the information there was about the syndrome. Ever since then we've been paying the cost of an annual checkup at the center for every person in the danger zone—air fare, doctor's bills, lab fees, the works. It adds up to several million dollars a year. When the trust terminates, the corpus fragments into dozens of shares, and all that effort to end this awful curse is over. That's why I'm so delighted that the trust property is now worth almost two hundred million dollars. That's why I put in fifty to sixty hours a week, trying to make the trust as profitable as I can. That's why this foundation fought the lawsuit." Her eyes were bright with the zeal of a crusader.

Loren wondered how much of this background Ben Richmond had known before he had voted to preserve the trust. He asked himself whether Lillian Bennell, with her contempt for John Philip Wood, might have offered Richmond a bribe to decide the case her way. He speculated whether Corinne Kirk, with her desire to see the fight against Bennell's disease go on, might have offered a bribe of her own. His impression of the accountant Emmet and the lawyer Taylor was that they were professionals who couldn't care less in a personal sense what the outcome of the suit was, but who just might have tried a bribe if they were afraid their own lucrative jobs with the foundation would end with an adverse ruling. But something more than these possibilities puzzled him. He closed his notepad and drew himself closer to Ms. Kirk.

"I'm confused," he said. "Are you suggesting that all the dozens of Bennells who would each take a piece of the trust property wouldn't get together, pool their resources and keep supporting the research?"

Harlow Emmet cleared his throat. "Some would, some not," he cut in. "Simple matter of cost-benefit analysis. If you're under thirty, or if you're over but have kids or want to have them, you probably would. Otherwise you might prefer to enjoy yourself with the money."

"The Bennell descendants are a microcosm of America,"

Roy Taylor croaked. "They are rich and poor, young and old, selfish and caring, liberal and conservative. They are divided among themselves, as we all are. They have to die eventually, as we all do. The difference is that they know this in their bones every day."

"Yes, Roy, but remember, some of the people who brought the suit were under thirty," Corinne Kirk insisted. "You see, Mr. Mackenzie, the ones in the danger zone are dissatisfied with the doctors' not having found how to control the disease. Some of them prefer to protect their health in their own ways, or just to forget it, have a ball, and if they die, they die."

"Wouldn't you love to marry a Bennell woman?" Harlow Emmet asked Loren without clearing his throat.

About ten minutes later, in the midst of a string of innocuous questions whose answers did not concern him in the least, Loren read the body language of the others in the room as telling him he had stayed long enough. Their shifting in chairs, glancing at their watches and one another—everything conveyed the message that they were tired of being interviewed and wanted lunch. He tapered off with some final pointless queries, thanked everyone profusely, promised to send an advance copy of his article to the foundation, and was escorted by Lillian Bennell through the breathtaking foyer to the front door. It was almost one o'clock. Novo must have checked in by now, he thought. He started his car, turned out of the drive and headed downtown.

Halfway to the Belvedere Inn he swerved off the boulevard into the lot of a fast-food restaurant and ordered a roast beef and melted cheddar sandwich and coffee. When the food arrived, he took his tray to an outdoor table on the tiny paved terrace and chewed on what he had learned this morning. He was convinced of several propositions. First, any one or any combination of the people who worked on the Bennell trust in that magnificent house might have offered Ben Richmond a bribe to decide the case so as to keep the trust in being. But then, a bribe might also have been offered by any one or any combination of the several Bennells who had fought the suit to break the trust. And if those political columnists were right, and Benneco's Latin-American interests were closely tied with the dirty-tricks department of the American intelligence agencies, the CIA itself could have offered the bribe if it, like Lillian Bennell, felt its operations threatened by the termination of the trust. Loren made a mental note to call Frank Bolish within the next few days and learn more about the CIA connection. With his network of informants within the government, Frank might be able to tell him whether it was CIA men who had tried to keep Loren out of the case by crippling him.

Loren sat on the terrace facing the stream of boulevard traffic, the sunlight beating on his shoulders. He felt a slow wet crawling down his spine—not sweat but an icy-cool sensation, the same feeling he had experienced in the sub-basement of the law library before the hit men had appeared. The feeling of eyes watching him. From somewhere. Everywhere.

He had shrugged off that feeling the last time, and the watchers had been there. He couldn't shrug it off again. He restrained the impulse to let out a yelp and bolt for the car. Very slowly he finished the sandwich and coffee, savoring the last bites as if he might never eat again. He tossed the wrappings into a garbage can and crossed the terrace to the double row of cars in the parking lot and slipped behind the wheel of the VW and watched the restaurant and the terrace through the windshield. People were moving about in all directions, from the lot into the building, from the building to the terrace, from the terrace back to the building or to the lot. Cars going in and out of the lot formed a perpetual traffic jam at the entranceway. There was no way of telling if any of the hundred or more people in his sight had a special interest in him.

He waited for a break in the traffic, gunned the VW out of

the lot, took the boulevard east to a side street and made a right, then another right and some lefts, driving haphazardly until he was lost, and satisfied that he must also have lost any followers.

That was when he realized that a professional who wanted to track him would simply have planted a homing device in or on the VW. The thought made him feel naked and vulnerable and more than a little frightened. He stopped at a service station for a fill-up and directions and then wove circuitously toward downtown, turning in the VW at the rental agency and hailing a cab back to the Belvedere.

The electric clock behind the registration desk read 1:55 when he entered the lobby and asked the clerk if a Mr. Novo had checked in. The sandy-haired clerk flipped through his card index with ink-stained fingers and looked up. "Yessir. Couple hours ago. Room nine-seven-eight."

Loren took the elevator to the fourteenth floor and the fire stairs down five flights, feeling like a secret agent in a bad movie, and tapped on nine-seven-eight. The door opened instantly as if at an electronic signal and a short powerful-looking man with tangled coal-black hair and a glowing pipe in his hand stood facing him warily.

"Tommy Novo?"

"I'm Novo," the other grunted.

"I'm Mensing," Loren said. "Hooft sent you with a package for me."

"Let's see some ID," the short man said. Loren handed him the driver's license and the law faculty card from his wallet. "Describe what's in the envelope," the short man demanded.

"Marc said a key and some writing. And it's not an envelope, just a sheet of scratch paper folded over and taped around the edges."

"The duck flies down with the prize in his beak." The short man motioned Loren into the room, shut the door, reached inside the pillow slip on the bed and handed him a sheet of paper. "Wish I knew what this charade was about."

"You and me both," Loren said. "Okay, now you let me see some ID." The other flashed a driver's license and a private investigator's license in the name of Thomas J. Novo and sat down on the edge of the bed, watching Loren with sentry's eyes.

"Anything happen to you after the blowouts?" Loren asked. "Did you have a feeling you were being trailed?"

Novo shook his shaggy head. "Someone bird-dogs me, I know it in five minutes. Anything else before I head for home?"

Loren thought quickly. "One more job. I want you to keep an eye on me for a while and see if I'm being watched. If you spot anyone, get a description and let me know. It should take you till evening."

"Shit," Novo said. "And my daughter's playing first base in the Little League game tonight.... Oh, hell, a job's a job. What's your room number and your schedule for the rest of the day?"

"Fourteen-nineteen. I'm going there now. When I leave, you'll see me." They shook hands inside the doorway and Loren darted for the fire stairs and climbed five flights, his hand in his pocket pressed tightly against the paper.

He chain-locked the door and sat in the chair, rested the sheet of paper on the Formica-topped table, and gently lifted the strapping tape from one sealed edge. A small steel key clattered to the tabletop. Loren inspected it carefully. It did not look like a room key, but it could have been the key to anything else—a locker, a deed box, a desk drawer. He turned the key over. There was a number etched in the tiny barrel: A536. He stripped the tape from the other edges of the paper and spread it on the table, written side up.

FIRST CAPITAL CITY TRUST CO. SAFE DEPOSIT BOX YOUR NAME.

That was the sum total of the message.

The handwriting was Ben Richmond's. Loren had seen it too often not to recognize it now.

He snatched the directory and the phone, found the number of First Capital City, spun the dial, and asked the answering voice how late the bank was open. A magnolia-kissed female voice informed him that the bank opened its doors every weekday morning at 8:30 and shut them every afternoon at two.

Loren checked his watch. The hands pointed to 2:14. He hung up the phone gently and bellowed unseemly words.

He lowered himself into the plastic armchair and buried his chin in his hands. At least until Val Tremaine reported back to him, there wasn't much more he could do, but he was damned if he'd waste the rest of the afternoon watching TV game shows. He stalked to the phone and dialed and listened to Dunphy's private line ring twelve times without answer. He checked the directory, dialed the court administrator's office, and was told that all seven justices were in conference and would remain so for several hours. He broke the connection, dialed nine-seven-eight and heard Novo's soft grunt on the other end.

"Me again," Loren said. "I've got an idea how you might get home in time for your daughter's game. Come on up."

Loren sat in the bathroom with the phone directory and a blank page of his pocket notebook balanced on his knees, working out a schedule while Tommy Novo systematically searched the rest of the suite for bugging devices. After Novo gave the all-clear sign, Loren straightened the chaos in the main room while Novo checked out the bath. By three o'clock he was satisfied. "No bugs. Of course, you don't need a device planted in a room or a car to bug someone, just the right equipment and a listening post hundreds of yards away. There's no way you can be sure someone isn't spying on you these days. You either learn to live with it or you go fruitsy. What's our next play?"

Loren motioned him into the bathroom and turned on the shower full blast. Behind the roar of water, and a continuous flushing of the toilet, Loren told him the rest of the plan. "I'm going out and be conspicuous for a while. You watch me and see if anyone else is. Be back in your room at 4:30." He shut off the water and they left the room, boarding separate elevators to the lobby.

For the next hour Loren wandered the streets, dropping into a bookstore on one block, browsing in a record shop around the corner, peering into furniture-store windows, stopping at a cocktail lounge for a quick scotch. Heavy gray clouds massed overhead, threatening a sudden storm. The temperature fell fifteen degrees in sixty minutes. Loren kept his eyes front, careful not to look around for a glimpse of Novo, not to act like someone who knew he was being shadowed. That casual hour of sauntering the city streets was one of the longest and most difficult of his life.

At 4:30 he reentered the Belvedere and took the elevator to fourteen and the fire stairs to nine. Novo flung the door open at the first light tap. "You wore a tail the whole trip," he announced as Loren slipped in. "Nice piece of tail, too. Did you spot her?"

"I didn't even spot you," Loren said. "Give me a description."

"Woman in her middle twenties, taller than average, dark-brown hair in a pixie cut, curled under at the neck. High cheekbones. Sort of cute face but not really beautiful. Built like a fashion model—small tits, not much ass. Wore a tan blouse and slacks and carried a brown purse. I'm amazed you didn't spot her. She's not a pro; did too many things a pro wouldn't."

The description sounded like no one Loren knew, and he wondered how many more unknown quantities might be mixed into this devilish case. And when had this woman begun to shadow him?

"When you started drifting back this way, she split," Novo

went on. "I trailed her down Kingsley for a couple of blocks, then she grabbed a cab and I lost her. Got the cab's number, though."

"Let me have it," Loren said. "Then you can go home. I've got a local operative who can take it from here."

Novo checked his watch. "If I skip supper and don't hit any radar traps on the Interstate, I can just about make it. Thanks for the break, Mr. Mensing." They shook hands and Novo locked the door behind the two of them and trotted toward the elevators while Loren used the fire stairs up to fourteen.

In his own room Loren tried the number Val had given him. It rang twelve times and no one picked it up. Nothing to do now but wait. When she called or dropped by he would put her on the trail of the shadow with the fashion model's body. He adjusted the deadbolt and chain lock, stripped off his outer clothing and dropped into a sorely needed nap. From somewhere beyond the mists of sleep, thunder rolled and rumbled violently.

The phone's harsh ringing jerked him awake. He rubbed his eyes, groped for the handset and muttered into the mouthpiece.

"Hi, Loren. Want an earful?"

He stared blearily at his watch on the night table: two minutes past six. He'd been out more than an hour. Rain beat harshly against the windows. "Come on up, Val," he said, and sprang to his feet and splashed icy water on his face and threw his clothes on with the speed of a fireman. She rapped; he unbolted and opened and smiled. Her hair was drawn back in the ponytail and she wore a pale print blouse and corn-colored slacks and Hush Puppies, and she was drenched to the skin, her clothes clinging to her. "I scored," she said brightly. She tapped the dripping vinyl portfolio that she carried under her arm; it was fat with unseen contents. "Bennell's disease, Benneco Industries, the foundation—the works. You just woke up, didn't you? Your shoes aren't laced."

Loren looked down at his feet and began to laugh raucously. "It's been a rough day," he said when he was able to speak. "And from the looks of that portfolio I'm going to be up half the night, reading. Sit down, dry off, and tell me what you found."

"Hey, could I grab a hot shower first? The temperature's gone crazy and my teeth are chattering so hard I'm afraid they're going to chip if I don't get warm and dry. And then a bite to eat; I got caught up in this stuff and skipped lunch."

Loren remembered that she'd had no breakfast either; the poor soaked kid must be starving, he thought. In his unlaced shoes he staggered to the phone and dialed room service and ordered two brandies and a jumbo-shrimp cocktail. Behind him he heard the closing of the bathroom door, the plop of wet clothing against the tile floor. Thoughts that had very little connection with the Richmond bribe and the Bennell family held his mind in a distinctly pleasant grip. He heard the muffled rush of shower water, visualized her under the soft warm spray, and tied his shoes and went to the closet to get his robe and toss it in to her.

And then almost as soon as it had started the roar of water died.

He heard the swish of the shower curtain being swept back, the pad of feet. The door flew open and she stood on the threshold of the bathroom. Tanned and naked. Water dripping from her body onto the tiles. Her face corpse-white under the tan, her eyes stunned and vacant. A small cake of hotel soap in her hand.

And tiny streams of blood mingling with the dripping water, crawling down her arms and breasts and belly.

"May I bor—borrow your styptic pencil, Loren?" she asked in a tight quivering voice.

SEVEN

The next hour was a blur of fear and frenzied movement. Val sat naked on the rim of the tub and cleansed the cuts with soap and warm water and dabbed at herself with the styptic pencil from Loren's shaving kit until the bleeding stopped. Loren studied the soap she had been using to lather herself. The glistening edge of a razor blade winked in the center of the off-white cake.

Someone had entered the room while he was at the foundation and substituted a razor-bladed cake of soap for the used piece already in the shower dish. And the sight of a used cake of soap in the shower was so commonplace that neither he nor Novo had thought to check it when the two of them searched the room. It was the easiest thing in the world to insert a razor blade into a piece of soap. Somebody had wanted Loren to cut himself to ribbons the next time he showered, maybe to sever an artery. His stomach churned with guilt that Val had taken the punishment meant for him, and with an unreasoning panicky sense that enemies were spying on him from every corner. He felt an urge to rip the room apart. He thought of the satisfaction Moraga and Rojas had seemed to feel at the prospect of maiming him, and clenched his hands in fury and fright. This incident bore their hallmark, that same quiet pleasure in terror.

When the cuts had closed, Val gulped down both of the brandies and washed off the clinging fragments of antiseptic pencil with warm water and a freshly unwrapped and carefully inspected cake of soap, while Loren mopped the blood with a sopping bath towel. "The airport hotel's a good place to move to," Val suggested. "My car's in the lot across the street; I'll drive you. We'll stop on the way at a doctor friend of mine. I want some shots in case there were germs on that blade. You sure you don't want to call in the cops?"

"What good would it do? First of all, I'd have to explain why it happened, and second, even if I did that, which I can't, they'd probably write it off as a nasty practical joke." And if he told them he thought CIA agents were responsible, they would likely try to put him into the mental hospital for observation. "No, the thing to do is to change locations and lie low." He sat on the toilet-seat cover and took her hand in his own. "Val, I'm sorry this happened to you. I feel as if I'd cut you up myself. Maybe you should bug out of this and let me handle it."

She gave him a wry little smile and squeezed his hand. "I don't think I'm scarred for life or anything. But God, I almost fell over when I looked down at myself and saw all the blood. Loren, you're going to tell me what the hell is going on here; and whatever the game is, I'm staying in it till I meet the son of a bitch who did this."

"You're sure? These guys aren't sexists; they'd take out a woman as fast as they would a man."

"I'm not giving you a choice," Val said calmly. "All right, get your things together while I dress, then check out. I'll meet you across the boulevard with the car."

Loren packed his two-suiter with an excess of care, like someone trapped in a snakes' nest, running his hands through his clothing with infinite gentleness. No more surprises awaited him. The last thing he did before zipping the suitcase shut was to shroud the bladed soap bar in the discarded wrapper from a fresh cake and stow it by itself in one of the two-suiter's center pockets.

They drove through the empty downtown canyons, through cool evening darkness and the dregs of the storm. Val turned the five-year-old Pontiac onto the ramp for the expressway, sped west to the outlying suburbs, exited after a few miles and wound through residential streets. In front of a low ranch-type house with a signpost on the immaculate front lawn that read PAUL W. SIEGEL, M.D., she braked to a stop. Loren waited in the car while Val ran in. She was out ten minutes later, rubbing her upper arm. "No problem with germs," she said as she slipped behind the wheel. "Paul says they can't live in soap anyway, but he gave me some shots just to be certain." She swung into a K-turn and headed back for the Interstate. "That was an incredibly vicious thing to do to anyone," she said, her profile pale in the dimness of the car. "Like those bastards who put razor blades in apples and give them to kids on Halloween. I was hired on a case like that last year. Caught the guy in half a day's work."

"What happened to him?"

She swerved onto the ramp for Interstate West. "The court gave him a suspended sentence. God, I hate lawyers! But not you, Loren."

The Pontiac left the highway at the airport exit. In the broad plain downhill to their right Loren could see the expanse of airport grounds, the parking lot east of the runways, the hundreds of tiny squares of light in the steel-and-glass tower of the new hotel half a mile west of the air terminal. He would have given years of his life if he and Val could take the next Transstate flight home and never think of the goddamned case again. He felt the outline of the tape cassette and the note and safe-deposit-box key in his pocket, and knew that Val was right. He wasn't given a choice. Val snatched a ticket from the machine at the entrance gate of the parking lot and they drove down row after row until she found and maneuvered into a slot. They locked the car and strode hand in hand to the kiosk, where the escalator took them below ground to the tunnel train station.

Loren had read about the construction of the new multi-million-dollar airport facilities, but all of his trips to the capital since the project's completion had been by auto. Beneath the parking lot the engineers had built a brightly lighted tunnel, through which an unmanned "people mover" click-clacked along an oval track on a perpetual circuit that connected the parking area, the terminal building, and the airport hotel. A train slid silently into the station and Loren and Val stepped into one of the tiny two-person cubicles. They sat side by side on the orange plastic seat as the train clicked through the long garishly lighted tunnel. "If anyone followed us they'll think you're flying somewhere," Val remarked over the robotlike sounds.

The lobby of the airport hotel, an escalator flight up from the point where they left the tunnel train, was a bright oval twenty stories high, carpeted in flame red, with low couches upholstered in rose velvet and glass-and-chrome tables beside giant plants in scarlet pots. Val registered them as Mr. and Mrs. V. J. Tremaine, and they rode with the bellgirl on an external elevator with sheet glass on all four sides, bordered with bright bulbs. As the cage rose to the sixteenth floor, the view of the airport with planes lifting into the evening sky grew more magnificent every second. Within the sound-proofed hotel the thunder of jet engines was a muted rumble.

Loren didn't bother to unpack. As soon as the bellgirl had pocketed her dollar and left, they went back to the elevators and rode to the revolving restaurant on the roof. They took a table on the slowly rotating outer rim and ordered Chateaubriand and a bottle of Burgundy and savored the view of the moving horizon and the purple-gray mountains in the distance. Unwinding. Trying to banish the horrors and perplexities for an hour. Talking of little things—music, movies, likes and dislikes. By the time they had finished their coffee and liqueur it was deep black dusk, studded with airfield lights like diamonds. They went down to the room and sat in matching soft blue armchairs, with a tiny maple table between them on which Val set her portfolio.

"Thanks for not rushing me," she said. "I needed time."

"You don't have to summarize the material for me; I can read through it tonight."

"I want to," she insisted. "When I'm finished, you'll tell me what it's about. I've been wretched all day, imagining how I'd feel if I'd been born a Bennell. I want to talk it out."

"I'm listening," he said simply.

"There was a man named Jabez Bennell who was a sailor," she began. "He jumped ship in Boston Harbor in 1832 and settled in Massachusetts. He was the first Bennell to live in America. He married and had a houseful of kids and ever since then his family has been subject to this disease. There's an unpronounceable medical name for it. Wait a minute, I wrote it down." She fished among the papers in the portfolio until she found her notes. "Here it is: 'autosomal dominant striatonigral degeneration.' Bennell's Disease, for short. A professor of neurology at the University of California Medical School identified it about five years ago. He got in touch with the Bennell Foundation and the foundation got court permission to use income from the trust to finance a gathering of all known members of the family out at the medical center in Los Angeles."

"I know about the meeting," Loren said. "I visited the foundation this morning and picked up a lot of details. Tell me, what are the chances of any given Bennell getting the disease?"

"There was a medical journal article I photocopied that's in there somewhere with those papers. It said that only someone who actually has the disease can pass it on to children, and each child of a diseased parent has a fifty-fifty chance of inheriting it himself. So if you know your parents escaped, you know you're safe, but if your parent had it, you've got an even chance of getting it, too. It's transmitted genetically and can't be detected till it's too late, and it isn't medically treatable once it is detected. The longest anyone's been known to live after developing symptoms is twenty months. Of utter hell."

Loren felt the trapped hopelessness he had felt at the Belvedere when he had stared at that razor blade gleaming through the cake of soap. But this time there was no enemy to hate, not even an unseen one. Just the common human fate of pain and death. He wanted to drive all that out of his head. He fought a perverse urge to tell her to shut up.

"Tell me about Benneco Industries and the CIA," he made himself say.

Val reached into the portfolio for a handful of photocopied newspaper pages held together by a paper clip. "There's very little in print on that delicate subject, but here are a few Frank Bolish columns and one or two by Jack Anderson. They're all pretty much on the same theme—that Benneco is sort of a two-way conduit for dirty tricks. Spies from the South American dictatorships where the company's established come to the states as Benneco employees and harass dissident students from the home countries, sometimes beating them up or framing them on criminal charges so they can be deported and tortured back home. CIA agents go down to those countries as Benneco employees, act as advisers to the local intelligence people, help the juntas stay in power and sabotage unfriendly neighboring countries."

"Do you believe it?"

Her shrug was a gesture of helplessness and disgust. "Anybody with power is going to use it to hurt people without it. That's why I love plants so much and most people so little."

Loren recognized the echo of his own cynicism in her answer, and wanted to embrace her like a newly discovered sister. Instead he settled deeper into the soft blue chair and thought of Moraga and Rojas. Was it possible that they were not CIA men but members of counterpart agencies from one of those dictatorships, using forged credentials either with or without CIA's approval? He lost himself in labyrinths of thought. Could Moraga and Rojas, using those same credentials, have approached Ben Richmond, demanded in the name of national security that the Bennell trust be kept intact as long as possible, and offered him the money that unknown to them he so desperately wanted for his mistress if he would swing the case their way? Knowing the judge as well as he had, Loren still could not decide how Ben would have reacted in such a situation. But if that were the answer, it would explain much: the shoebox full of money, the attempts to maim Loren.... Much, but not everything. There was still the mystery of the woman with the pixie hair who had shadowed him downtown, and the matter of how Moraga and Rojas had learned almost instantly that Dunphy had called Loren into the case. He would have to mull over those items later.

"You're dreaming again, Loren." Val's voice jerked him back to reality. "I said now it's your turn to explain things to me. That was our deal, remember?"

"I remember," Loren said, and reluctantly dug into his pocket for the Richmond cassette. He set it on the maple table beside Val's portfolio and drew a long ragged breath. "This is going to hurt me," he said, "but here goes, from the top."

He talked for almost half an hour, describing his own clerkship under Richmond, the multiple debts of gratitude he owed the judge, Ben's death, the call from the court to investigate the shoebox, the incident in the underground garage that almost cost him his legs, the tape that had been slipped into his suitcase—every development before he had followed Hooft's advice and retained Val to help and the later developments like the safe-deposit-box key in the lawbook. The only thing he refused to do was to play the tape for her. He had to stop three times and gulp down glassfuls of water from the bathroom sink. When the story was over, his voice was hoarse and raspy and his throat felt arid and cracked.

"So even though you started out refusing to believe the

judge could have taken the money, you're convinced now that he did, and you hate yourself for not still having blind faith that he didn't sell out, and now you have to find out who bribed him and tell the whole story to the court."

"That's it," he said. "Still want to stay in the game?"

"More than ever. I owe a debt now, too." Tenderly she felt her ribs beneath the print blouse, then she raised her arms high overhead and stretched catlike in her chair, and gasped at the stab of pain. "God, I'm worn out," she yawned. "Okay, what's the menu for tomorrow?"

Loren drew from his wallet the scrap of paper on which he'd jotted down the number of the taxi Novo had seen taking the shadow woman away this afternoon. "Find the driver of that cab," he told her. "Between four and four-thirty this afternoon he picked up the woman I described, a couple of blocks from the Belvedere. I want to know where he took her. And another thing, send one of your people over here about nine in the morning with an agency car. I'm borrowing my wheels from you for the duration."

"You got it." She eased to her feet and Loren stood in turn, and she kissed him softly on the mouth. "I'm glad we're together," she whispered.

He put his arms around her very gently, remembering the razor cuts, and nuzzled her lovely neck. "Sure you don't want to stay?" he said softly into her ear.

"Wouldn't be fair," she said. "I'm feeling sore as hell already and it's going to be agony tonight. We have time."

They kissed again at the door, and Loren watched her walk down the red-carpeted corridor, holding herself a little stiffly. When the elevator door cut off her tiny figure at the end of the hall, he locked himself in and sat down again in the silken depths of the blue chair and sifted through the pile of photocopies she had left. He tried to read but his mind refused to make connections between one sentence and the next. His body seemed to be charged with tension and his nerves quivered as if a part of him that had been paralyzed had come alive again. He wanted her back so badly. Just to look into her eyes, to talk with her about life and people and what counted and what didn't count in the long painful crawl from womb to grave. He wanted to hold her naked against him and water plants with her and show her the book he was writing on the Third Reich and forge something real with her.

And she had narrowly escaped being murdered today and carried on her own body the scars that were meant for him.

He threw off his clothes and stood under the roaring shower, first scalding hot then biting cold, until his mind was together again and he could think objectively. He lay in bed in his pajamas, pillows propped under his neck, and spread the papers around him and began to read.

Until, at 11:27 by the digital clock on the night table, the phone rang.

The only person in the world who knew he was in this room tonight was Val. He scooped the receiver up in the middle of the second ring.

"Mr. Mensing?" It was a woman's voice but not Val's. A voice he didn't recognize. A ball of cold fear formed in his stomach. He tried not even to breathe into the phone, groped desperately for what he should say. After what seemed hours but was actually no more than five seconds, he cleared his throat.

"I ... I'm afraid you have the wrong number," he said. "This is Mr. Tremaine."

"Mr. Mensing, it's vital that I see you tonight," the woman insisted. "I know it's you; I followed you and the blond woman from the Belvedere. I'm downstairs in the lobby. Please let me come up."

Loren banged his fist against the night table in fury and self-disgust. With the haste and panic of their escape from downtown, they hadn't bothered to look for the woman shadow again when he had checked out, but she had been there and stuck with them and had not been fooled by their maneuver with the tunnel train.

"Oh, please, Mr. Mensing," she begged, and he thought the desperation in her voice was real.

"Are you a tall slender brunette," he asked, "about twenty-five, and do you wear your hair curled under at the neck?"

"Yes," she said.

"What's your name?" he growled.

"Marisa. Marisa Bennell."

Bennell. A voice in his head predicted that the last wisps of doubt about the connection between the Bennell case and the shoebox would soon dissolve. "Give me five minutes," he said, and dropped the phone in its cradle and made a dash for the clothes closet. Half dressed, he stuffed the photocopies back into Val's portfolio, which he then stowed inside his two-suiter. He slipped the Richmond cassette within the folds of an unused towel on the bathroom shelf, and was just fitting the safe-deposit-box key onto his ring when the knock sounded on the door. "Just a second," he called, and fumbled with his shirt buttons and belt buckle. Standing to one side of the door, he unhooked the chain and twisted the knob slowly.

The young woman in the entranceway fitted Novo's description precisely, except that she had changed to a blue-denim jumpsuit. She darted into the room and Loren slammed the door behind her. She turned to face him, holding out her hand. "Thank you for seeing me," she said. Her voice was soft, subdued but intense, her hand moist and almost clammy. Something about her reminded him of a frightened fawn.

"Sit down," he said, "and tell me how long you've been following me, and why, and what brings you out of the shadows." As they crossed the room to the blue armchairs, he studied her face. Her eyes seemed feverishly bright and there was a touch of unnatural color to her high cheekbones. She sat on the edge of the soft deep chair as if afraid of relaxing. Loren wondered when she had slept last.

"I've been following you the last two days," she said. "Yesterday I couldn't make too much sense out of where you went, except that the blonde you had lunch with at the Midwood Mall is the same woman who visited you at the Belvedere this morning and drove you here a couple of hours ago. You spent most of yesterday afternoon at the law school and most of this morning at the Bennell Foundation. I lost you after you gunned out of the roast beef place but picked you up again at the hotel."

"It's always nice to know when your privacy's been invaded," Loren said. "Mind telling me why?"

"Because the man I work with asked me to. That's why I'm here now. He wants to see you tonight. You probably know his name if Lil gave you the usual pitch at the foundation today."

"Let me guess," Loren said. "John Philip Wood? The communist hippie who's trying to tear down the South American juntas?"

She gave him a forlorn little smile. "Lil would be funny if she weren't so pathetic. She handed me that same version of the lawsuit over the trust when I went to work at the foundation."

Loren fought to absorb what she was saying and its implications. "You work at the foundation? But you certainly weren't there today, or you couldn't have followed me. . . . Ah. You must be the graduate student who's doing the thesis on Stanford Ives Bennell. Lil said you were sick with flu."

"That's right," she said. "I've been playing dedicated grad student since February, while being Woody's spy in the enemy camp."

Loren surrendered to the cushiony embrace of the chair, leaned back and closed his eyes and concentrated. "But your friend Woody *is* working to terminate the trust? I take it that at least that much of Lillian's account was true. Which means that you must be working for the same end, and since you're a Bennell, you must be one of those who were on the losing side of the suit."

"I wasn't a named party but you can certainly say I lost by the court's decision, yes. When that trust is broken up I am entitled to one-eighth of the proceeds, probably something like twenty million dollars, and Woody is entitled to the same amount. We want our shares now, Mr. Mensing. We believe we were cheated out of them. We won that suit all the way until the supreme court ruled against us by one vote. I don't think that just happened."

Loren said silent thanks that he'd hid the cassette before she had knocked on the door. He wondered how much the woman really knew. Very cautiously, keeping his voice neutral, he ventured a question. "How do you account for the court's decision?"

"Someone was paid off," she said. "Maybe more than one. You're a law professor and a sort of unofficial detective. I believe you know or suspect that what I'm saying is true and that's why you're in Capital City. Woody and I can help. We don't know who took the bribe but we do know who paid it."

"Tell me," he said, his heart racing.

"Woody has to tell you himself. It's a long story. Won't you please let me take you to him?"

"Why can't this Woody come here?" Loren demanded.

"He could be killed if he comes out of hiding," Marisa answered calmly. "There have been three attempts on his life and one on mine in the last few months. I can't force you to come with me, Mr. Mensing; in fact, I can't even phone Woody from here and have you talk with him, because there's no phone where he is." She held out both hands to him in a desperate pleading gesture. "Please trust me a little?"

Loren felt the cool moisture of her hands again, studied the dark smudges under her too-bright eyes. "Are you sure you're all right? Maybe a doctor's office is where I should take you."

"No doctor can help me," she said simply. "My father died of Bennell's disease when I was a child."

Loren gripped her hands tighter, searching for the right words to say and knowing there were none.

"It's all right," she said. "It's like being in a war: you get used to it after a while. If I die tomorrow, I've lived and loved and been loved and *wanted* things more intensely this last year than in all the rest of my life. I guess that's why being in danger doesn't mean so much to me. I have Woody, who's been in worse danger longer, and every day I may develop the symptoms of Bennell's disease and die anyway." Almost involuntarily she smiled. "Funny, most kids in their twenties hate the thought of that thirtieth birthday. I've got five more years, but if I make it to that day, I'm going to run through the woods and sing and dance and just go out of my skull with joy and Woody and I are going to celebrate like no one's ever celebrated anything before."

"Save me a ticket to the gala event," Loren said, and released her hands and took a long breath and a chance. "Okay, I'll go with you to see Woody. I hope you have wheels because I'm fresh out."

"My car's in the airport lot. Easier to bury it in the crowd of cars there. We can take the tunnel train. It's a bit of a drive."

An escalator took them from the lobby to the subbasement that housed the train tunnel. It was near midnight and the station area was deserted. They sat on a bench in the garish light and waited for the distant clacking of the train to come closer. "It's never more than an eight-minute wait," Marisa said. "The trains run all night even when there's no one riding them. Like ghost trains."

They rode the half mile to the parking lot in a tiny white cubicle and took the escalator to ground level. Several hundred cars stood neatly parked in their slots, rows of steel hoods gleaming in the moonlight. They wove through the serried ranks, Marisa darting careful glances about, as if searching for watchers in the deep shadows. She unlocked the passenger door of a Volvo and slid into the driver's seat, and when Loren had followed her in and slammed the door, she turned the ignition key and the car sped out of its slot.

She took the expressway east, toward the city, turning off at the Lord Avenue ramp that hung precariously on reinforced pillars between blocks of brick tenements and dilapidated brownstones. At the first major intersection she made a right into an ill-lighted street scarred with potholes, lined with ramshackle storefronts, bars, soul-music shops and fast-food joints. Loren read a sign on the wall of a brick building: SUNDRIES-BAR-B-QUE-BAIL BONDS. The sidewalks were crowded with black men and women and children, running, walking, strutting, playing, delighting in the cool night breezes. Marisa swung off the main drag into another long block of abandoned houses, with knots of black teenagers playing in the garbage-littered yards.

"Woody taught me this trick," she said. "Drive through the ghetto for ten minutes and you can lose any whites if you know what you're doing. ... *Watch out!*" She hit the brake pedal, then fed gas and shot forward. Loren threw out his hands to keep from slamming into the windshield. Out of the corner of his eye, through the side window, he saw a black youth heft a rock in his hand, then hurl it at the Volvo full force. It smashed against the wing window six inches from Loren's head with a thunderclap explosion. Cracks radiated through the shatterproof glass. The Volvo roared past the suddenly emptied lot. The rock thrower had dematerialized.

Marisa made a quick left and then a right, turned into another main street of the ghetto. Loren was all but choked with rage. The Volvo swerved onto the next access road to the expressway. "They know the route I've been taking," she said quietly. "I can't go that way anymore."

Loren fought down the last of his anger, tried to think again. "What are you saying? That the black punk with the rock knew who you were, that he was trying to kill you specifically?"

"They've probably paid other kids to watch for the car

and do the same thing if they spot it. I'm sorry it happened while you were with me, Mr. Mensing, but it gives you some idea of what Woody and I are fighting."

Loren lapsed into silent puzzlement, while Marisa turned off the expressway and drove down a dark narrow street dotted with warehouses and concrete loading bays. Beyond the warehouses the lots fronting the street were empty, the earth leveled and sterile. Waiting for something that wasn't going to come. "Urban renewal?" Loren asked.

"They tore down everything in the area," she nodded, "and then the money ran out. Here we are." She braked a block beyond the devastation, next to an empty storefront, the glass in its show windows long since smashed. Across the street was a massive brick and stone structure with its front doors boarded up. Loren could barely read the letters cut into the stonework above the doors: HUMBER. The only sound was the ticking of the Volvo's motor. "Quick now," Marisa said, and darted out of the car and across the street. Loren followed her into the doorway of the old building. With swift deft movements she unboarded the door, inserted a key into a padlock and, when the door was open a few inches, reset the lock and readjusted the boards.

They stood in a high-ceilinged lobby, ghostly dim, smelling of long disuse. A stone fountain loomed in the center of the cracked tile floor. At the far end of the lobby Loren saw two steel doors.

"This is the old Humber Hotel," Marisa said. "It's been deserted for years. Even the derelicts won't camp here; there's a rumor it's haunted. We've got twelve flights of fire stairs to climb. Want to take the east stairs or the west?"

"West," Loren said.

She tugged open the steel fire door in the west wall and they climbed, the slap of their shoes on the stairs eerie in the thick semidarkness. Loren was panting by the sixth flight. They rested for a minute and resumed at a slower pace. Finally, when it seemed he had been climbing stairs half his life, she held out a hand to halt him, and they went through another fire door into a long narrow corridor, with moonlight filtering through a window at one end. He heard a chittering, scurrying sound that made him think of rats in the walls, and shuddered. They followed the corridor in the other direction, away from the window, stopped at a solid-looking door with 1208 in grimy brass figures on the topmost panel. Marisa knocked loudly, four quick raps. No sound came from the other side of the door. Then Loren heard a low padding noise, like someone approaching in felt slippers. Marisa whispered her name. A key scratched and the door opened. On the threshold stood a thickset man in T-shirt and jeans and moccasins. He held a gun pointed at Loren's middle.

"It's all right, Woody," Marisa said. "This is Loren Mensing. Mr. Mensing, John Philip Wood. Woody, someone tried to smash Mr. Mensing with a rock as we were going through the ghetto. Three blocks south of Bender, on Conners Street. We have to work out a new route."

"Jesus," Woody muttered. "Anyone hurt?" His voice was deep but curiously gentle and compassionate. It reminded Loren of the voice of a priest he once knew.

"Just the wing window in the Volvo," she said. "Let's go in, shall we?"

It was one of the strangest rooms Loren had ever entered. Thick blackout curtains muffled the tall windows. Coleman lanterns on the floor and hanging from wall hooks threw grotesque shadows. Two sleeping bags lay side by side on a threadbare Oriental rug. A stack of cardboard cartons on each side of the sleeping bags served as night tables. Rows of canned foods stood in neat military order on improvised shelving, flanked by two thermos jugs. Twin canvas chairs faced each other against the corridor wall, near a sterno unit on which a coffeepot bubbled merrily. An M-16 rifle rested on an old olive-drab file cabinet, within easy reach.

"Mr. Wood, is this your full-time residence?" Loren asked in amazement.

"Woody to friends," he replied. "No, it's one of three holes I have, but this is the safest. It's not bad when you get used to it. Hell of a long walk to the john, though. What are you drinking? I've got some scotch you can have straight or with water from the thermos, or coffee."

"Just tell me why you wanted to see me," Loren said. "It's late, I'm tired, and it's been a rotten day." They sat in the canvas chairs while Marisa knelt over the spirit lamp and poured Woody a cup of coffee. He fondled the thick china mug in his powerful hands and drank greedily.

"You've been in the city two days now," Woody began, "so I assume you have a working knowledge of the Bennell trust, Benneco Industries, the lawsuit and Bennell's disease."

"Enough to get by. Marisa said you and she will each take a one-eighth share when the trust terminates. Another distant relative of yours explained why you were so concerned to claim your share now."

"Dear old Lil," Woody said. "Long-haired radical freak wants all the Benneco stock so he can infiltrate the management and blow the patriotic activities of our gallant CIA. And you know, she's absolutely right."

"I've heard her side," Loren said. "I'm willing to listen to yours."

"Have you ever been in Argentina, Professor? Or Brazil, Uruguay, Chile since our government murdered Allende? Any of the other fascist dictatorships down there? The Philippines?"

"I've never felt an urge to leave any tourist dollars there after the books and Amnesty International reports I've read." In fact, he had long ago reached the decision that not only could he not in conscience spend his money in such places, but he couldn't spend it in America either, a decision that for practical reasons he had never implemented.

"I've been in all of those countries," Woody said softly. His eyes seemed to burn in the shadowed gloom. "Underground most of the time. Working with the people, doing journalism for the movement. I've seen the secret police arrest and hold friends of mine indefinitely, just for speaking against some stinking dictator. Men, women, children. No rights, no due process, no nothing. Members of the opposition political party, former congressmen, workers, students, journalists, clergy, poets, trade unionists. They're taken to secret interrogation centers, beaten, burned, flogged, flayed, given electric shocks, mutilated for life. Your tax money supports these horrors, Professor, and every time you pull into a Benneco station and tell the guy at the pump to fill her up, you're putting a few more bucks into the operation."

"I'm not going to argue with you, Woody," Loren said.

"I knew a woman in Uruguay," he said, his voice low, hypnotic, falling upon the darkness like rain. "She was living with a poet who opposed the regime. She was four months pregnant when the local Gestapo arrested her on suspicion. They stripped her naked in one of those prison cells and made her hold a forty-pound block of ice against her stomach until the baby died. I knew a pastor in Manila. Marcos' secret police grabbed him three years ago. For six weeks they wouldn't give him a drop of water, made him drink his own urine. He's either still in the slam or dead. Dead, I hope. I've seen teenage boys with their mouths and penises barbecued by cigarette lighters. There was a girl in Argentina named Dolores whom I cared for very much. She was eighteen years old, Professor. They grabbed her, gang-raped her, shaved her head, knocked out all her teeth, and cut off her nipples with an electric saw. This is as common in those countries as buying a newspaper to read on the way to work, and the fucking pigs that do it go to Mass and Communion every day. Do we want to use the leverage of all that Benneco stock in the trust, and all the cash that's coming to Marisa and me, to rub the world's nose in that shit until somehow they make them clean it up and put away the people that have made torture of the helpless a patriotic act? You bet your ass we do, Professor."

The intensity of his voice was almost a physical presence, and Loren remembered what Lillian Bennell had said—that Wood could hypnotize the gullible as a snake hypnotizes a bird. Listening to his words, watching his thick powerful hands clench and unclench in the wavering light, seeing his eyes burn, with something like tears at their corners, Loren wanted Woody to win, wanted him to take the money and use it to blow all that filth and horror into atoms, whatever it took to do it. And he wondered if he too was being hypnotized. He knew that Woody would not have hesitated to offer Ben Richmond a substantial cash bribe if it would gain him and Marisa the money and stock for their fight. But then he remembered that it was Woody's side of the case that had lost the suit.

"Who do you think is trying to stop you?" Loren asked. "CIA?"

Marisa, sitting Indian fashion at Woody's feet, answered for him. "Not directly," she said. "They know what's happening, but in case things go wrong and we come out on top, they need to preserve their deniability."

Woody reached down to stroke her hair lightly. "It's a team of hit men from these dictatorships. A joint effort of three or four countries down there with Benneco connections. I don't know how many are in the group. They were let into this country for the express purpose of doing whatever has to be done to keep Benneco's status the way it is. CIA turns its back, like they do when the Korean spooks corrupt our congressmen or the Iranians carve up a few dissident students. If the hit men get caught, why, no one ever heard of them, they were just your ordinary nonpolitical killers. If they put Marisa and me out of the way, they're heroes, probably get some medals."

"Do you have any of their names?" Loren thought of Moraga and Rojas, with their CIA credentials and their casual approach to crippling another human being.

"Just one," Woody said. Something cold and deadly crept into his voice as he spoke. "But he's the one that counts. The head honcho. The boss of the team. Did you ever hear of Bruno Ernesto Schreyach?"

Loren rummaged through accumulated memories of his reading over the years, books and articles and reports about abuses of human rights in various countries. Somehow that name seemed dimly familiar, so that he was half certain he had encountered it before, but try as he might he couldn't remember where. "Better fill me in," he said when he had given up, and tried to get more comfortable in the canvas chair.

"Schreyach is a specialist in intelligence and security." Woody kept his voice under tight control. "He's one of the best in the field. He ran the secret interrogation centers in Uruguay and then later in Argentina, and he also handled personal security for a couple of military dictators. We'd call him the chief of the secret service. He's been underground for the last couple of years, they say. I know where. Right here in this city, somewhere within a few square miles of us. He's the one who found a way to get the supreme court to rule against breaking the trust. He's hunting me right now, just as I'm hunting him."

"Why would you want to hunt him?" Loren asked.

Woody's voice cracked; his answer was almost a sob. "Because he's the filthy son of a bitch that tortured Dolores!" He lowered his head, turned away from Loren and Marisa. Loren heard the muffled sounds of his grief. Marisa crossed the room, filled another mug with scotch, set the mug in Woody's hands. He rocked back and forth in the canvas chair in a silent rhythm of mourning. "They let her go after they were through with her," he muttered. "I saw her the day they released her, in a filthy little hut in the poorest section of the city. I threw up all over when I saw the repulsive horror they'd turned her into. Somewhere she'd found a knife. She cried and begged me over and over to kill her and I couldn't do it, I was just too sick and torn up to do it. She gasped out some kind of prayer and plunged that knife into her own heart in front of my eyes. I made her and myself a promise while she died there. I swore that some day, ten, twenty, thirty years if it had to be that long, I would take Doctor Schreyach alone with me to some place miles from anywhere, and I would break his arms and legs, and cut his eyes out with a knife, and skin him alive strip by strip. I'd keep him alive as long as I could, and piss in his face while he was dying." He began to laugh, as if he already had Schreyach in his hands. Sharp, wild, frenzied laughter. Loren had heard that kind of hysterical laughter before, in the violent ward of a mental hospital. But he remembered his own rage and grief over Lucy, and thought that he almost understood. He tried to shut out the frenzied sounds by burrowing into his memory, straining to recall exactly where he had read that torturers in various countries insisted on being addressed as "doctor," as if they were practitioners of an old, established profession.

Woody gulped the rest of the scotch, choking the laughter off. "Sorry," he said. "You fantasize things like that when you see the pieces of someone you loved. I know the difference between dreaming and the real world. When I see Doctor Schreyach, it's going to be me against him, *mano a mano*, very quick and bloody. Luck has been good to me; it's brought him within reach. I'll do the rest."

The intensity of Woody's hate was like a flaming torch, and Loren recoiled from its heat. With the remnants of his rational faculties he rejected the whole story as an impossible mad fantasy. Two mortal enemies fighting a primitive silent war to the death in an American metropolis was a concept that refused to mesh with the elements of the familiar universe. But it generated a sense of its own reality that Loren could *feel*, and that turned his stomach to ice. He had to get away from it for a few minutes. Change the subject. More data, that was what he needed. Nice, clean, objective data that would chase the blood and nightmare away.

"Tell me more about yourself, Woody. Lillian said that your mother was one of the eight remaindermen—er, remainderpersons—named in Stanford Ives Bennell's trust. Did she—forgive me for asking personal questions—but did she die of Bennell's disease?"

"Yeah," he said. "When I was a kid. Marisa's father did, too. The doctors didn't know what it was then, of course. But

I had the same fifty-fifty chance of dying from it as Marisa. I guess that's why I took a lot of risks when I was younger. I knew I might begin a long painful dying any minute."

"You were in college when you turned twenty, I guess," Loren prodded him. He had a compulsion to know about those years of Woody's life, with each day lived in the shadow of death. He wondered if there was something sick about his wanting to know.

"Twelve years ago," Woody said, remembering, "I was a junior at the University of Connecticut. My parents were dead; I had no close family and no friends. No one wanted a potential corpse for a buddy. It was like in combat, where people don't dare care about the other guys in the unit too much because anyone can die any minute. I was a loner at Connecticut. I did a lot of reading about the conditions of life, how the wretched of the earth lived, how the people in power stepped on everyone else. Somehow I made up my mind that I should do something to change that. Maybe I was afraid that if I made it to thirty, I'd have a hell of a lot of money and power someday too, and needed to train myself not to use them to hurt. It was a very quiet, lonely kind of training, like becoming a priest or learning karate, but different. When the Vietnam war got hot, the more I read about it the more I knew that was part of what I was fighting. I led peace marches. Broke into draft boards. Some spooks photographed me at a rally and a couple of weeks later my own board appraised me that I'd just been reclassified one-A. Maybe I could have fought it out in court on medical grounds or conscientious objection—I don't know. I didn't. I split. I wound up down in South America and saw closeup the same kind of rotten sadistic dictatorships we were supporting with blood and money in South Vietnam. I got into some urban guerrilla action. My Spanish was good enough and I learned how to use a gun and a knife and a Molotov cocktail. There's still a price on my head in three or four of those countries, under different names I assumed. After the amnesty I came back to the States. I did a little checking into Benneco and the estate and discovered that if old S. Gordon Bennell died or signed away his rights in the trust, the foundation would have to break up and we could all take our shares in the trust property. I wanted that block of Benneco stock in the trust so I could use it to expose how the company and the CIA have been playing footsie with those military dictators. I paid old S. Gordon triple his annuity to assign his rights, and then organized some of the other Bennell relatives and they started the suit. Along the way I met Marisa. We've been a team for a year and eight months now, right, kid?" He tousled her hair with a playful hand, and she held it to her mouth and kissed it.

"All the way, darling," she said. "Till death." And she gazed up at Woody with such a depth of love in her eyes that Loren felt a pang of utter loneliness. He needed to retreat from the radiance of her love as he had needed to back away from the flame of Woody's hate. More questions—that was it, more questions.

"Did you two, ah, meet at the family conference where the doctors told everyone the facts about the disease?"

"Hell, no. I was wanted by the FBI when they held that, but I heard about it later. Marisa was there. We met much later than that."

"But wait a minute." Loren looked down at Marisa, the lamplight glowing on one side of her face. "You must have met and talked with Lillian Bennell at that meeting, right?"

"I suppose so," she said. "There were so many people and we were all too frightened to do much socializing."

"But four months ago you were able to present yourself at the foundation under a false name and persuade her to let you do this phony graduate thesis with the Bennell family papers! Didn't she remember you from the meeting?"

"It's not phony!" Her voice rose in a spasm of anger. "It may have started out as a cover story, but I've really gotten interested in the whole family. I guess reading *Roots* had something to do with it, but I've been taking a lot of notes, and if I can stay another year or two, I'll have enough for a history of the Bennells."

"You'll make another mint on top of the mint you'll get from the trust," Loren grinned. "You still haven't answered my first question."

"Next time you look into Lil's eyes, you'll see the answer," Marisa told him. "She's got about twenty-eighty vision and refuses to wear glasses. Besides, I look more respectable now than I did when I was twenty."

Uncomfortable as the canvas chair was, Loren felt himself drifting into sleep in it. He had been through more than enough for one day and night. And when he remembered that he had to get up early in the morning and visit the safe-deposit vault at First Capital City Trust, he knew it was time to make a move. He struggled out of the chair and stretched his cramped muscles and yawned prodigiously. "Let's call it a night," he said. "I'm dragged out."

"Me too," Woody confessed, and stood up and offered his hand. "Keep pulling in the same direction, buddy. Between us we'll nail the bastards to the wall." His grip was like that of a steel vise. "Honey, before you take the professor back to his hotel you maybe ought to show him where your place is just in case he has to get hold of you in a hurry."

"Good idea." She held out her hands and Loren lifted her to her feet. In the flickering shadows of the oil lamps she seemed extraordinarily lovely. Woody unlocked the door and walked them down the musty corridor to the fire exit. "Stay in touch," he said, and the steel door creaked shut behind them as they began the long trudge down twelve flights in the dark.

EIGHT

They wove through empty streets in the empty night. Downtown was a ghost city, with phantom lights blazing in its towers. Loren twisted in his seat and tried to watch through the rear window for signs of any following cars but he could barely keep his eyes focused. His head drooped and the buzzing in his ears refused to go away. Twice he shook himself out of a waking doze.

Marisa turned into a street dominated by high-rise apartment buildings, then down a narrow driveway at the side of one brick structure, with a low attached garage at its end. She pressed a button on the Volvo's dashboard and an electric eye raised the overhead door. She maneuvered into a numbered slot and tugged at Loren's arm. "We're here," she said gently.

"Ah, but where are we?" he muttered through a mammoth yawn.

"My place. Come on, let's go upstairs. I'll fix you a drink and a map of how to get here from the airport."

A double brandy, he thought, would push him over the edge of sleep. He stumbled out of the Volvo and their footsteps clattered hollowly on the concrete floor. A self-service elevator stood open at the far end of the garage. Marisa pressed 4 and the cage hummed as it lifted them. She inserted a key from her purse in the door directly across the hall from the elevator, eased the door open with one hand and with the other snapped on an overhead light from the switch just inside the foyer.

And screamed.

A long beige snake with dark brown markings lay coiled lazily on the area rug a foot from the doorway, its head lifted, forked tongue probing the air.

Loren thrust her out into the corridor and slammed the door just as the snake darted to strike. Marisa stumbled against him, gagging, eyes wide with horror, making little whistling moans as she clung to him. He fought back a shudder and held her tight, muffled her cries against him. Through the haze of his own panic he thought, Schreyach has found her place and left a calling card, like the razor when he found mine.

"Come on," he whispered in her ear. "Back to the car. It's all right, it's all right..." His mind raced; fear shot adrenalin through his body. He stabbed the elevator button and the humming cage lowered them to the garage. He led her through the silent steel jungle of parked cars, keeping her close against him, his own nerves screaming, straining for every sound. *What was that ticking?* Then he realized that it had to be coming from the Volvo, cooling down. He took the key ring from her stiff hands, helped her into the passenger seat, let himself in and gunned the motor. The electric eye released them into the driveway. He sped through the grave-yard streets, not knowing where he was, searching for signs that would point him to the expressway. Marisa hunched in the corner of the seat, a wad of tissue against her mouth, her eyes still haunted. Loren held her with one hand and drove with the other.

Ten blundering minutes later he found the signs, turned left, then right into a boulevard with an access ramp to the highway. He tore west on the expressway, got off at the airport exit, parked in the lot as Val had parked earlier, led Marisa across to the escalator. Below the earth they waited for the next tunnel train to the hotel. Loren kept his arm around her shoulders, could feel the shuddering of her body. The train clicked to a stop, all but empty, and they sat silently in a cubicle as the gleaming white walls slid by. The escalator lifted them to the bright lobby, warm with red furniture and soft music, and they crossed to the glass elevator. Loren had to look at the key in his pocket to remember the number of his room. In the sixteenth-floor corridor he lowered her into a plush settee while he unlocked his door and cut his hand up to the light switch. His stomach churned with fear. If they had found Marisa's hole, they could have found his, too. He flew through the room, opening drawers, lifting pillows, inspecting the bathroom. What he was looking for he didn't know: another snake, tarantulas, scorpions—it could be anything. He made himself complete the search and found nothing. Not even his shaving kit was out of place. He led Marisa in from the corridor and locked and chained the heavy door behind them. "You're safe now," he told her.

"Oh, Loren, that was hideous. I've been frightened to death of snakes ever since I was a child. . . . Loren, I have to tell Woody."

"You have to get some rest," he said. "And so do I. And Woody can't help us now. There's not a square foot of space outside this room we can be sure is safe. So you're staying here with me."

He had to soothe her another ten minutes before she regained any semblance of control. Then he went into the bathroom and ran a tub of water almost too hot to touch and gingerly unwrapped a fresh cake of soap, making very certain it had not been tampered with before setting it in the porcelain recess in the wall. When the tub was ready, he handed Marisa his robe and told her to lock herself in, soak and try to relax. As soon as he heard the squeak of the bathroom lock he undressed, struggled into pajamas, took some blankets and a pillow from the king-sized bed, collapsed into one blue armchair and lifted his feet to the other. Within two minutes he was dead to the world.

He had no recollection of changing beds during the night. There was a blur of dream motion at the back of his mind, a rustling whisper of garments, a sensation as of falling onto a soft fleecy cloud that magically supported his weight, but nothing he identified as happening to him. It was only when he stirred awake for a moment, and saw the luminous figures 5:46 on the digital clock on the night table, and felt the mattress beneath him and the sheets covering him, that he knew. Thick window drapes held back the sunrise, kept the room in semidarkness, but he could feel Marisa curled snugly against him, warm and lovely and breathing softly in her sleep, with her hair spread on the pillow, caressing his cheek. *Oh Christ, I couldn't have!* Then he realized that he was still wearing his pajamas, and that Marisa was still wrapped tight in his robe, and he knew that he hadn't.

The muffled roar of a jet making altitude penetrated the room. He felt Marisa stir, saw her eyes come slowly open beside him. "Morning," he whispered.

"Hi," she said. "I was afraid to sleep without someone next to me. Did you mind?"

"My pleasure," he said, still groggy and not thinking clearly, and brushed his lips against her cheek.

"Thanks for, well, for nothing," she went on. "I didn't think you were the kind that would take advantage of the situation."

"We were both too pooped," he said. "No, that wasn't it. I guess it was the way I saw you looking at Woody last night. Come on, let's go back to sleep."

"My brain's awake now. I've had it. Loren, how can I ever get back into my apartment?"

Loren considered for a minute; then he knew the answer.

"That blonde I was with yesterday is a private detective. When it's a decent hour, I'll call her and have her send an operative who knows how to handle snakes. He can check the place out for other gifts. I think you'd better find a new apartment, but I'll get you a private room on this floor till you're settled."

"Let me stay here," she said. "Please, Loren? I'm—I'm frightened so much I'm clammy all over. I was so careful renting that place! And there's twenty-four-hour security-guard service and you can't get into the garage without a device they give you for your car that gets you past that electric eye, but they found the place anyway and left that awful snake and I have to go for my tests in three weeks.... Loren, I just don't have any defenses left."

"Test?" For an errant moment he thought she was making some reference to her cover as a graduate student. Then he remembered. Lillian Bennell had mentioned that the trust paid all the expenses of a special medical checkup each year for each Bennell descendant subject to the disease. "Oh, in California, you mean."

"It's like an early-warning system. They have machines they put you under that can tell if you're likely to show the symptoms over the next twelve months. It's not infallible but if you pass the tests you can at least plan a little ahead. If you flunk..." Without warning the tears flooded out of her, and she shook and clung to Loren tightly enough to scare him a little. "Oh, God, why do I have this thing inside me? Why?" She sobbed against him and he held her close and stroked her hair and tried to comfort her as if she were a child afraid of the dark, saying words that meant nothing but let her know that he was with her.

It was almost seven before she fell asleep again. Loren set his internal alarm for eight and lay down himself. When he woke again, he noted that it was six past eight and inched out of bed as stealthily as possible so as not to disturb her. He picked up the phone and carried it into the bathroom, easing the door shut behind him, and set the receiver on the toilet-seat cover and himself on the rim of the tub, and made a call.

"Hi, Val. Sleep okay last night?"

"Awful," she told him. "And I'm sore all over today. What's up?"

"Couple of changes in your schedule. Forget about tracing the cab driver who picked up that woman. I've already found her, and when she wakes up, I'm sending her to your office. Give her protection. Meanwhile, contact every place within a hundred miles that keeps snakes and find out if any of them sold or lost a pet recently. When you locate the one that did, tell them to send someone that knows how to handle snakes to sixty-four-seventy-two Murray Drive. The girl who's coming to your office lives there. Both of you go out to her place and let the handler into apartment four G. After the snake's gone, search the place for any other surprises. When she's packed and left, see what you can learn about the snake. I'll call you later and explain. Another thing I want you to do is to get me as much background as you can on a man named John Philip Wood." Quickly he summarized all that Lillian Bennell and Woody himself had revealed about the young rebel's life. "And don't forget that car for me this morning."

"I hope you know what kind of a bill you're running up," she said. "What are you going to be doing today?"

"Bank business," Loren replied, and fingered the deposit-box key on his ring. "Good luck."

He shaved and dressed noiselessly and waited till 8:45 to wake Marisa and explain what she was to do. While she was dressing, the phone shrilled. It was the desk clerk, reporting that the man with the car was waiting at the curb. "I'm off," Loren called into the bathroom. "You stick with Miss Tremaine till you hear from me." He took the elevator to the lobby and pushed through revolving doors into the harsh sunlight.

A blue Ford compact waited with its motor running in the semicircular loading zone in front of the hotel. A young black man with a Clark Gable mustache was sitting behind the wheel. Loren almost fell over with surprise when he opened the passenger door and heard the overture to Tchaikovsky's *The Tempest* on the car radio. "Did Miss Tremaine send you to pick me up?" he asked, recovering.

"Sure did, man. I'm Bob Jackson."

Loren offered his hand to the young man. "How did Val find out I was a classical music nut?"

"Shit, man, this is for *me!* My mama was a cleaning woman at Carnegie Hall; she snuck me into concerts when I was little and I got to dig 'em. Want me to drive us downtown and then I'll grab a cab back to the shop?" He didn't wait for Loren to answer but gunned the Ford out of the parking area and made a screaming left into the road that led to the expressway. They were silent for a few minutes, both exulting in the wild splendor of Tchaikovsky's storm music. Jackson hung a sharp right onto the downtown exit ramp.

"Working for Miss Tremaine long?" Loren asked.

"Three years now," he said, and merged into the thick commuter traffic on Terhune Boulevard. "She took me out of the juvenile offenders' home and gave me a job. Another year or so and I'll go to work as an investigator for the public defender. She's the baddest white chick I ever met, but she don't pay enough for me to keep up my record collection. Hey, I see some cabs in front of that hotel, you take the wheel and I'll split." He tore across the intervening traffic lanes into a no-parking zone, threw Loren a mock salute and slammed the driver's door, leaving Loren to slide across and start the Ford again and rejoin the stream of autos before a cop came by.

Twelve minutes of bumper-to-bumper driving later, Loren swung into an overpriced parking lot between two steel-and-glass business towers a block from his destination. First Capital City Trust was a tan stone fortress with slits of windows recessed into its front wall. He strode into the welcome chill of air conditioning and bent over a Formica writing surface in the center of the high-ceilinged chamber, pretending to fill out a deposit slip while he oriented himself. Tellers' cages lined the north wall, loan officers' cubicles the south. Above the line of cages a long strip of surrealistic mural had been painted on the wall, illustrating the history of money. A half door with a counter at waist level cut off part of the west side of the floor space. Loren detached the key from his ring and crossed the carpeted floor to the stern gray woman behind the counter. "Mr. Mensing," he said. "Box A-five-thirty-six."

The woman thrust a ledgerlike volume across to him. "Would you sign in, please," she said.

Loren hesitated a moment. From the estates he had handled for his father's firm he knew the standard procedure. A person who rents a safe-deposit box must make out a signature card, and must sign again whenever he wants to enter the vault where the boxes are located, with an attendant checking the signature against the original each time. Most banks have an employee who reads the obituary notices in each day's local papers and checks the names against the master lists of depositors. Once the bank learns that a customer is dead, his account is frozen and any safe-deposit box he may have rented is sealed, not to be opened except in the presence of someone from the inheritance-tax bureau. As a lawyer Richmond would have known all that. He wouldn't have dared take out this box under his own name in his home city. That was why he had used Loren's name. But how could he have worked things so that Loren could pass the signature scrutiny and be allowed access to the box after Richmond's death?

Then Loren knew what the answer had to be. He smiled, and signed his name as he had thousands of times before, and the gray woman compared the signatures and pressed the buzzer that released the door lock.

He'd been right. Wily Ben had simply taught himself to

forge Loren's signature, no doubt using as models the hundreds of genuine signatures on the memoranda Loren had written when he'd been the judge's clerk. Richmond had used not just Loren's name but his handwriting. Loren marched down the black marble staircase to the lower level and showed his key to the vault attendant, who escorted him to the wall of boxes and inserted his own key into one of the holes for box A356 while Loren placed his in the second. The box in his hand, Loren followed the attendant to an alcove hidden behind a gold-trimmed black curtain. The attendant parted the drape and Loren was alone in the tiny cubicle with the box. The box he dreaded to open. He threw back the gray steel lid.

The box was packed tight with money, twenties and fifties and some hundreds. Loren forced himself not to think about what the money might mean, and riffled through the bills, counting.... Nine thousand two, nine thousand three, a total of ninety-four hundred dollars. And beneath all the money, at the bottom of the box, he found a long white envelope, blank except for "Loren Mensing" in Richmond's handwriting across the front. He tore the flap open with a fingernail, and a sheet of plain white bond fluttered to the table. Loren used an ornamental paperweight on the table top to anchor the sheet without leaving his own prints on its surface. Carefully he read the handwritten letter.

> Dear Loren:
>
> Your reading this means several things. First, I am now worm food. Second, you've received the cassette I arranged to be sent to you after my death. Third, you've found the key to this box and the second message which I left for you in the spine of Volume 2 of Story. I was confident that you'd read these words one day.
>
> I want you to take what you find in this box and give it to the woman I described on the tape. It isn't much money but it was all I could raise without having

embarrassing questions asked. I hope she'll understand that this is my way of saying how thankful beyond words I am that we had each other.

I realize that under the law of wills this transaction is illegal, since this letter lacks the proper testamentary formalities, and also that no estate taxes will be paid on the money you transfer. I beg you nevertheless to do this for me, Loren; to remember what I did at various times for you, and do this for me, and then to destroy this letter.

The money is to be given to Corinne Kirk, who at this writing is employed as an investment analyst by the Bennell Foundation in this city. Please tell her how grateful I am for the times of peace and happiness she gave me.

Thanks from the bottom of my heart, Loren, and goodbye.

Fondly,

BEN

Loren felt as if a bomb had gone off inside his head. Suddenly everything he thought he had known about the origin of the shoebox money and all the other aspects of this nightmare had been shattered into atoms, and a hornet's nest of fresh puzzles let loose. Had Corinne Kirk seduced Ben, either on her own initiative or on behalf of the foundation, in order to influence his decision in the Bennell case? Was there a connection between Ben's affair with Ms. Kirk and the activities of Bruno Ernesto Schreyach and his goons? If the money Ben wanted the Kirk woman to have was the money in the safe-deposit vault, then where in the name of common sense had the much larger sum of money in the shoe box come from? And what was Loren's ethical responsibility in the matter of Ben's posthumously received request?

He remembered the list of the serial numbers on the shoebox bills, the list that Abelson had compiled and given him Tuesday evening, and dug the folded sheets out of his hip pocket. Then he spread the deposit box money on the table in front of him and scrutinized the serial number of each bill, hunting for patterns, consecutive numbers, connections between the numbers on the shoebox bills and the numbers on the money before him. He found nothing but three brief consecutive runs of twenties and one of fifties. None of the numbers even came close to the figures on the long runs of consecutively numbered shoebox bills. One more fiasco.

The first question that confronted him was what to do with the money. That was an easy one. The safest place in the world to keep the ninety-four hundred dollars was, for now, in the deposit box. He returned the bills to the steel container, stowed Richmond's letter in his breast pocket, and rang for the vault attendant. Together they relocked the box in its wall niche.

Loren took the marble staircase to ground level and strode out of the bank into the noise and pollution of a business day. He needed to consult with someone on how to handle the money, and Dunphy was the only logical person to see. Besides, it was about time he visited Conor on another matter.

The ancient elevators in the lobby of the State House boasted sculptured arches over each cage entrance, doors polished to the gleam of a Marine recruit's belt buckle, and elderly operators who manipulated buttons and levers from the comfort of padded secretarial chairs and called out the floor number whenever the cage came to a stop. Loren stepped out at the fifth floor, where the justices had their chambers. A security guard took his name and pressed touchtone buttons on an interoffice phone. While the guard was still on the line a paneled door at the end of the hallway slowly opened. Loren glanced down the corridor. Conor Dunphy was pushing his way through, his shillelagh in one hand and a briefcase in the other. Loren half ran to meet him.

"I thought ye'd dropped through the earth!" Dunphy's eyes were alight behind his thick spectacles as he stuffed the briefcase under his arm and held out a powerful hand. "They said at the Belvedere you'd checked out about dinnertime yesterday and no one knew where you'd gone. What's been happening?"

"More than I like to think about," Loren answered. "I'll need at least an hour to fill you in. Are you free?"

The chief justice's broad Irish face shadowed over with disappointment. "Loren, you couldn't have picked a more godawful time. A limousine's coming in two or three minutes to take me to the governor's mansion. There are problems with the budget appropriation for the court and I'm hopelessly hog-tied the rest of the day."

"Well, the report can wait," Loren said, "but there's something I have to ask you that can't." He lowered his voice so that Dunphy could barely hear him. "It's about Ben."

Dunphy nodded slowly, and something in his eyes told Loren that he already knew what the question would be. He gestured to a door set in the wall, with EXIT in black letters painted on a red glass box over the lintel. "Walk me down the fire stairs to the street," he suggested. "That will give us some privacy." Loren held the door wide, let Dunphy lead the way and set the pace. The chief justice made the descent with extreme caution, planting his shillelagh carefully at each step before leaning his weight on the stick and going down another stair. A thump of wood against metal punctuated every step of the way. "Ready when you are, young sleuth," he said brightly.

"Conor," Loren said, "I know you put that cassette in my suitcase."

Dunphy stood motionless. His fingers gripped the stick more tightly, then loosened again, and he took another hobbling step. "Caught with my pants down," he said, not unhappily. "I had a feeling you'd not be puzzled by my little mystery for long."

"Ben wouldn't have entrusted that tape to anyone but a very close friend, and among the people in the house Tuesday night, the closest friend he had was you," Loren explained. "Want to tell me about it?"

When they reached the third-floor landing, Dunphy paused to catch his breath, then continued his slow descent. with a step-step-*thwack*, step-step-*thwack*. "I did what Ben asked me to do," he said. "Three weeks ago yesterday I happened to be rummaging through a file cabinet in my chambers for some damn thing or other when I noticed a funny-looking envelope wedged against the far corner of the drawer. Well, I knew I hadn't put it there; I'd never seen it before in my life. My name was on the front in Ben's handwriting. So I opened it, and inside there was a tape cassette and a note."

"Do you have that note?"

"Upstairs, hidden away. Ben reminded me of how long we'd been friends, of all the favors we'd done each other over the years." Just as he had in his note in the deposit box, Loren thought. "Then he begged me to do him one final favor, something he described as the biggest he'd ever asked of anyone. He asked me to keep the tape hidden till eight months after his death, and then I was to mail it anonymously to you. I was not to play the tape myself under any circumstances, or let anyone else have it."

"I had a hunch it might have been like that," Loren said. "At the time you found the tape, what was your reaction?"

"I tried not to think about it at all. I suppose if I had had to make a guess I'd have said there was a woman involved in it, but that would have been pure speculation. Then when this other mess came up involving Ben, the shoebox and all that, I decided that you should be called in, because I had a kind of sick intuition that the tape and the shoebox might be connected. That's why I jumped the gun by a month and slipped the tape into your suitcase Tuesday."

"Then you still have no idea what's on the cassette?"

"Do you think I'd violate my best friend's dying confidence?" Dunphy burst out. Then, more calmly: "But I take it you have played the tape, so I have to ask you something I dread to hear you answer." He halted again, cane planted firmly, and gazed with savage intensity into Loren's eyes. "Does Ben confess that he took a bribe?"

"No," Loren said. "Until I played it I thought just what you did, but there's nothing Ben says that seems to connect with the shoebox."

The chief justice expelled a rush of air. "Thank God," he murmured. "I've had nightmares about having to make Iris and Jeanette listen to Ben admitting his own corruption. I'll sleep sounder tonight for what you've just told me. I . . . I guess it's none of my business what he did say on the tape."

"I can't be sure yet," Loren said. "But I do need to tell you at least part of the story, because Ben has thrown a hell of an ethics problem at me from his grave and I need some advice." He held open the ground-floor fire door and stood aside as Dunphy hobbled through into the ornate foyer. "When are you free? Sometime this weekend?"

"Try me tonight," Dunphy told him. "You've got my home number. There's the limo for me. Thanks ever so much for relieving my mind, Loren." They shook hands at the State House entrance and the governor's chauffeur held the rear door open as the chief justice maneuvered painfully into the limousine.

The clock in Soldiers' Memorial Tower sounded eleven mellow booms and the first wave of lunchgoing government personnel streamed out of the State House. Loren merged himself with the human tide that moved in the direction of his parking lot. It was time to arrange a confrontation with Ben Richmond's woman.

He drove aimlessly about the city, the car radio turned just low enough to hear as he worked out a plan. Halfway to his destination he remembered Val and Marisa and the snake, and hunted for a place to park that would be reasonably near a building with a pay phone, and couldn't find one. He headed out of the business district to the area of elegant residences off Duke Boulevard. Five blocks from the intersection of Duke and the private street that housed the foundation headquarters he pulled up to the curb, fed a meter and entered the cool dim artificial twilight of a palatable-looking restaurant with COGBURN'S in neat blue script above the recessed entranceway. He closed the phone-booth door behind him and dialed the number of the Tremaine Agency. After the fifteenth ring he hung up and tried the foundation's number.

Luck was with him. Corinne Kirk was still at her desk.

"Ms. Kirk, my name is Mensing. I'm an attorney and I've been asked to handle certain . . . aspects of the estate of the late Justice Ben Richmond. You knew the judge, I believe?"

The silence at the other end seemed endless. Finally her voice came over the line, sounding dim and far away, not at all like Japanese wind chimes. "I knew him," she said.

"The judge left something for you," Loren said smoothly, hating himself. "Something I don't think he would have wanted Mrs. Richmond to know about." He paused, but she said nothing, and for a moment he was afraid she had left the phone. "It would help if we could talk about it," he said.

"Would you like me to come to your office, Mr. . . . Mensing, was it?" Her voice was poised and calm now, the voice of a woman in control.

"Well, actually I'm just a few blocks from you right now, and if you can make it I'd appreciate it very much if you'd join me at Cogburn's for lunch." Again there was hesitation from the other end. "It's extremely important, for everyone's sake."

"Give me half an hour," she said, and hung up.

Loren looked up the number of the *Democrat* in the directory anchored to the wall between the phones, then sealed himself into his booth again and fed coins into the slot. A bored and raspy voice answered on the fourth ring.

"Frank Bolish around?" Loren asked.

"Who wants to know?" the rasp demanded.

"The name's Loren Mensing. Frank knows me." And indeed he did. Bolish had built a national reputation as a hard-hitting muckraking political journalist, exposing lies, cover-ups, corruption and dirty dealing on every level from a smalltown magistrate's court to the Pentagon and the White House. It was rumored that three out of every four government officials who knew him offered regular prayers that he be struck by a bolt of lightning. During the nightmare years of Vietnam and Watergate, Loren had given Bolish a few tips that had led to major exposés in the journalist's syndicated column. Now it was time to ask a favor in return.

"Loren, you stupid bastard!" The same old Bolish voice, deep, raucous and blustering. "What shithouse did you pop out of? Where you calling from?"

"Right in town, Frank. I see by the papers you're still tearing the clothes off the emperors three times a week?"

"World without end, baby," Bolish roared. "In fact I've got a hot column in the Olympia and a 2:00 deadline, so I can't shoot the shit with you right now."

"This is a business call. Frank, remember those columns you did a while back about the CIA using Benneco Industries operations in South America as a cover for sabotaging local governments that were too far left?"

"What about them?"

"I have reason to believe," Loren said carefully, "that it's still happening. And furthermore, I believe there's an extremely nasty person from below the border who's up here with CIA's silent backing to help keep those activities from being blown. Ever hear of Bruno Ernesto Schreyach?"

"Jesus!" Bolish bellowed. "When I was in Uruguay for Amnesty International about five years ago, I saw some of the son of a bitch's handiwork. Group of teenage students who'd been locked up without a trial for belonging to the wrong organization. God, they were like butchered meat....What makes you think he's in the States?"

"Not just in the States but right in this city. I have my

reasons, Frank. The main one is that he's tried to cripple me twice since Tuesday. Want to help me nail him?"

"You're on, brother," Bolish said solemnly. "What do you need?"

"Mucho information. Check all your contacts in Washington; comb through your files; put together everything you can on Schreyach. Description, background, likes and dislikes—the works. Shoot for some kind of verification from your whistle-blowing pals in D.C. that the CIA knows about Schreyach's mission. This may net you a month of red hot columns if you get the breaks. How soon will you have some facts for me?"

"Hell, on a story this big I'll stay on the phone all day. Where can we meet for dinner tonight?"

"The Steerhorn Lounge, out at the airport hotel. I'll see you in the bar, say about eight?"

"Deal," Bolish said. "You're buying. And you better know what you're talking about, baby. Ciao."

At 12:19 by Loren's watch she entered the restaurant, standing in the entranceway, peering into the dimly lighted room as if searching for someone. Loren decided that the situation called for him to take a risk. He rose from his booth in the rear, stood conspicuously in the aisle and beckoned her over. She wove through the irregularly spaced tables and approached him, looking cool and enticing in a lime-green pantsuit, her reddish-blond hair falling loosely to her shoulders. When she was close enough to recognize him, he saw a puzzled expression steal across her face. "Why, Mr. Mackenzie!" she said. "Haven't you gone back to New York yet?"

That was the reaction Loren had hoped for. If she were tied in with the other side, she would have known by now not only what Loren Mensing looked like but also that there was no such person as Jack Mackenzie from *Businessways* magazine. Loren did not think she could have faked the proper response on a split second's warning; if she had, she was the premiere actress in the city.

"Sit down, please," Loren said. "I'm Mensing, the man who called you. Mackenzie doesn't exist."

Her confusion was replaced by anger. Her face seemed to grow taut with it and her eyes blazed.

"I'm sorry I had to deceive you the other day," Loren went on. "But what I told you on the phone just now was the exact truth. Ben did ask me to give you something."

With her head tilted birdlike to one side she scrutinized him through caution-hooded eyes. "Is your first name Loren?" she asked.

"That's right."

She lowered herself into the booth opposite him with a graceful fluid motion. "Ben talked about you several times," she said. "In some ways I think he thought of you as a son. I can believe that if he left something for me, he'd leave it with you."

They ordered cocktails and Loren began to tell her of the cassette and the safe-deposit box and the money, keeping his voice soft, trying to suppress all emotion from his tone. She listened intently, her Bacardi untouched on the snowy white tablecloth, her eyes glistening with tears she refused to shed until Loren told her what Ben had said on the tape about her abortion. Then her head lowered and she groped for her napkin and pressed it against her face. Loren could hear the low passionate sobs.

"I think he felt guilty and grateful to you at the same time, if that makes any sense," he said. "But he was never very good at showing feelings. He was raised the old way, which dictated that a man never displayed feelings, and the legal training and his being a judge reinforced that repression. But I know he was a very tender and sensitive man."

"He was the most sensitive man I'd ever met," she told him. "I think that was why we cared for each other so much, because I'm the same way. You can't play a man's game like investment counseling without turning yourself into a male stereotype, or maybe I should say the stereotype of the pushy bitch businesswoman. But with Ben I didn't have to play that role; I could be me, and he could talk about his feelings ... Do you know how many times I prayed that his wife would leave him, or crawl into a hole and die and let us have a few good years together? And then that awful night Ben came to me and told me he had cancer. That was the night I learned what hell was all about."

Loren left her in the darkness of her silence, alone and reliving pain. Around them cutlery chinked against plates, drinks and meals were ordered, waiters scurried, two dozen conversations buzzed. Loren wished he knew how to ease her grief. He had learned most of what he had come here for, learned it by tearing open Corinne Kirk's emotional wounds. He despised himself, but he had become convinced that she was not one of the enemy. Whatever doubts he had had about her feeling for Ben had dissolved in the sounds of her weeping. There was only one thing left to ask, and he waited until a semblance of self-possession came back to her.

"Ben said on the tape that you and he first met about eight months after he came on the court. That was quite a while before the lawsuit to break the trust was filed."

"I suppose so," she said, and wiped her eyes again and drank deeply from her water tumbler.

"What was Ben's reaction when the case was appealed to the supreme court?"

Fury possessed her face and voice again. "Do you mean did I take advantage of our love to brainwash him about how important it was to keep the trust going?"

"No, not that way," Loren said. "Before this talk I guess I suspected something like that. But not now. I'm just trying to see the situation as Ben must have seen it. He couldn't give you up; he couldn't let you influence his vote; he didn't dare do what he should have done and disqualify himself from the case because he was afraid someone would ask why and that would be the end of the world for him. A conflict like that would have torn him apart, but he'd never show it. He'd take it like the Spartan boy in the story who let the fox tear his guts out without making a whimper."

"He showed it to me," she said quietly. "He tried to stop seeing me once he knew the case would come before the court. It didn't work. We just couldn't keep away from each other. But we had to be twice as careful as ever before that no one saw us, and we never never talked about the case. I swear it, not even once."

"But he knew how you felt about it? He must have."

"No one in this world can say if he did, or if it had any effect on his decision. He never talked about it. After it was over and done with we broke our necks arranging our schedules so we could sneak away for a weekend together, and I've never in my life seen anyone looking as relieved as he was those two days. It was as if a mountain had been taken off his back. We laughed again and loved again."

Loren felt a sharp pang of loneliness gnawing in his own belly. "And it was only a few months later that he learned about the cancer," he said.

Her eyes filled with tears again. "Oh, please, Mr. Mensing, don't ask me anything more. I didn't want him to leave me the damn money, I didn't know he'd do anything so foolish. I don't want a penny from him. Keep the money. give it to charity—anything—just let me alone." She looked at him through her haunted eyes. "Please."

"It was Ben's way of saying thank you for all the happiness you brought him," Loren said. "Not a good way, but all he could do. I'll see that the money gets into Ben's estate."

"Does that mean it will go to—?" She did not finish the question, and Loren wondered whether she had made a decision never to pronounce Iris Richmond's name.

"Some of it," he said. "I think I could persuade her to donate her share to the American Cancer Society, if that would make you feel better about it."

"Ben would have liked that," she said. "Would you please go now, Mr. Mensing? I have to be by myself for a while."

Loren tossed down some money on the table, rose and stood over her. "I wish there were some way I could have avoided hurting you like this," he said, and touched her shoulder tentatively in a gesture of farewell.

The urge to get away from Corinne Kirk's silent agony overpowered him and he drove toward the expressway without thought of the speed limit. Just short of the entrance ramp he swerved sharply into a gas station where he ordered a fill-up and asked where the pay phone was. In the open enclosure he dialed the Tremaine Agency and caught Val in the office.

"Feeling any better?" he asked.

"Not as sore as this morning," she said. "I'll survive. I like Marisa a lot, Loren. Thanks for sending her."

"Where is she now?"

"She's moved out of that apartment and for the time being she'll stay at that house I'm building out in the sticks. I'm having a phone put in today and I'll be sleeping out there myself till this mess is over."

"What about the snake?"

"I found where it came from with three phone calls. It's a trans-Pecos rat snake, a very ugly and vicious-looking brute but not venomous. It's found in the Big Bend region of Texas, along a stretch of the Rio Grande. The one in her apartment was stolen from an animal-supply house in the city after closing yesterday. With the right equipment it's easy enough to drive past that electric-eye device into her garage, and you can beat her apartment lock with a credit card."

"Not a poisonous snake," Loren repeated. "Whoever planted it didn't mean to kill Marisa, just terrorize her."

"Unless they didn't know it wasn't poisonous," Val said. "At any rate, a handler came from the supply house and took it out of there with no trouble, and I searched the place and didn't find any more booby traps and Marisa couldn't find anything missing so she packed some things and moved out."

"I don't suppose there are any clues to the person that did it?"

"The police have been to the supply house. I doubt they've come up with anything. No one called them to report what happened last night, so now that the snake's recovered they'll probably drop the investigation. The supply house people don't want the publicity and would just as soon forget it."

"So would I," Loren said. "In case I need to see Marisa, would you give me directions to your house?" He found a scrap of paper in his wallet and scrawled notes as Val dictated the route. "Okay, I think I can find it. Right now, except for digging up some poop on John Philip Wood, your part of the case seems to be at a dead end, so relax for a bit."

"Surely you jest!" she exclaimed. "If you knew how much you've disrupted my routine business ... well, I work better under pressure, so what the hell. See you later, Loren."

Loren paid the attendant for the gas and steered the Ford onto the expressway ramp without paying attention to the road. He drove downtown all but unconsciously while his mind raced. He had to be sure there was rational basis for his conviction that whatever the explanation for that shoebox full of money, Ben Richmond had not sold out. On that cassette and in those posthumous letters, Ben had stripped himself naked to Loren, baring the secrets of his life as he had never done before. If one of those secrets was that he had taken a bribe in the Bennell case, Loren was positive he would have confessed that, too. His torment over having to reach a decision in the case while remaining the lover of a woman involved indirectly in the litigation had been genuine; Corinne's description of Ben's agonies was too real to have been faked. Now that Loren had talked to Corinne, all the extraneous elements that had seemed to condemn the judge—the fund-juggling, the renting of the safety box in Loren's name, the convoluted series of communications designed to reach Loren after Ben's death—now made sense.

The only thing that didn't fit was the shoebox. That and the Schreyach gang's role.

It was time to check out an angle Loren had had no chance to consider until now. The odds were against him, but it was the only lead to the shoebox money he had left. He felt in his pocket to make sure he still had Abelson's list of serial numbers from those bills, and turned off the beltway at the ramp that fed into the downtown business district.

NINE

The senior vice-president of the Federal Reserve branch in Capital City was a rotund and red-faced gentleman named Sanford J. Bissonette. Behind his gleaming walnut desk in the corner office on the third floor of the bank building he sat like a genial Napoleon, exulting in the quiet efficiency of the operation he commanded. Loren had spent forty minutes convincing the little banker that he was a well-known mystery writer who had come to research a novel about a murder in the Fed's money vault. Spontaneous and totally imaginary as the plot and all its ramifications were, the idea seemed to have a huge appeal for Bissonette, whose head bounced gleefully up and down during Loren's recital like the head of a boy at a Fourth of July picnic bobbing for apples.

"Marvelous," he repeated nasally, rubbing his palms together in a frenzy of delight. "Simply marvelous, Mr. Hoch! I swear, where in the world you writers get your ideas is beyond my comprehension."

"Then you don't mind giving me some technical assistance?"

"Well, I certainly wouldn't want any errors to creep into your little fable. Exactly what would you like to know?"

"Well," Loren said, crossing his legs and balancing his notebook on one knee, "let's begin with the body in your vault. The police find a big bundle of currency stuffed in the dead man's pocket. Naturally they want to learn all they can about the history of this money. So they come to you. Now, just from looking at those bills, could you tell them anything about when they originated, whose hands they'd gone through—anything along those lines?"

Bissonette deposited his spectacles on the leather desk blotter and began to polish them with a tissue. "What I could tell your investigators," he replied precisely, "would be of very limited help. Given the serial number of any Federal Reserve note, we could check back with the Bureau of Printing and Engraving and find out from their records when the bill had been printed and when it had been shipped from the Bureau to the appropriate Federal Reserve agent, and then check with the regional bank and find out when the F.R. agent had released the bill."

Loren halted his furious scrawling of notes and raised a hand in bafflement. "I'm afraid you lost me somewhere. Could we backtrack a bit and go through it more slowly?"

The banker beamed, obviously pleased to be a part of the creative process. "Too much information too fast, eh? You see, Mr. Hoch, when the Bureau of Printing and Engraving in Washington sends out a shipment of new money, it goes by truck to whichever of the Federal Reserve's twelve regional banks the money is intended for. Do you have a dollar bill?"

Loren dug a single from his wallet and handed it to Bissonette. "The serial number of this bill," the banker announced, "is D35641643A. The *D* in the serial number means the same thing as the *D* in the seal in the center of the bill's left half and the same thing as the printed figure four you see in several places on the face of the bill, namely that this piece of currency was originally shipped by the Bureau to the regional bank in Cleveland. As I said a moment ago, the Bureau's records would indicate when this bill was shipped to the Cleveland F.R. agent."

"What," Loren asked politely, "is an F.R. agent?"

Bissonette gazed at Loren with a slight smile of superior knowledge. "The Federal Reserve Board has an agent in each of the twelve regional banks who is also the chairman of the board of directors of that bank. The bills are shipped to the appropriate agent and he in turn holds them in escrow, so to speak, until they are collateralized—that is to say, until they're actually released to the bank itself. The regional bank's records will show the date the F.R. agent has released a given bill. In due course the money will go to a commercial bank and from there into public circulation, but beyond the point where the F.R. agent releases a bill there are no reliable records of its history. You can't search the title to a piece of currency as you can to a piece of land." The banker allowed a tinge of sadness to darken his shining smile. "I do hope I haven't just ruined your plot for you . . ."

Loren sat bolt upright in his green leather chair, his eyes blazing as the implication of Bissonette's lecture suddenly struck a spark. The bills in the shoebox looked new enough. The brainstorm just might work. He groped for Abelson's list of numbers taken from the shoebox money. "Let me make sure I understand. If I gave you the serial number of a recently printed bill, you could check with the regional bank, tell me the date that bill was released by the F.R. agent into the system, and be absolutely certain that no one could have gotten hold of the bill before then?"

Sanford J. Bissonette bobbed up and down affirmatively.

"Then you have just given me a whale of an idea," Loren almost shouted. "Would you mind if I put it to a test? Suppose I give you a few sequences of serial numbers I happen to have jotted down recently, and you tell me when the bills were released. All right?"

The banker allowed a moment of doubt to settle upon his roundly glowing features. Then his face brightened again and he beamed like an indulgent uncle. "Well, it's a Friday afternoon, and I've never helped write a mystery before. All right, let me have your numbers."

Slowly Loren read off the first and last numbers in each of the consecutive runs of bills Abelson had written down on the sheet. Bissonette copied the numbers carefully on a crested notepad, then excused himself and left the office. Loren sat and drummed his fingers against the chair arm. Waiting, waiting, wondering if this could be the break in the case. Five minutes, ten minutes. He crossed the room to a low walnut table, neatly decorated with copies of several banking journals, and tried to find something in their pages that would occupy him until Bissonette returned. Nothing worked. He paced to the window, studied the patterns of street traffic, tried to read the marquee of the movie house four blocks down the boulevard, paced some more, sat some more. Twenty minutes after he had stepped out of the room Bissonette bounced back into his office. In his hand he carried a sheet from the same notepad, its surface filled with neatly penciled numbers. He settled into his brown leather executive swivel chair and leaned back expansively.

"The bills whose numbers you gave me were issued over a period of several years," he announced. "The earliest sequence was printed in October of 1970; then we have a sequence that—"

"Pardon me," Loren said, "could we jump ahead to the latest sequence, please? That's the one that's most relevant to the...ah...the story idea I had. When were the bills released that are the newest of those I read out to you?"

"Well, there are two sequences that I could best characterize as neck and neck." He read out the first and last serial numbers of two of the runs of bills Loren had dictated to him. "The first sequence was released to the Fed in Chicago last December. The second was released to the St. Louis Fed in January of this year."

January of this year. *At least two weeks after Ben Richmond's death.* Then someone had paid forty-nine thousand dollars to a judge who not only had long ago rendered his vote in the Bennell case but was dead to boot. It was all a scam, a posthumous frame-up, part of someone's elaborate scheme to discredit the court's four-to-three ruling in the Bennell case. And Loren could prove it.

"Ah, Mr. Hoch? Still with us? Have I demonstrated what you need to know?"

"You most certainly have," Loren said abstractedly. "I'm more grateful than I can tell you." He thanked the beaming vice-president with a profusion of heartfelt superlatives and made his departure. In the corridor outside Bissonette's office he pressed the button for an elevator, and when a cage sighed open for him, he hit the button for the fifth floor, where according to the downstairs directory the bank's law library was located. He needed a quiet place where he could think, where he could try to reassemble the once again shattered fragments of the case.

He found the small vacant room where the bank's research collection was housed, took a chair in the obscurest corner and sat with his elbows on the library table and his chin cupped in his fists. His ecstasy at finding irrefutable proof that Ben Richmond had not compromised his integrity was matched only by his hopeless confusion at what that proof implied. For if Ben had been the victim of a posthumous frame-up, the only conceivable purpose of the persons responsible must have been to let the shoebox be discovered in the expectation that it would lead to the reopening of the Bennell lawsuit. And if that were true, then the forces Loren had come to think of collectively as the enemy—the foundation, Benneco Industries, the CIA, Bruno Schreyach and his terror specialists—couldn't be behind the frame, since the side they favored had won the suit and they had no reason in the world to want the judgment questioned. No, it had to be someone on the other side—the side that had fought to end the trust, the losing side—who was the engineer of the frame. The side of Marisa and Woody.

Loren recoiled from that conclusion as he had from the snake in Marisa's hallway. It was too wild, too chancy, a strategy of desperation. But he could not shake the conviction that both Marisa and Woody believed so religiously in the rightness of their cause that they might not have scruples about destroying a dead man's reputation if it served their high purpose. There was only one thing wrong with Loren's theory: it did nothing to explain why the Schreyach forces had tried first to cripple him and then to have him cut himself to shreds in the shower when logically they should be on his side.

Loren decided to verify one matter without further delay. Assuming that the frame had worked, and that Loren had eventually reported to the court that Ben had almost certainly sold his vote in the Bennell litigation, would the court have the legal power to reopen a matter that had been *res judicata* for more than a year? He scanned the shelves and pulled down several volumes of the state statutes, the supreme court rules of practice and procedure, and Fleming's five-volume treatise on the law of trusts and estates. He read furiously, scrawled notes, cross-checked, skimmed relevant cases, made more notes. By 4:00 he had established the existence of at least three theories the court could use effectively to reopen the litigation and reexamine the propriety of terminating the trust within the lifetime of the healthy octogenarian S. Gordon Bennell.

He still wasn't satisfied. A part of his mind that refused to work on strict reasoning rebelled at accepting the notion that Woody and Marisa were the adversary. He needed more data, more tangible elements to work with. He had to find out exactly how that shoebox had wound up in Ben's closet. He buried his head in his arms and concentrated fiercely.

And after a while, he saw the answer.

At first he couldn't accept it; despite the basic simplicity of his solution it was too baroque, too complicated. But this time he could perform the crucial test of his theory at once.

He swung out of the chair, hunted through the room for a telephone directory, thumbed through the Yellow Pages under *E*, ran his eyes down a particular alphabetical listing. APACHE, ARCO, BILLY'S....That was it! All the proof he needed. He tore out of the tiny library, stabbed the elevator button, raced through the deserted ground floor corridor of the bank to the lot where he'd left the Ford, crawled through the nightmare congestion of downtown traffic and the even worse nightmare of the homebound bumper-to-bumper brigade going west on the expressway to the residential suburbs. Three times in four miles a single stalled car forced an entire lane of traffic to a grinding standstill. Loren shifted lanes like a madman, pounded his horn raucously and cursed. An eternity later the traffic began to thin, and Loren turned off the highway and wove among the two-lane blacktops, stopping twice at gas stations for directions, and finally he saw it. Cut into the hill on his left was the steeply rising private lane, flanked by twin rows of whitewashed stones like the borders of a rock garden. As he crested the hill the huge stone house lay dead ahead. He braked in the macadam driveway, between a gleaming Fleetwood that he hadn't seen before and a blue Toyota he recognized as Jeanette's. He hit the bell, and heard the hollow echo of chimes within the house and the sharp rapping of footsteps on the parquet floor. Iris Richmond stood in the doorway, tall, wrinkled, patrician, wearing a long black dress and a look compounded of curiosity and mild anger, a glass of frothy green liquid in one hand.

"Why, Loren, how nice to see you again. Please come in and join us. Jeanette and Norm have stopped by for cocktails."

"Excellent!" Loren said, and, marveling at that stroke of luck, he followed her down the hall to the spacious front room of his Tuesday-night conference with the justices. He hoped he had not looked strangely at Iris when she had answered the bell. He knew so much more now about her private life and Ben's than he had known three days ago, so much that he wished he had never had to know and that he would never let her know that he had learned. He felt as he imagined a child might feel after happening upon its parents making love.

Jeanette and Abelson sat in twin velvet chairs with a pitcher of the foamy green drink on the low table between them. "Hi, Loren," Jeanette called. "Just in time for a grasshopper." Abelson grunted a greeting and wrung Loren's hand in his strangler grip while Iris poured Loren some of the thick syrupy beverage.

"I have good news for all of you." Loren leaned back in the barrel chair he had sat in Tuesday evening. "Ben did not take a bribe, and I can prove he didn't. The money was put in his closet after he was dead."

He studied the rush of emotion to the women's faces. Iris' features came alight with an almost unbelieving excitement and joy; Jeanette's dark eyes gleamed with silent gratitude. Abelson kept his poker face but Loren thought he detected a hint of cool satisfaction, and he felt very good indeed. Instantly they bombarded him with demands that he explain his statement in full detail, and settling back and sipping his drink, he described his visit to the Federal Reserve and what he had discovered there, being careful to drop not even a hint about all the other aspects of the case that had plagued him.

"My God," Abelson muttered solemnly at the end of the recital. "I never knew you could tell so much from serial numbers."

"Neither did whoever planted the money," Loren pointed out. "So now we come to the question of who that somebody was, and I think I know the answer to that one too. Iris, remember all those questions I asked you Tuesday about visitors to the house and people who had access to Ben's suite?"

"Of course," she answered carefully, like a witness on the stand. "You were extremely thorough, but I thought we had reached a dead end as far as trying to establish that someone could have slipped the shoebox into Ben's closet."

"We did," Loren said, "and I've thought it over again and I'm now more convinced than ever that no one had the means and opportunity to smuggle the box in and upstairs."

Jeanette Richmond leaned forward, her knees almost touching Loren's, her eyes intense. "But, Loren, that doesn't make sense! You say Father was innocent and then you say no one else could have—"

"No *one* else could have," Loren interrupted, "but two people could, and did."

A buzz of exclamation rose from the three listeners. Loren sat back and let them absorb what he had said, and when the room was quiet again, he went on. "Let's take the second step first. How did the box get upstairs? Well, as I remarked Tuesday night, there is an obvious suspect. The maid, Angella Carmer, who cleaned that suite regularly and without supervision after Ben's death. Sometime before she quit last month, supposedly to get married, she put that shoebox in the closet."

Iris Richmond's face turned as chalky white as if she herself had been the person accused. "Loren, that's impossible," she insisted. "I specifically told you Tuesday that Angella never once brought anything into this house that was large enough to hold a shoebox."

"Exactly," Loren said. "Knowing your memory for details, I took your word for that and ruled the maid out on that basis. But I didn't consider the possibility that she had an accomplice. Someone else who actually smuggled the box into the house to a place where she could pick it up and hide it behind Ben's suitcases."

He paused again and finished his drink. There was not a

sound in the room until he set down his empty glass.

"Once again, there's an obvious suspect for the first step of the job. Remember that exterminator who came here in March with a story about Ben's having ordered an inspection for termites before his death? Iris, you told me Tuesday that that man carried a tool kit or equipment bag of some kind around with him on his inspection. Remember? Now tell me, was that tool kit large enough to hold a shoebox?"

She sat motionless in her chair, fingers clutched together, eyes far away in concentration. It was as if she were willing herself back in time to the day three months ago when the exterminator had come to her door. Then, very slowly and deliberately, she raised her head until her eyes were level with Loren's and staring intently into his. "I believe it was," she said. "Yes! I'm sure of it now. It was a big monster of a bag with a flap over the front so you couldn't see what was in it. I recall thinking it was large enough to contain a vacuum cleaner, and wondering if that was how they got rid of termites."

"Now, you told me Tuesday that this man did not go upstairs at all, but that he did take his kit down to the basement with him. Right?"

"That's right," she said.

"Did you go down to the basement with him?" he demanded.

"I did not," she answered firmly.

"*Voilà!* That was where he hid the shoebox. Angella simply picked it up later and sneaked it upstairs into Ben's closet when the chance came along. A neat little two-step. It's the only theory that covers all the facts."

Norman Abelson sprang from his chair and paced across the rug in front of Loren like an attorney addressing a jury. "Mensing, that's insane," he shouted. "Why in the hell would an exterminator do any such thing?"

"The answer's implied in the question," Loren said. "He wasn't an exterminator. And I can prove it. Someone get me the Yellow Pages." Jeanette half ran across the room to the ornately carved shelf on which the directory and the telephone itself rested. "Iris," Loren continued, "tell me again—what was the name of the exterminating company the man said he worked for?"

The widow retreated into dazed reflection for a moment as her daughter came back with the phone book in her hand. "Why, it was Ajax, I think. That's right, Ajax Exterminators. It was on the side of his van and on the back of his overalls. And it was on the business card he gave me, and the bill his company sent, the one I showed you Tuesday evening."

"Anybody can get a business card printed." Loren declined to mention that he had done so himself within the past seventy-two hours. "Anybody can get a name painted on a truck van or stitched on overalls or printed on a phony bill form. Jeanette, open the Yellow Pages to the *E*'s and start reading the alphabetical list under Exterminators and Fumigators. Aloud, please."

Jeanette dropped into her chair, balanced the thick directory on her knees, bent her head to read the fine print. "ABC Pest Control," she recited. "Aardvark Exterminators. Allied. Antimite, Apache, Arco, Billy's Bugsaway . . ."

"That's far enough," Loren said. "There is no Ajax Exterminators. Ever since you mentioned that name, Iris, I've had the nagging feeling that it sounded a bit too much like the names of all the fictitious businesses in all the B movies I've ever seen. There's your proof that the termite inspector was a fake. When we check the company's address, we'll find a vacant lot."

Norman Abelson sank back into his chair and sat uncomfortably on its foremost three inches. "You've convinced me," he said. "It's not mathematical proof but it sounds plausible enough to be worth pursuing with everything you've got. What's the next step?"

"One I should have taken a couple of days ago but never had the time for." Loren crossed to the phone, opened his pocket notepad to the city address and phone number of Angella Carmer as Iris had dictated them Tuesday evening. He spun the dial and listened to a muffled ringing before an operator's recorded voice broke into the line.

"I'm sorry, the number you have dialed has been disconnected..."

Loren slammed the phone down, dialed directory assistance and asked for the current number of Angella Carmer, spelling both names precisely. The operator advised him that no number existed under such a name, which was exactly what Loren had expected to hear. He replaced the receiver and turned to face the room.

"There's no phone in her name anymore. Of course, it's possible that she got married and moved, as she said she would, and that her new number is in her husband's name, whatever that may be. I'm going to find out." He dialed the Tremaine Agency and waited for fifteen rings before he hung up and checked his watch. Nine past six. She must be on her way to that house of hers in the sticks. At first he was tempted to follow the directions she had given him over the phone at lunchtime, drive to the house, set her on the missing maid's trail and have another talk with Marisa. Then he saw that the timing was all wrong. He needed rest, Val needed rest, he had to make his report to Dunphy before his eight-o'clock dinner date with Frank Bolish, and he was reluctant to talk to Marisa as long as he suspected her of complicity in framing Ben. Let the two women spend the night undisturbed, he decided; later he could tap Val's impressions, find out if she thought Marisa might be hiding anything. He would have given much if he could be certain she wasn't involved. He couldn't reconcile the way she had clung to him last night, her trembling desperation to live unshadowed by the threat of physical degeneration and death in her twenties, with the suspicion that she had coldly schemed to destroy a dead man's integrity.

He declined Iris' invitation that he stay for dinner, accepted the heartfelt thanks of the Richmonds and Abelson and drove back to the expressway, where he turned east, exiting at the airport ramp. He set the chain lock on his door, stripped off jacket and tie and enfolded himself in the blue armchair, organizing his thoughts. Then he hunted through his much-thumbed notepad for Conor Dunphy's home number.

Luck seemed to be in his corner for once. Not only was Conor at home but from the sound of his voice he seemed reasonably sober. The phone cradled against his shoulder, Loren gave the chief justice a complete if concise report on one carefully isolated subject, the only aspect of the case he was ready to reveal to Dunphy or any other outsider at this stage of the game. The Bennell connection, the silent war between John Philip Wood and Bruno Schreyach, the private emotional torment in which Ben Richmond had lived—these Loren kept strictly to himself.

At the end of his explanation of how he had established Ben's innocence in the matter of the shoebox money, Loren waited for Dunphy to react. He heard nothing, not even Dunphy's loud ragged breathing. The silence seemed to drag on for hours. Then an ear-shattering roar of joy exploded over the wire. "Glory hallelujah!" Dunphy burst out rapturously. "You pulled it off again! God, that is the best single item of news I've heard since I came on the court.... So what happens now, if I may be so bold?"

"Now," Loren told him, "we go on the offensive." He went on to summarize the case he had constructed against the mysterious termite inspector and Angella Carmer as the grass-roots agents who had planted the shoe box, and the steps he planned to take to have the maid located and questioned. "Once we get a statement from her, find out who hired her, we simply pull on the chain till the last link's in our hands."

"Gorgeous! Gorgeous!" Dunphy exulted. "Well, you go ahead then, young sleuth, and yank that chain for all you're worth. I'll be pacing like an expectant papa till I hear from you again."

"It may take a few days before there's anything to tell. Sleep tight, Conor."

The digital clock on the night table read 7:48. Twelve minutes to grab a shower and change for dinner. Loren spun the phone dial again. No one answered at Val's house. After twenty rings he slammed the receiver down. Mild curiosity about the absence of both Val and Marisa was giving way to a subtly gnawing fear.

He showered, changed to a pullover and slacks, and just before leaving the room, he tried Val again. Same result. Nothing. He cursed, banged the receiver into place and told himself very firmly that Val was a capable, feisty woman who could take ample care of herself and did not need the male equivalent of a mother hen fretting about her. The thought did nothing to decrease his anxiety. He locked the door carefully behind him and made for the glass-walled elevator.

Scanning the long oval bar from the entranceway to the Steerhorn Lounge, he spotted his man instantly. With his six-three height, huge shoulders and chest and thick gut, Frank Bolish was a hard man to miss even in a mob. He sat hunched forward on a high stool at the far end of the dimly lit room, a gigantic stein of dark Bavarian beer half empty on the bar in front of him. Anyone who didn't know him would have taken him for a longshoreman or a truckdriver and would have conjured up the mental picture of a bruiser whose every other word was what used to be called "unprintable," who cherished his union card and drank like a fish and had never read anything more complex than an Executioner paperback. This was precisely the impression that Bolish worked like a dockhand to convey, allowing no hint of the realities—that he was fluent in both the cultivated dialect and the gutter slang of four languages, that he had two master's degrees under his belt and had read widely in Marx and Nietzsche and Freud and Sartre without benefit of translators—to penetrate the macho persona through which he glared balefully at the world.

Loren edged through the congregation of drinkers, peanut munchers and ripe-breasted barmaids, and as he came into view Bolish set down his stein and thrust out a damp hand at him. "Hey, man, you look good," the journalist rumbled. "What are you guzzling?"

"Make it a Southern Comfort on the rocks." Loren snatched a just then vacated stool three drinkers down the bar and squeezed it into the space between Bolish and the wall, and for fifteen minutes that went by like fifteen seconds they drank and swapped yarns and ogled the waitresses. Then they ordered fresh rounds and took their drinks with them through the bead-hung archway that led into the restaurant area. A red-jacketed attendant led them to a table in the far corner and they ordered prime rib with baked potato and a bottle of Château La Pelleterie 1970 and made a pilgrimage to the well-stocked salad buffet in the center of the room, where they piled their plates high.

"Okay. Frank," Loren said as they attacked their salads. "Time for you to pay your share of this feast. What have you got on Bruno Schreyach?"

Bolish popped an overloaded forkful into his mouth. "There's not a whole lot known about the guy's life. He's about forty, Argentinian by birth, but he's lived and operated in eight or nine countries. The first time anyone heard of him was about 1962, when he went to work as a sort of high-class bodyguard for some old Nazis who were hiding in Uruguay and got scared shitless by the Eichmann kidnapping. There are rumors he took out a couple of Israeli agents around that time, but no one ever found the bodies. In the middle sixties he turns up as a unit leader in one of those death squads the juntas keep handy in fascist dictatorships. You know, to kill dissidents for the government. That job led him into interrogating prisoners, and he did that for five or six years.

You've seen the reports; I've seen some of the people he cut and burned, and believe me, you don't want details while you're eating."

Loren remembered the quiet fury in Woody's voice as he described the butcheries Schreyach had presided over. "What does he look like? Any photographs floating around you could snag for me?"

"Nothing less than fifteen years old. He's sort of medium build, Latin in appearance, soft-spoken so I'm told. Doesn't slobber at the mouth when he's at work, like a sadist in a comic book, just does his job quietly and efficiently, like a good cop." The waiter served their main course and they put the salad plates to one side. "I can tell you how you'll know him if you ever see him, though," Bolish continued.

"Let's hear it," he said.

"By 1974 Schreyach was involved in handling security arrangements for some of the top honchos in the Uruguayan government. In June of that year two carloads of urban guerrillas went out to get the minister of internal affairs, who I'm told was a sadistic bastard even worse than Schreyach. The minister and Schreyach were in the back seat of a chauffeured limo when they made the hit, right on one of the main boulevards of the capital. The limo was peppered with machine gun fire and the driver and the minister were riddled in three seconds. Schreyach leaped over into the front seat and kicked the driver's body out of the way and gunned that limo out of the area at ninety kilometers per hour. A block away he smacked into the back of a freight truck and his head sailed right through the windshield. The impact literally sliced the nose off his face, and blood just gushed down out of those empty holes into his mouth. He didn't let it stop him. Somehow he got the limo started again and tore out of there till he'd lost the guerrillas."

"You sound as if you were there," Loren said.

"I interviewed the truck driver and two of the hit men," Bolish said. "For a while everyone hoped Schreyach was dead, too, but he got to a hospital in time—carrying his severed nose in his hand, they say—and the doctors sewed it back on. But that's how you can recognize him if you ever see him close up. There's a fine network of little white lines around the edges of the nostrils, and they stand out against the tan of the rest of his face, unless he's taken to darkening them with greasepaint."

Loren squinted his eyes almost shut, trying to reconstruct the face of the man in the law library basement who had called himself Moraga, and who was of medium build and Latin appearance and soft-spoken, and who had set about his job of crushing Loren's legs with the quiet efficiency of a good cop. Had there been tiny white lines around the nostrils? Loren sealed himself into a vacuum of thought for several minutes, while his food grew cold on his plate, and for the life of him he simply couldn't be sure. The splash of coffee into his cup as the waiter poured him a refill brought him back to his surroundings.

"Hello again," Bolish said. "It's a good thing I know your moods or I might have called for a doctor. Anyway, Schreyach's kept a very low profile since that shoot-out. Actually he hasn't been seen once in public after that, as far as I can learn. The word is he's been transferred into secret intelligence work—liaison with CIA and that sort of game—but I can't get verification of that."

"I take it, then, that your contacts in Washington haven't been able to confirm that he's here in the States."

"Not so far," Bolish said, "but I've still got lines out. Of course, if he is here, as you claim, and if he's on some covert operation CIA knows about, the facts are going to be buried pretty deep. But you give me two more days and I'll have the answer one way or the other.... Now when are you going to let loose with what this shit is all about?"

"When I find out myself," Loren said. "What are you having for dessert?" And over deep-dish apple pie and another several cups of coffee they lit the lamp of memory, rekindling the embers of old friends and enemies, old wars and loves, until an apologetic waiter hovered over their table and politely pointed out that it was after midnight and that the restaurant had closed ten minutes ago. Loren apologized and left an especially large tip under his napkin, and exchanged final handshakes and goodnights with Bolish in the dim deserted lobby. As soon as he had chained himself inside his room again, he snatched up the phone and tried Val's number.

And once more the phone rang twenty times at the other end without being picked up.

TEN

He couldn't sleep. His mind kept rearranging everything that had happened into crazyquilt patterns and refused to let itself be shut off for the night. The five cups of coffee he had drunk while reliving old crusades with Bolish jangled his nerves to a state of almost painful alertness, like that of a safecracker's sandpapered fingertips. He tried lying perfectly still in bed and imagining he had no body. It didn't put him out. He tried focusing his concentration intensely on the gentle hum of the air conditioner and letting the monotone lull him to rest. It didn't put him out. The tiny click of the digital clock as one minute number gave way to another was like a bomb going off every sixty seconds. The luminous figures blazed at him like the eyes of a predator. And the crazy patterns kept forming in his mind, so that finally when the clock read 3:26, he gave up, lurched from the bed to the blue armchair, and, dead tired as he was, analyzed the thoughts that were keeping him awake.

The train of ideas began with a supposition: Suppose one of the people at the Bennell Foundation—Lillian; Harlow Emmet; Roy Taylor; even, arguably, Corinne Kirk—had been siphoning funds from the trust over a long period of time? If so, the suit to terminate the trust, instigated by Woody, would have been a frightening prospect indeed, because if the action should be successful, there would have to be a final and meticulous outside audit of all the trust accounts prior to the distribution of the property, and the embezzler's dippings would almost certainly be exposed. If the hypothetical embezzler had happened to discover Corinne Kirk's affair with Justice Richmond, or if the embezzler was Corinne herself, would it not have been an irresistible temptation to use that knowledge to force Richmond to rule in favor of maintaining the trust? A double-edged offer, perhaps—cash payoff if Ben cooperated, public disgrace if he didn't.

There was just one thing wrong with that lovely theory: A substantial chunk of the hypothetical payoff money hadn't been put into circulation until after Richmond's death.

But suppose the shoebox cash wasn't the payoff money? Suppose the explanation behind that money was still unknown, and that the real bribe money had been the cash Richmond had put in the safe-deposit box? Again, Loren found a hole in that theory. Having admitted so many other damning things in his posthumous communications to Loren, wouldn't Ben have admitted having been blackmailed or bribed if either event had in fact happened?

Loren tortured his brain, paced and slumped in the armchair and agonized in the cool dark silence of the room, but he could not devise a plausible alternative to his earlier suspicion. It must have been Woody and Marisa who had planted the shoebox money as a step in seeking the reopening of the Bennell litigation.

And then, as if in a burst of light, he saw that it didn't have to be that way at all. He saw another possibility. Wild, yes; untested, yes. But conceivable. Suppose the hypothetical embezzler was Lillian Bennell. After all, as the only resident director, she would be in the best position to manipulate money, and, more important, she was the only one of the four Loren had interviewed at the foundation who had given vent to an unquenchable fear and loathing of John Philip Wood and all his works. With the outcome of the lawsuit she had been lucky: the court had defeated Woody's move to end the trust, by a four-three vote, rendered lawfully and impartially. But Lillian would never assume that Woody would tuck his tail between his legs and abandon his quest just because of one serious setback. She would expect him to try again by other means, and again, and again. Aggressive infighter that she was, she would hardly be averse to a single bold stroke that could blunt in advance the threat of any future moves Woody might make. What bold stroke? Why, bribing the Richmonds' maid and paying a phony termite inspector to plant the shoebox full of money in Ben's house after Ben's death. Money whose serial numbers would demonstrate conclusively that it was *not* a bribe Richmond had taken in his lifetime! Money which would therefore be readily accepted as having been planted by Woody after Richmond's death in a desperate attempt to discredit the court's ruling and have the case reopened. In other words, the purpose of planting the shoebox was to frame Woody on a charge of having framed Ben!

The theory accounted for every element in the case Loren could think of, except that it didn't explain the role of the Schreyach goons in the matter. Loren could surmise only that they did not know the real story behind the shoebox money and were fighting tooth and nail to keep the foundation intact for their own reasons. In the lonely darkness the theory did not seem totally insane.

Of course, the jolly octogenarian, S. Gordon Bennell, might die of natural causes any day, and his death would automatically end the trust. Loren asked himself what he would do about that if he were the putative embezzler. And the obvious answer struck him squarely in the face. If he had it in his power, he would arrange for the old man to disappear, in such a way that his body would not be found and his death could not be legally established, so that the seven-year waiting period mandated by the law would have to run out before S. Gordon would be presumed dead and the trust property distributed. Seven years was much longer than the probable remainder of the last annuitant's life, and, more important, it was a fixed length of time. The embezzler would have bought that time in which to skim off as much additional trust property as possible and then make tracks for parts unknown.

When he remembered how well S. Gordon Bennell was being guarded by private detectives hired by the foundation, he began to wonder whether an official of the foundation might still be able to spirit the old man away and dispose of him in a quiet place. He decided that when he finally reestablished contact with Val, he would have her check with those operatives in St. Louis and find out if any unusual incidents had taken place around S. Gordon's home. On impulse, and hoping that she was not the type to get angry if awakened in the middle of the night, he picked up the phone and tried Val's number again.

And once again got no answer.

He stumbled back to bed and tried to smother the nagging sensation that all his neat hypotheses had hopelessly missed the mark and that somewhere buried in his experiences of the last ninety hours was the key that would magically unlock the door. As the first wisps of light filtered under the bottom edge of the drapes and touched the corners of the room with pale gray, he drifted into a sluggish and unrestful sleep.

A droning wheeze in the corridor woke him a little after nine: the maids, vacuuming outside, damn them. His body felt drained and bone-weary; his mind rebelled against further thought. And when he was more fully awake, he realized with a start that it was Saturday morning and he had nothing to do. The case had become a waiting game. He must wait for Val to call so he could put her on Angella Carmer's trail and find out why she hadn't been home all night. He fumbled for the receiver, tried Val's house again and for the sixth time in a little more than twelve hours, was greeted with no answer.

After a shower and shave he decided to take advantage of the lull in the action. He slipped on a light pullover and the swimsuit he had had the foresight to pack, rode the glass-walled external elevator to the mezzanine level, which opened on the Olympic-size hotel pool. He spread a towel over a white plastic lounge and lay stretched flat on his back under the already broiling sun, closing his eyes, letting the sweat roll off him, savoring the lethargy in which the only realities were the splash of divers and the squeals of children and the roar of planes overhead. He drifted to the edge of sleep but never quite lasted for more than a few minutes' nap at a time. He hauled himself to his feet and jumped into the cool bracing water and swam furiously and went back to his lounge, where he lay on his stomach and squinted out of one eye at the three goddesses in string bikinis who had appropriated the lounges next to his own.

He slipped in and out of sleep again, and was beginning to wonder what time it was when he felt a cool shadow fall over him from behind. He turned and there was Val, perched on the edge of the lounge, looking down at him with a kind of friendly mockery in her gray-blue eyes. "So this is how the great detectives work," she whispered.

"I've been trying to call you all night," Loren told her peevishly. "Where have you been and what's been going on?"

"Tell you upstairs. Your shoulders look barbecued; it's time you got out of the sun, anyway." She looked up at the moving bubble that glided down the hotel's outer wall from the top floors. "Come on, we can grab that one."

They had the cage to themselves and Loren studied her as they ascended. She leaned against a wall as if desperately tired, and her eyes were drawn and her mouth taut. Something told him she had been up all night. "How did you know I'd be out at the pool?"

"You forget they gave me a key to the room, too, when we checked in, Mr. Tremaine," she said. "I came by, saw the agency car in the lot and all the spare towels gone from the bathroom. It figured. Loren, I had to see you in a hurry; all hell's broken loose again."

Loren let them into the room and chained the door. "Tell me," he said.

"I got to meet Woody last night. Those hit men had half killed him. They pulled him into an alley and nearly strangled him with a piece of piano wire."

"Is he all right?"

"He's got a vicious cut all around his neck and he talks like a frog but otherwise I think he's okay. He'll tell you the story in a few minutes. I told him and Marisa to park in the airport lot and take the train over. They were supposed to come half an hour after me and take the elevator up here if I wasn't waiting in the lobby. What's been happening at your end?"

"I found out who planted the shoebox." Rapidly Loren summarized the developments since his post-lunch phone conversation with her yesterday, and when he had brought her up to the present, Val scooped up the phone and dialed. "I'm putting Bob Jackson on it," she said as she waited for an answer. "He can canvass the maid's neighborhood and pick up the— Oh, hi, Bob. Got a job for you, starting like an hour ago." As she was giving Jackson the details, a sharp, staccato tattoo sounded on the door. Loren put his mouth against the paneling. "Marisa?"

"Let us in, Loren!" Her voice was high and tight with fear. He unfastened the chain lock and opened the door and they slipped in, Woody chain-locking them in with a swift blur of motion. He looked gaunt and haggard, his clothes were hopelessly disheveled, and there was a wild look in his eyes that Loren had not seen in them before. It was the look of one who has tasted death. He collapsed into one of the armchairs, and Marisa, white-faced and trembling, rushed to the bathroom and ran tap water into the drinking glass and handed it to Woody. He held the glass between his bruised and shaking hands, gulped the water gratefully. As he threw his head back to swallow, Loren saw the deep red gash that ran across his neck like a bloody ornament. He sat on the bed's edge, waiting for Woody to regain control. When Woody had set the empty glass on the bureau, Loren decided that it was time to ask questions. "Can you talk about it?"

"Not much." His voice came out cracked and hoarse, almost with a note of hysteria. "Last night, maybe eight o'clock, I got hungry. Took a chance on walking to a bus stop and hitting a cafeteria downtown. They got me on the way back. I was trying to catch a return bus and like a damn fool I took a shortcut through an alley. Two men must have been following me all along. They raced up behind me and threw piano wire around my neck. Show him, honey." Reluctantly Marisa opened her purse and handed Loren a long thin noose of fine wire, its bright surface smeared reddish brown. She touched it with abhorrence as if it were another snake. "Go on," Loren said.

"I got lucky. Didn't have much wind left but I kicked the front man in the balls and then got to work on the bastard who was tightening the wire behind me. Broke some ribs for him. They got away but they'll feel pain for a while. I beat it fast before a prowl car came by. Then I phoned the place where Marisa calls to leave messages for me and got word I should give her a ring at Miss Tremaine's house. I told her what happened to me and she told me about the snake Thursday night."

"Val and I had been out to dinner and stayed talking till around eight-thirty," Marisa continued. "We'd been home only a few minutes when Woody called. We drove to the Humber right away. The wire was so deep in his neck we had to cut it out with pliers. He refused to see a doctor or call the police. We stayed there all night, taking care of him and telling Val the whole story."

"At least you know they haven't found the Humber yet," Loren pointed out.

"They're panicking," Woody croaked triumphantly. "They've never come out in the open like this before. We've got 'em on the run, honey! Three more days and I'll have Schreyach's hide in my paws."

Val hung up the phone and slid along the bed to sit beside Loren. "Bob's on his way," she said. "All right, now you know what happened last night and why we couldn't get hold of each other. Frankly, Loren, I don't think I can hold out on the cops any longer. They can check out all the medical facilities and find those thugs a lot faster than my people can."

"Don't you touch it!" Woody shouted painfully. "For God's sake, this is my hunt. Give me till Monday, anyway. I have contacts of my own. I'll have him by then; I swear to God I will."

"Mr. Wood, you want me to just buzz off and let you and this creep Schreyach have a private duel. I can't oblige you. I've got a license and legal obligations."

Marisa Bennell sprang out of the armchair and clutched Val's hands in supplication. "Oh, listen to him, Val. Give us just till Monday morning. Please?"

Val patted the other woman's hands, thought the request over, her eyes narrowed. "Tell you what," she said. "This is not the kind of story I want to explain to some cop who's a stranger to me. I've got a close friend in the detective bureau; he was our best man when Chris and I got married. He's out of town now but he's due back on the job first thing Monday morning. I give you till then. That's when Loren and I open the bag and let it all spill out."

Marisa threw her arms around Val and hugged her fiercely. "Oh, you're a doll, Val."

"A damn fool, you mean. Now, there's one condition: Marisa, I don't want you to be near Woody over this weekend. You can go back to your place or stay with me, but I will not let you get caught in any crossfire between him and Schreyach."

"I don't want her around," Woody said. "Honey, this is

the last act. You drop me off a half mile or so from the Humber and leave the rest to me. Go stay with Val." He bent over and kissed Marisa's forehead. "I know what I'm doing, kid."

"I'll go." Marisa's eyes glistened with a combination of gratefulness and anxiety. She embraced Val again, and hand in hand she and Woody crossed to the door and let themselves out. "I'll phone the house later to make sure you got back safely," Val called down the corridor after her. Loren fastened the chain lock again behind them. Now that they were alone, Val seemed unable to stand up anymore, and Loren was afraid she might keel over from exhaustion. "God, what kind of impossible nightmare have we all stumbled into?" she demanded.

"One that's almost over," Loren whispered, "I think. Look, why don't you grab some sleep? Nothing's going to happen for a while, and we've both had some rough sledding lately."

Val crossed the room to the far wall, moving slowly and dreamily, as if walking through water. She tugged at one of the thick drapes, let a wedge of bright hazy sunlight into the room. The light shone gold around her. Then she drew the drapes tight shut, plunging the room into sudden half-darkness, her back still turned. Loren wondered what she thought she was doing, and felt a stirring deep inside him, and he knew. She swept her hands behind her neck and unfastened the band around her ponytail, letting the hair fall freely below her shoulder blades. The next moment her shoulders were shaking and she was wriggling out of her bright print blouse, which fluttered slowly to the carpet at her feet. Loren gazed at her naked back. He was almost afraid to breathe. He took a few hesitant steps across the room, and she stood perfectly motionless in the dimness. When he was next to her, he bent to kiss her shoulders and neck and her hair, and his arms encircled her waist, caressing her belly with feather-light strokes, feeling the little puckers of flesh where the razor blade had cut her. The muscles of her stomach writhed and pulsated under his hands, and with a thrill of delight he knew that she was performing a sort of belly dance for him, and pressed his lips against her neck. His hands rose along her midriff, fondling tenderly, until they cupped her adorable breasts, and she swayed back against him and moaned with urgency and she tore at the fastening of her slacks and wriggled them down her legs and kicked them away and squirmed in his arms until she was facing him and her body was molded fiercely against him and her lips parted to receive his kiss. And, still clinging together, they glided across to the bed and reached for each other in a slow peaceful rhythm of offering.

He had no idea how long it lasted. The digital clock on the night table didn't exist anymore. They coupled, and slept awhile, nestled together, and coupled again, and slept some more. Restoring each other. In the dimness he couldn't see the razor marks but felt the tiny scars against his lips when he kissed her breasts and belly. She lay in his arms, relaxed and totally at peace and unbearably lovely in her nakedness. The brushing of her thighs against him made him want her again fiercely, but when he remembered the horror she had seen and that she'd had no sleep last night, he couldn't find it in him to kiss her awake. He closed his eyes and disengaged himself from her and yawned. When he blinked himself back to awareness, he noticed, for the first time in hours, the luminous figures on the clock: 8:22. They'd spent almost eight hours sleeping and making love, and beneath her aggressive shell she was so lovely and sensitive and giving that he wished they could stay here eight days, or even eight months. And in a strangely detached way, he began to wonder if he had stumbled into love.

Then, shelving that thought as if afraid of it, and having nothing else to do and nowhere to go, he began to think about the case again. He propped pillows under his shoulders and closed himself off in his private mental space, rooting around in all the events and all the words that had been said since Tuesday afternoon, just about one hundred hours ago, when the gunmen who called themselves Moraga and Rojas had led him out of the law library. He let the train of events run through his mind—the nightmare in the underground garage, the summons from Dunphy, the meeting with the justices at the Richmond house, the tape Dunphy had slipped into his suitcase, all the way to the attack on Woody last night in a downtown alley. There was something buried in that pile of events. Something that kept nagging him, as if taunting him to find it. Something too small to see, or perhaps too large. He squeezed his eyes shut so tightly he saw white rockets and pinwheels blazing behind his eyelids, but the more he strained to capture that elusive something, the farther it seemed to recede.

There was a rustling of sheets and he felt the shift of weight on the mattress, opened his eyes and focused blearily in the dimness. He could make out Val, sitting up now and watching him, and he could imagine what he must look like to her. "Was I that lousy?" she asked him playfully. "You look like you just swallowed a quart of castor oil."

He slid over against her, kissed her mouth softly. "You were too good," he whispered. "Just out of this world. I can't put it into words. You make me want to keep you next to me forever."

"My big gentle loving bear," she smiled. "Oh, you'll never know how good inside I feel with you." She held his hand between her own and drew it to her breasts. "You were thinking about the case again, weren't you?"

"A little," he admitted, and made tiny love bites on her rounded shoulder. "There's something I've seen or heard that's gotten to me like a splinter under a fingernail. I can feel it but I can't find it; it's just too tiny for me to see." He rubbed his mouth against her breasts. "Ah, this is so much better. So much."

"Have you thought about giving yourself an incentive to find whatever it is?"

"What kind of incentive?" he mumbled absently.

"Something I read in the newspaper once, or maybe it was

a self-help book." She ran her nails lightly down his back as he fondled her. "The trick is, you deny yourself something you want very badly till you remember whatever it was you've forgotten. Say it's booze if you're a heavy drinker, or a cigarette if you smoke a lot."

"Suppose you're a sex maniac?" Loren asked, and stroked her thighs with long smooth caresses.

"We won't discuss that," she said, laughing. "Anyway, when you remember whatever it is, you treat yourself to a heaping helping of whatever you denied yourself—like a prize."

Like a prize. A prize. A prize.

"That's it!" he roared, pulling away and leaping to his feet. In the dimness outside the cone of golden light from the bedlamp he fumbled on the floor for his hastily discarded swim trunks, then started pacing back and forth past the bed, feverishly, enfolded again in a private universe. Systematically he ran the sequence through his memory again, in fast motion, with the events of a day compressed into seconds of concentrated analysis. It fit; everything in the monumental pile of circumstances fell magically into place. It was bizarre—some of it was almost impossible to accept—but it formed a coherent whole, firm and clear and horrible. He paced faster and faster, fitting each piece of the puzzle into the next, connecting one sequence with another until he perceived the shape of the picture.

Suddenly he stopped in his tracks and with a shock he saw that Val had jumped out of bed and was standing in his path, naked, her fingers digging frantically into his shoulders. He smiled at her inanely and laid his hands on top of her own, disengaging her. "I get sort of caught up like this now and then," he said. "Don't worry—it's not a fit or anything. You know those 'I Found It' bumper stickers? Well, I could use one. I got what I was after, and you gave me the key. Do I get you as the prize?"

"Whoa, boy! I'm not so sure I want a whirling dervish for

a lover. Maybe you'd better calm down and explain what set you off."

The phone screamed then and Loren rushed for it, barking hello into the mouthpiece. He listened for a few seconds and beckoned to Val. "It's for you. Bob Jackson."

She perched on the edge of the bed and took the phone from him. "Yes, Bob ... You did? ... She was *what?* Oh, dear God. Hang on a minute." She dropped the phone on the pillow, and in the lamp glow Loren saw that her face had gone white. "Loren, Angella Carmer's been murdered. Strangled with piano wire."

Loren reached past her, snatched up the handset. "Bob, this is Mensing, the guy you picked up here yesterday morning. Give me the whole story, quick. When and where did it happen? Who found her?"

"Ain't much to tell," the youthful voice reported. "I went out to the chick's old neighborhood and asked around, found a gal friend she'd stayed in touch with. Angella had told this gal she was calling herself Samantha Bradley now and was living in this big highrise over on Wyndmoor Avenue. I found this building but didn't get no farther than the lobby when a cop stopped me and asked me what I wanted. I shucked him, and then I commenced to asking myself a few casual questions, like, why was there a cop in the lobby? The doorman was a black dude, so I bought him a few beers when he got off and picked up a fair amount of poop from him. He told me there was a chick got herself strangled with piano wire in nineteen-D."

"When was the body found?" Loren demanded.

"This morning. The window washers were doing the outside of the building today. One of them was in his harness rig outside the front-room window of nineteen-D and he happened to look across the room and saw this chick lying all twisted on the floor, and he climbed in the nearest window he could open and called the fuzz. From what the doorman told me they ain't got clues nor suspects nor nothing."

"You didn't tell the officer that stopped you that the dead girl used to call herself Angella Carmer?"

"Didn't tell him a thing, man. But the cops know their onions in this town. They'll be onto that other name tomorrow, no later. So what's my next move?"

Loren returned the phone to Val, resumed his pacing while she listened to Jackson's story. "Good job," she said finally. "Now go home and forget it; we'll carry the ball for a while." When she had hung up she slid across the bed and rummaged in the darkness for her clothes.

"Did you catch the time of death?" Loren asked. "I forgot to ask Jackson."

"The doorman told Bob that the police think it was between seven and nine last night," Val answered. "Same general time as the attack on Woody with the same method. Looks like Schreyach's trying to take out anybody who can tie him into this." She froze in her tracks, her blouse half buttoned. "Oh, God, and Woody's all but disabled and alone in that empty hotel! Loren, we have to warn him."

"Relax," Loren said. "He's in no danger, believe me. Sit down. Listen to me. I've got a horror story to tell. Wait a minute; I have a call to make before I begin." He lifted the receiver and dialed the number of Val's house, counting the rings, hoping that Marisa would be there and pick up the phone. Seven, eight, nine—then he heard the sound of the receiver being raised on the other end, and let out a long breath. "Marisa?"

"Yes?" Her voice was hesitant, still fearful.

"Loren. Listen, I want you to drive back here to the hotel. It's important.... No, nothing's happened; no one else has been hurt. Val and I are still here and we'll be waiting for you. Lock the house tight and leave now, okay? We'll expect you in forty-five minutes or so." He hung up, crossed the room to Val, who sat in one of the blue chairs, watching him anxiously, as if uncertain he still had his wits. Loren dropped into the twin chair and looked at her intently, wondering how to begin. "Have you ever met one of these word nuts?" he asked finally. "Someone who insists you speak precisely and gets mortally offended if you use 'may' for 'can' or 'infer' for 'imply'?"

"I know a few professors like that," Val said carefully. "And I hope I haven't met another this week."

"You haven't," he grinned. "But what just struck me a few minutes ago, and what I realized was the tiny thing I couldn't get my hands on before, is precisely that. A verbal blunder. *The same blunder twice.* The first was on paper; the second I heard. Put 'em together and the case is solved."

"I'm waiting," she said, and leaned forward tensely, a frown of concentration on her forehead.

"When a corporation or institution is considering hiring your outfit for an investigation, have you ever been told that you'd be *apprised* of the board of directors' decision in due course, or words to that effect?"

"I suppose everyone in business has. What's wrong with that?"

"Not a thing. But have you ever been told that you'd be *appraised* of the decision?"

Val closed her eyes and seemed to be thinking into her past professional life. Loren didn't wait for her to answer his question. "'Apprise' means to inform, and 'appraise' means to evaluate. The words are just close enough in meaning so that a careless speaker might mix them up. And some careless speakers habitually confuse them."

Val sprang to her feet with the tawny grace of a lioness. "This sounds like it's going to be a long story, and I'm thirsty, not to mention that I haven't eaten all day." She walked to the mirrored bureau and stretched out a hand for the used water glass on its polished surface.

"Freeze!" Loren yelled. "Don't touch that!"

Val whirled, her face ablaze with anger. Loren rose and put an arm around her waist, led her back to the chair. "I didn't mean to shout, partner, but that glass is important.

Use the clean one in the john, okay?" He waited until she had returned from the bathroom with a full tumbler of water in her hand.

"As I was saying, that particular verbal confusion is one I've encountered twice since I came to this city. The second time was Thursday night at the Humber Hotel. Woody made some remark about the draft board reclassifying him after they were *appraised* of his antiwar activities. I don't embarrass people by correcting their language, so I didn't say anything and just barely registered it in my memory. Then, just now, I realized that I'd seen that mistake before. Literally seen it. It was on the cancelled bill that the mysterious termite inspector had sent to Ben Richmond's widow. 'If you see any more signs of termites, please *appraise* me.' "

Val phrased her question with exaggerated care. "Are you trying to tell me that the fake termite inspector was Woody himself?"

"None other," Loren said. "What do you think?"

"I think it stinks! That is one of the flimsiest arguments I've heard a grown person put forward in my life. Why, any number of people might confuse 'appraise' and 'apprise.' I might myself!"

"I don't like it any more than you do, and for the same reason I gather you don't. We both have a weakness for people with a rage for decency. That's the way Woody struck you, wasn't it?"

"He's almost a fanatically compassionate person," she said. "That isn't just my own impression, Loren. Marisa and I had a long woman-to-woman talk yesterday, before Woody called. She loves him so much it hurts. She'd die for him. I will not believe she could be wrong about something like that."

"I think I can show you how she could be," Loren said. "Just how much do we know—really objectively know—about John Philip Wood?"

Val drummed silently on the chair's upholstered arm.

"When you asked me to check on him yesterday, you mentioned that Lillian had said she'd had the Kurtz agency investigate Woody. I was able to sneak a peek at their report. There's no doubt that Woody was a leader of the student-protest movement at the University of Connecticut, that the draft board reclassified him one-A in retaliation and that he went underground and lived in various parts of South America before the amnesty."

"How do we know the man who went into exile is the same man that came back?" Loren interrupted her.

Amazement widened Val's eyes until Loren was almost afraid they might explode. "An imposter," she whispered.

"Why not? There's enough money at stake so a really clever con man who was about the same size and age as the real Woody might take a long chance. It's quite possible that the guy we know as Woody killed the real Wood in South America a few years ago and came back when it was safe, hoping that as Wood he could collect Wood's one-eighth interest in the Bennell trust fund. I wouldn't be surprised if he made a trip to St. Louis to see if he could speed the transfer a bit by killing S. Gordon Bennell. We know how well the foundation keeps the old boy guarded, so it's safe to assume Woody gave up and settled back to wait for him to die naturally."

"You've got no proof, Loren," Val told him fervently. "None!"

"If he has a record anywhere, the fingerprints on that water glass he drank out of will give us the proof. But I'm not finished yet. Somewhere along the line, our man— whether he's the real Woody or a fake—met Marisa."

"Loren, if you try to tell me she's mixed up in this . . ." Val cut in.

"Only as a victim," Loren said. "He met Marisa, found out that she would inherit her own one-eighth share when the trust folded, and saw a way to double his take. He used all his charm to get into her confidence, and then he pulled one of the most fantastically ambitious long-range con schemes in human history. He created a completely imaginary spy-thriller universe, and made her believe in it. He played on her loneliness, her sense of death being always with her, her social sympathies. My God, he played her the way Casals played the cello. He made her his partner in a one-hundred-percent fictitious crusade against political filth. The scenario had all the tried and true ingredients: sadistic torturers from fascist dictatorships, CIA dirty tricks, love, danger, vengeance—the whole ball of wax. Months of buildup spiced with a few carefully rigged pseudo-attempts on each of their lives and she bought the whole farm, right down to the bit about the silent *mano a mano* between Woody and Schreyach. She was so completely a part of this imaginary web of intrigue that she could take a totally extraneous incident, like that black kid's throwing the rock at her car while she was driving through the ghetto, and assimilate it into Woody's scenario. And, damn it, I believed it, too, for a while. He knows how to make people believe."

A look of detached objectivity had replaced the emotions on Val's face, and she seemed to shrink in her chair. "Loren, don't you think maybe it's you who is dreaming up a fantastic universe? There are just no facts that support this elaborate structure you're building!"

"Let me finish building it," Loren insisted. "We'll get the facts later. All right, somewhere along the line he has to get Marisa to marry him. That's the linchpin of the whole scheme. For all we know, they've been secretly married a long time. The idea is that after the trust is finally terminated and they each collect one-eighth, there's going to be one last attack by Schreyach and company, and that one will be a success."

"Loren, you can't believe what you're saying," Val cried.

"But then Woody becomes impatient," Loren went on, as if he hadn't heard her. "S. Gordon Bennell refuses to get sick and die, and Woody knows he can't kill the old man. So he devises another fantastic scheme. He offers the old boy triple his annuity for the rest of his life if he'll relinquish his mini-interest in the trust. Then he organizes the Bennell relatives who benefit by termination and they band together and bring their lawsuit. Of course, he has to tie this in for Marisa's benefit with his crusade against fascism, so he explains that his real purpose is to get his hands on the Benneco stock in the trust and use the leverage that will give him to expose the company's links with the CIA and the corrupt juntas. He makes her feel even more like a character in a spy movie by arranging a cover identity for her and getting her into the Bennell Foundation. Everything goes like clockwork. They win on the trial level; they win on the intermediate appellate level. And then the whole magnificent scheme goes boom, because of a four-three reversal in the supreme court! Imagine how Woody must have felt about Ben Richmond when that decision came down."

"Loren," Val said quietly, "you're almost getting me to believe in this nightmare."

"And now we flash forward six months," Loren said. "Ben Richmond dies, and Woody hits on a last desperate gamble to reopen the litigation. He works out a scheme to plant a shoebox full of money in Ben's house, wait for it to be discovered, and then lay a false trail to show that the winning side in the case, the foundation or Benneco or whoever, bribed Ben to vote the way he did. He played the part of the Ajax exterminator himself—the 'appraise-apprise' slip shows that—and he paid Angella Carmer to do the rest. And notice that he shelled out big money on this last gamble. Forty-nine thousand in the shoebox, enough to Angella so that she was able to move into a fancy highrise in the Wyndmoor section, plus incidentals like renting a truck. But if the gamble paid off, he'd have made thousands of times his investment. Are you still with me?"

"It's a rough ride, but I'm hanging on," she said.

"Once the box was discovered and the court brought me in, Woody and his goons, Moraga and Rojas, went into high gear. First he sends them downstate to throw a scare into me. Now, observe one interesting thing about the apparent attempt to cripple me in the underground garage. Remember how those women students of mine got me out of that? Gael Irwin told me that the two men acted so sinister when they asked for directions that she immediately concluded something fishy was up. And, Val, that was precisely the impression those men wanted to leave. They didn't want to cripple me. They *wanted* to be stopped before they ran me over, and if the girls hadn't come along, they would have pretended they'd heard people approaching and buzzed off without leaving a mark on me. The idea of that little exercise was simply to plant some seeds in my mind, to get me thinking about Latin-American dictatorships and CIA conspiracies and spies and torture, so that later on, when I began looking into which of the court's decisions might have been involved in the bribe, I'd have a huge shock of recognition when I encountered all those elements again in the Bennell case! This was how they programmed me to identify the Bennell decision as the one in which Ben had been supposedly bribed. Am I still making sense?"

"I'm afraid to answer that," she said.

"Woody knew I was investigating early in the game. Remember, he had Marisa tailing me as early as Wednesday, and he wanted me to get suspicious that I was being watched. Then he started softening me up, like with the razor blade in the soap. Just to scare me, cut me a little, build up an atmosphere so that when he made the big pitch, I'd be primed for it. The big pitch, of course, was Thursday night, when he had Marisa bring me to meet him at the Humber. He had to sell me on the reality of his war with Bruno Schreyach and all the rest of his imaginary universe. He had to make me a believer. You must have seen him at work when you met him last night. He is frighteningly good at it."

"I know," she said. "There was something bugging me all the while I was listening to that intense hypnotic voice of his and watching those weird shadows from the Coleman lamps.

You just put your finger on it, Loren. It was like being at a faith-healing rally, or in a revival tent."

"That's exactly it. We were both being subtly manipulated to believe in something that in the cold light of reason we'd reject in half a minute. As was Marisa. All right, let's talk about snakes for a while. Marisa and I finding that snake right inside the door of her apartment was the *coup de grâce*; we couldn't help but accept Woody's crazy scenario after that. But look at the facts: A, it was a nonpoisonous snake; B, Marisa is deathly afraid of snakes; C, Woody specifically suggested that Marisa should stop off with me at her apartment that night before she drove me back here. The idea was not to kill or maim either of us, just to scare us both, and to demonstrate to me that there were terrorists out there who didn't want me or Marisa or Woody to win.

"But he made one huge mistake, and I caught it yesterday. The money he put in that shoe box included one run of consecutively numbered bills that were so new they hadn't been issued at the time Ben Richmond died! So much for the hypothesis that Ben had been paid off by the foundation or by Schreyach or whatever. That discovery of mine explains why the other side has hit the panic button. Woody and his goons killed Angella Carmer last night, and then he had them literally strangle him half to death with piano wire right afterward, which gave him the best possible alibi and threw off any suspicion I might have been developing about him. And that, partner, is how we come to be here today. And when Marisa knocks on that door, in ten minutes or so, I'm going to have to destroy her whole world, her faith in Woody, her love, her reason for living. It's going to be just about the cruelest thing I've done. I hope you can soften the blow for her. Excuse me, I've got to make another call." He picked up the phone again and dialed the Richmond home, and was momentarily disconcerted when a young woman's voice answered.

"Jeanette? Loren. How are things with you?"

"Maddening," she said. "I've been waiting to hear that you've located Angella Carmer and that she's talked."

"We located her," Loren said, "but she isn't talking. But I think we're in the homestretch anyway. Let me talk to your mother, please." There was a silence followed by some whispers and rustling noises, and then he heard Iris Richmond's high thin quaver.

"Loren, did you just tell Jeanette that the investigation is almost complete?"

"Something like that. Things have been happening fast since yesterday. Look, Iris, I want you to come down right away to the airport hotel, room sixteen-oh-four. Please take the station wagon."

"Why is this necessary, Loren?" Ben Richmond's widow demanded. "The weather report predicts severe thunderstorms all evening and I really don't like to drive at night, even in perfect weather."

"Jeanette can drive you, then." Loren tried to conceal the edge of impatience in his voice. "It's very important; believe me. I want you to go downtown with us and see if you can identify someone I'm going to point out to you."

"Identify *whom?*" He could detect the irritation in her tone.

"Iris, I just can't tell you now, but please leave as soon as possible. And remember the station wagon. We'll be waiting for you."

"Well," she hesitated, "if you absolutely insist...."

"Thanks a million, Iris. I'll see you in an hour." He hung up the phone and motioned across the room to Val, who still sat in the blue chair as if stunned by Loren's arguments. "Your turn on the horn," he said. "Have Bob Jackson meet us here an hour from now. Don't take no for an answer."

"My God," Val murmured, bounding to her feet, "you're forming a war party. I take it we're going to storm the Humber Hotel and see if Mrs. Richmond can identify Woody as the exterminator?"

"You hit it. And if she says he's the man, Jackson can hold him while you call the police, or vice versa if you want to play it that way. There may be some action."

"If Woody's the son of a bitch that had that razor blade put in the soap, I'll show him some action." She sat beside him on the bed, snatched up the receiver, but her finger spun the dial only once. "Room service.... Yes, this is Mrs. Tremaine in sixteen-oh-four. Please send up two complete steak dinners as soon as you can. Medium rare." Loren whispered a correction into her ear. "No, make that one medium rare and one medium. Two bowls of French onion soup." Loren nodded. "Baked potatoes with plenty of butter and sour cream." He nodded even more enthusiastically, and grinned with delight at how she had divined his tastes after only one quick luncheon. "How soon can we be served, please? ... Fifteen minutes? Dandy." She depressed the disconnect button and turned to Loren.

"Now that the important business is out of the way, I'll give Bob a buzz. Even the Marines get to eat before they go into combat, lover."

ELEVEN

Marisa arrived with the first thunderclaps of the storm, as Loren and Val were finishing their meal. She and Val sat in the matching armchairs and Loren perched on the bed. Thunder exploded savagely outside while Loren repeated the substance of the case against Woody. Marisa fought like a fury against his indictment. When he accused Woody of having been responsible for the snake, she screamed and flew at him and tore at his eyes with her nails, and it took him and Val together to subdue her, the three of them writhing on the bed, Val holding her arms in a vise and stroking her soothingly at the same time. When Loren returned from dabbing iodine on the scratches on his cheeks, Marisa lay collapsed on the bed like a heap of dead rags, sobbing softly against Val's breast. He waited in the short corridor that led to the bathroom, staying out of Marisa's sight while she cried her soul out, waiting for Val to come and signal him that she was ready for another assault. After a few more minutes he stopped hearing the sounds of crying and ventured around the corner. She sat erect now but motionless, as if catatonic. In the lightning flashes that burst in the dim room he could see the tears welled in her eyes. It was as if she had withdrawn into a private place where she could not be hurt anymore, and Loren knew it was useless to continue talking to her. He could not have despised himself more if he had just raped her and slashed her to bloody ribbons. He stepped into the front room again and patted her shoulder and said stupid things that were meant to comfort her.

A timid rapping broke into his mood and he stalked to the door and flung it open. Jeanette and Iris Richmond stood at the threshold, sopping wet in glistening raingear. Without explanation Loren motioned them into the short interior hallway, out of sight of the other women. He couldn't endure to go through the recital a third time in one night, and fortunately it wasn't necessary to tell the Richmonds anything at this juncture. "Just wait here a few minutes," he said. "Once the last person in the group joins us, we'll be off. You came in the station wagon, I hope?"

Jeanette shook her rain hat against her knee and stared at him curiously. "Just as you asked. Does that mean it's going to be a large group that's riding downtown?"

"Six of us," Loren said. "We three, the two women in the front room and a young man who should be here any minute."

Iris Richmond looked full into Loren's eyes, her own glistening wetly. "And just who are those young women?" she wanted to know.

"One's a private investigator who's been working with me. Let's forget the second girl for the moment." Another knock on the door relieved him of having to explain further, and he opened it to admit a drenched and miserable-looking young black man whose slicker was alive with falling water and whose wide-brimmed hat was sodden from the downpour. "Hey, man, the whole damn city's just one big duck pond tonight. I surely wish I was in my pad with Shostakovich and a six-pack."

"When the gig's over I'll buy you the new recording of his Tenth Symphony and all the Michelob you can drink," Loren promised. "This job may be a lot nastier than the weather."

Jackson's eyes searched the room and widened a bit as he took in the abundance of women. "Hey, do I count *four* chicks in this party?"

"Four it is," Loren said, "and they're all coming with us. We have a date with a remarkable man."

Rain pounded on the station-wagon roof, spattered the windshield in thick heavy drops, so that they couldn't see more than a foot or two ahead as the wagon slithered downtown. Jackson drove, keeping the car at a steady, cautious thirty-five with the rain shimmering under the high beams of the headlights. The streets had turned into man-made creek beds. Loren and Val sat in the rear, Marisa between them, the Richmond women in the front with Jackson. Thunder exploded, deafening as artillery, and Loren felt a sick tightness in his stomach. They made a detour to the Midwood Mall where Val ran into her office for two high-power flashlights and a Colt Combat Commander. Then they swung north to the blighted area of downtown, their faces tense. No one spoke. The big station wagon rocked under the whistling wind, shuddered with the assault of the storm.

Jackson turned left into a long narrow street, dark and ghostly, the thick bulk of warehouses looming on both sides. "We're close," Loren said. "Another four or five blocks." They passed the leveled area Loren remembered from Thursday night and he saw the lone dark finger of the Humber Hotel, stark against the surrounding emptiness in the glare of a lightning flash. "Make the next right," Loren directed. Jackson spun the wheel and they skidded into a dead-end street and parked at the curb. Loren studied Marisa's face, white and numb in the clammy darkness. "It's time," he said softly, taking her hand. They locked the car and huddled under umbrellas and trudged quickly across the street through the murk and emptiness and fiercely falling rain.

"Suppose he spots us from up there?" Val whispered as they came within fifty feet of the hotel. "I saw at least one army rifle in his room last night."

"He's got nowhere to go," Loren said, "and no help anymore. My guess is he paid off his goons last night and they're thousands of miles away by now. And he's hurt badly enough so he should probably be in the hospital. You and I and Bob and your gun should be enough to handle him." They took shelter in the hotel doorway from the wall of falling water, and Loren pulled down the boards across the front door as he had seen Marisa do Thursday night. He was about to ask Marisa for her key when he pushed lightly against the door and it gave under his weight. "Unlocked," he said. "Woody's getting careless."

"Or else he done flown the coop," Jackson added. They tiptoed into the musty lobby, Val spearing a path along the filthy tiled floor to the west fire stairs with her flashlight beam. Loren tugged the steel door open and they crowded into the area at the foot of the stairs, trembling with cold and something more than cold.

"It's too rough a climb for Iris." Loren glanced up the high stairwell uneasily. "Let's make him come down. Iris, you and Jeanette wait here with Bob. Don't move; don't talk; just wait. Val, you and I will roust him."

"I'm coming," Marisa said.

Her voice was a flat determined monotone, her head oddly tilted, and Loren wondered if she was still in shock. He wrestled with the thought for a moment, then decided she had a right to be there. "Okay," he said. "Forward, march." And the three of them began the long exhausting climb.

They took the stairs slowly, in total silence except for the soggy slap of their shoes on the concrete, pausing every other flight to breathe and rest for a minute. Thunder echoed through the hollow tower as if resonating through a drumhead. Marisa shuddered at every clap, and Loren held her tightly about the waist. Six to eight, and a rest. Eight to ten, and a rest. Two more to go. They climbed the last two flights in a headlong rush, as if frantic to get to the top and break the silent tension. Loren eased the door open and squinted down the long bare corridor. When Val tried to slip past him, he held her by the shoulder. "Wait," he whispered. "No flash now. Wait till the lightning comes again."

There was a bang of thunder and at almost the same second a sheet of lightning tore through the window at the end of the hall, etching the corridor in acid white. Loren blinked unbelievingly. Then the flash was gone and the corridor was plunged in eerie darkness. "Did you see it?" he whispered to Val.

"See what?"

"Woody's door. It was wide open. Something's wrong here, Val. Give me your light and stay back." He slid silently down the corridor behind the cone of wavering light from the flash. When he reached the open door, he hugged the wall to one side, waiting for something to happen, to hear something. Total silence. He threw the beam into the room, crouched low in the doorway.

And saw Woody lying twisted in agony on the floor.

Eyes open, mouth gaping. Head thrown back so that the ugly gash on his throat stood out black in the flash beam. Bubbles of blood still trickling down his chin from a corner of his mouth. Hands clutched to his belly, stained dark and wet.

Loren raced past a neat row of suitcases and dropped to one knee beside him, feeling for a pulse. None. He rose, ran to the doorway, his eyes questing up and down the corridor.

"What's happened?" Val's voice came loud and tight from out of the dimness.

Loren jogged up the corridor to her side. "He's dead. Shot in the stomach. It couldn't have happened more than a couple of minutes ago. The killer must be making a getaway down the other fire stairs."

Marisa shrieked, a high, piercing, unbearable scream, again and again. With her head thrown back and saliva dribbling from the corner of her mouth she rocked and shuddered helplessly, and Loren and Val grabbed for her to keep her from falling. She screamed and her fingers tore at the empty darkness, and Val and Loren took the brunt of her helpless fury and held her tightly until the spasms subsided and she swayed against them, moaning and sobbing low.

"Come on, Val, he's getting away!" Loren roared.

"I'm not going to leave Marisa. Let him go, Loren. Let the police find out who killed him."

"I can't," Loren said, and took Val's pistol and flashlight from the filthy floor where he had dropped them to hold Marisa, and raced back down the hallway, the beam darting ahead along the walls, almost at ceiling height, until he picked up the dirt-choked EXIT sign on the east wall and made for the other fire door. He threw back the door, stood on the landing with ears straining for a sound other than the thunder and the rain. It took him half a minute for his hearing to adjust. Then he heard it. Somewhere on the stairs below, several flights beneath him—how many he couldn't guess. The quick wet slap of retreating footsteps. Slupslup-*tump* slupslup*tump*. Not racing but moving quickly, as if afraid of losing footing and stumbling in the darkness. Loren grabbed the rotting banister rail and leaned far out over the staircase, aiming his flash beam down the long well between the flights of stairs. He saw only what might have been the edge of a moving shadow, five or six flights below.

Pistol held ahead of him, safety off, he began to run down the steps, racing, breathing raggedly, taking them two and three at a time in the semidarkness, risking a turned ankle or worse at every step. He had to see who it was. He had to know if the rest of his suspicions, the suspicions he had not divulged even to Val, were right. Hit a landing, turn, leap down another flight, hit a landing, turn. God, God, if only he had a walkie-talkie or some way to communicate with Jackson, get him to block the other end so the killer would be trapped! Then he knew he couldn't do that; the killer had a gun and Jackson didn't. The slap of the other's steps was louder now, Loren was gaining—slupslup*tump* slupslup*tump*.

He leaned precariously over the banister, shouted down the stairwell. "This is the police! The building is surrounded; you can't get out." No answer but more footsteps. Loren sped down the staircase, lurching in the blackness, counting the landings as he raced down—six, five. . . .

And suddenly his feet weren't under him anymore and he felt himself falling through empty space. He cried out, dropped the flash and the gun, threw his hands out to break his fall. His palms slammed against the wall and he fell in a heap, picked himself up, groped for the light, felt something wet and sticky on his hands. There was the boom of a steel door closing below, and Loren cursed and knew the other had made it to the lobby. He raced through the fifth-floor corridor, the light beam darting ahead, showing him the rotten floorboards, the spiderwebbed doorways. Above his footsteps he heard the scurrying of rats in the walls, the chitter of little furry rodents. He tore the west fire door open, cupped his bloody hands to his mouth. "Jackson!" he roared. "You and the women get up here. Now!" He panted hoarsely, rubbing his mangled palms against his wet raincoat, gulping deep grateful breaths of the fetid air as the clatter of several sets of footsteps rose along the stairwell. "Hurry, damn it, hurry!" he wheezed. Jackson left the women behind, ran the last two flights three steps at a time. "Val's upstairs with Marisa. Marisa's in shock. There's a dead man on the twelfth floor. Shot a couple minutes ago. Killer just got out. Down the other fire stairs. Through the lobby. See anyone? Hear anything?"

"Nothing," Jackson said, panting, as Jeanette and Iris stumbled up the last flight.

"All right. You two stay here. Don't move. Bob, go up to twelve and help Val. Give me the car keys. I'm calling the cops and an ambulance." He spun around and raced the questing flash beam down the last five flights to the dim lobby and the street door. The door was open to the raging night, the protective boards cluttered in the entrance as if thrust out of the way by the escaping murderer. Loren wasted no time examining the scene. The killer must have had a car nearby, parked in one of the other side streets. He ran through the torrent of rain to the station wagon, fumbled with the front-door key, finally got in. He slid into the driver's seat, started the car, gunned it into a U-turn and skidded into the empty main street he had come from. There had to be a phone somewhere. He rocketed down the street at fifty, straining to see the lights ahead that would mean people, a bar, a restaurant, a gas station. A phone. The leveled blocks, the blocks of dark abandoned building hulks, stretched on without end. At each intersection he scanned the cross street right and left for lights.

It seemed hours later when he found them. Snakelike blue and red neon tubing in the window of a low brick structure. Corner bar. He spun the wheel, braked at the curb, splashed through the curtain of rain to the doorway. The long narrow bar was all but empty: bored barman mopping the counter with a rag, a couple of seedy-looking men nursing beers, an ax-faced old crone in a corner booth hunched over a bloody mary. Loren half ran across the debris-strewn floor of the bar to the scarred wooden phone booth in the far corner, next to the washroom door. He pushed into the narrow cubicle, dug coins from his pocket, fumbled them into the slot and asked directory assistance for the city police. He dialed the number he was given and asked the desk sergeant for the homicide detail. There was a series of clickings that sounded like tiny explosions, then a low disinterested growl. "Homicide."

"There's a dead man in the old Humber Hotel," Loren said. "Shot twice in the stomach. Up on the twelfth floor. . . . That's right, the old Humber, on Weston, just north of Hunt. . . . I know it's deserted. Besides the dead man there's a woman in shock, so send an ambulance fast. . . . My name?

Jon Smyth, no *h* in the Jon, no *i* in the Smyth." He banged the receiver into its cradle, studied his palms. The blood had dried into a red crust. He turned up his raincoat collar and returned to the street and the filthy night. He gunned the station wagon into the empty center lane. Going south. Away from the Humber. Into the residential district across town.

He slid into a vacant space across the street and half a block from the stucco highrise and turned off the motor and waited. Rain drummed on the roof in a fierce tattoo. From the driver's seat he peered up through the streaming windshield at the windows of the northwest corner suites, counting balconies as his gaze lifted. Three showed lights; so did four and five. Six was dark.

Loren knew the darkness proved nothing. The man could be asleep or out on an innocent errand, or Loren might have beaten him back to home base. He hunched down in his seat, wet and miserable inside and out. The smell of sodden clothing filled the confined space.

He thought of the women he had left at the Humber. The prowl car would be there by now; the beat cops would be taking their stories. The ambulance for Marisa should have arrived. He thought of how in a few short hours she had lost everything that had been holding her precarious life together, and he ached for her. He knew they'd be hunting for him soon, that they'd put out a bulletin with the station wagon's number and after that any cruising black-and-white might spot it. The only thing that gave him time was the ferocity of the storm. Accidents, lines down, other emergencies would keep a lot of the cars off routine patrol. He needed at least a couple of hours. He had to do this alone. No Val, no cops—just he and the other, until the last shred of doubt was gone.

The glare of headlights in the rearview mirror almost blinded him. He sprawled across the front seat, below the level of the windows, waiting for the car to pass. It slithered by and its taillights glowed like match flares as it slowed and turned into the basement garage of the highrise. A late model Chrysler with a license number he couldn't make out in the rain. That had to be him. Loren trained his eyes on the windows at the northwest corner of the sixth floor and counted the seconds.

Two and a half minutes from the time the Chrysler had disappeared into the bowels of the building, the sixth-floor darkness blossomed into pale gold light. A tiny shadow flitted along the windowpanes. Back and forth and away, back and forth and away. Flitting like a black moth against the light. Loren waited. He thought he knew what the other was up to. If his hunch was right, the man would come down again soon, with suitcases, and drive away again. He decided to wait twenty minutes.

He kept his eyes on the light and the darting shadow six floors up, holding his wristwatch up to his eyes at intervals. Ten minutes swept by on its luminous hands, then four more.

Headlights stabbed the mirror and Loren crouched again. Another car swayed and hissed through the rain-soaked street. When it had passed, he raised his eyes to follow its retreat. A blue and white dome light whirled lazily on its roof. Cops. The car made a right two intersections down the street, vanished.

Loren stared up at six northwest. The lights were dead. The man must be on the way down. Loren began to count the seconds again. Give him three minutes. He straightened in his seat, fingered the key in the ignition switch. Three minutes crawled by. Nothing. Was the elevator slow getting up to him this time? Could he just have turned out the lights and gone to sleep? Loren cursed when he thought of the possibility that there might be a rear exit from the basement garage.

He had his hand on the door handle, ready to cross the street and go up to six and force the issue, when he heard the muffled roar of a motor and the Chrysler shot to the top of the ramp from the basement and made a sharp right into the street, heading away from Loren as the police car had. Loren gave him two blocks' start, then twisted the key and spun the wheel.

The car ahead made another right, then a left onto a six-lane boulevard, taking the broader avenue at a steady thirty-five, making no attempt to shed a tail. The beat of the rain seemed to diminish; Loren could see clearly through the windshield now, between the blurs of the wipers. The signs along the boulevard gave him the answer to where the Chrysler was headed. The car ahead lurched onto the sharply curving ramp that connected with the westbound lanes of the expressway. Loren gave him time to build up speed again, then made his own turn onto the ramp. On the expressway he fed gas, cruised at fifty, until he spotted the Chrysler again, then slowed to thirty-five, keeping several city blocks back of the other car's taillights. Four miles from where it had picked up the highway the Chrysler's right-turn signal light winked in the darkness like a ruby. Airport turnoff. Above the clouds Loren heard the drone of a plane. He gave the Chrysler a bigger lead, made his own exit, followed the access road to the entrance to the huge parking lot. Cut his lights.

Beyond the entrance gate he saw the lights of the Chrysler as it passed twin rows of dark drenched parked cars. He turned into the lot, opened the window to snatch a square of pasteboard from the automatic ticket dispenser, coasted along the same lane the Chrysler had used. He eyed an empty slot and swerved into it, locked up, jogged on a diagonal line through the lot, sloshing through puddles in the gravel. Veering toward the bright mouth of the tunnel into the earth.

He caught sight of the other, approaching the kiosk from a different angle. Lurching through the rain and wind. Loren crouched behind a parked car until the figure had vanished down the escalator. He ran to the top of the moving stairway, waited till the other had stepped off at the bottom. Then he began his own descent. He felt naked and vulnerable, alone in the fierce glare of the incandescents set in the roof of the white-painted boarding area, as the escalator lowered him gently.

The benches bolted into the floor of the station area were empty. But Loren saw the man, leaning against a tall pillar, looking down the track, back turned to Loren. As Loren reached the foot of the escalator, he heard a sudden *click-clack* as the tunnel train slid into the station. The dark figure hefted the suitcase at its feet. The long white line of train doors gently whispered open and the man stepped into one of the compartments.

Loren bounded across the platform, caught the edge of the closing door against his palm and entered the same cubicle. The door shut behind him. The man seated on the white plastic bench stared up through a thicket of reddish-gray brows. Behind his misted glasses his eyes seemed vacant and unfocused. Loren looked down at him miserably.

"Evening," the other grunted. "Pity the poor brutes who have no place to lay their heads on a night like this."

"Pity," Loren said quietly.

The train clicked through the long white tunnel. The men in the tiny cubicle were silent, motionless. The quiet stretched taut between them. They were like two frozen statues in the steady glare of the underground light.

"You know," the other said. His voice was detached, emotionless.

"All of it," Loren said. "It's over, Conor."

The chief justice of the state supreme court squeezed his eyes shut, and Loren could not be sure if the moisture that trickled down the sides of Conor's nose came from the rain or tears. "I knew it was over as soon as I did it," he said. "I don't know where I was going; I swear before God I don't. The gun's in the suitcase. When I got somewhere, I think I would have used it on myself."

"It's too late for that," Loren said.

The train slid into the airport station and the doors whispered open. No one stepped in; no one stepped out. The doors swung shut and the train clicked away down the long tunnel.

"Christ, I'm tired," Dunphy said, his head bent. "I wish I could sleep. Pretend none of it ever happened, never wake up."

"Too late for that, too," Loren told him.

"I know," Dunphy said.

"Want to tell me about it?" Loren said.

"Sit down."

Loren dropped onto the bench beside the chief justice, and they sat and stared at the empty white wall of the cubicle. The train slid into the hotel station and the doors whispered open. No one stepped in; no one stepped out. The two men might have been the last people alive in the world. The doors shut and the train swung around the bend in the track and clicked away up the long tunnel.

"How long have you known?" Dunphy's voice was low, toneless. He might have been talking about an abstract problem in epistemology.

Loren tried to remember when he had felt the first faint pricklings of suspicion, but couldn't pin it down. "I guess I suspected that something was fishy a couple of days ago, when I analyzed that extremely realistic attempt to crush my legs in the law-school garage. What struck me was that whoever sent those goons after me must have known about the court's sending for me to investigate the shoebox almost as soon as the decision had been made. Who were the first ones to know I'd been sent for? Iris and Jeanette Richmond, Abelson, and the justices themselves. Then, Tuesday night after our conference, I checked into the Belvedere Inn, and by Wednesday morning Woody had already instructed Marisa to pick me up at the Belvedere and shadow me until further notice. Same deduction, same suspects. By Thursday afternoon, the other side had not only found me but had been able to slip a razor blade into my shower soap. Further confirmation."

"The razor blade wasn't my doing," Dunphy muttered. "I ... don't want you to think I'd have you hurt."

Loren thought of Val, stumbling naked and bloody out of the shower. "You didn't care who you hurt," he said coldly. "There were a lot more pointers you left behind. One of them was the similarity between the bogus attempt to cripple me downstate and the real accident that crippled you. Another was that lawsuit Woody supposedly instigated, to terminate the Bennell trust prematurely. I couldn't buy that; the strategy of the suit was just too sophisticated for a nonlawyer like Woody to have thought up all by himself. It pointed to someone in the background with legal training. Then there was a third clue. Tuesday night, when I was questioning Iris about the exterminator's visit—which at that time looked perfectly innocent and aboveboard—I asked if she had been present when Ben called the extermination company. She said she hadn't personally heard any such call but that she hadn't been the least suspicious when the exterminator came, because one night at a restaurant before he went into the hospital he'd expressed concern about the possibility of termites in the house. Who was present at that dinner? Just the Richmonds themselves, Abelson and his wife, and you.

"Around 8:00 last night I really began putting it all together and seeing how Woody must be a fake and how there had to be someone behind him—a lawyer, and one who was intimately acquainted with the court and the Richmond family. Frankly, I thought it was Abelson. I didn't want to believe it was you. I should have known that those goons who went after me at school knew a hell of a lot about the building layout, the connection with the underground garage and all of that. Abelson had never been connected with the law school. He couldn't have briefed them on where to go and what to do for that charade. You're the former dean, Conor—the only one of the inner circle who could have done that.

"My reason kept prodding me that it had to be you and I kept fighting it. I told myself it wasn't airtight, that I couldn't be morally certain, that I might be hopelessly wrong. I kept my suspicions completely to myself. Until tonight, when I chased you down those fire stairs. Then I was morally certain. That peculiar noise you made racing down those stairs as fast as you could with one foot. Two squishy footstep sounds and a thump, two squishes and a thump. That was your shillelagh, Conor, and that triple sound was almost exactly the same sound I heard Friday lunchtime when you and I walked down the fire stairs of the State House, from the fifth floor down to the street.

"And right when I knew it was you, I tripped over my own feet and took a tumble, and that gave you the chance to get away. I'll never know if that was pure accident or if subconsciously I didn't want to catch you there and willed myself to slip."

The train clicked to a stop and the doors flew open and no one stepped in or out. Loren had no idea how many times it had traversed its endless circuit while he was speaking, or even what stop it was making now. They might have been alone in that dank stuffy compartment for years. The doors slid shut and the train clicked into the long hollow tunnel.

"Conor, what in God's name happened to you?" Loren's voice was broken with anguish. He couldn't look Dunphy in the eye but stared vacantly at the blank wall of the cubicle. "You gave me my start in teaching. You fought like a tiger to get me tenure, you've been a better father to me than my real father ever was, and here you've murdered one man and been an accessory in the murder of a woman and you've planned and schemed to destroy your best friend's reputation and leave his widow on the brink of a nervous breakdown. And for what? What could you do with the Bennell money that you couldn't do with your salary as chief justice?"

"It wasn't for the money," Dunphy growled feebly, and tapped his knobbed cane against the toe of his right shoe. "The money was secondary. You'll never know the pain I live with every day and every night, physical pain and mental pain. My foot that isn't there throbs all the time, as if every little bone in it were being crushed over and over again. I have to drink a bottle a night to get any relief." He sunk his chin into the depths of his sodden raincoat. "That police car did it to me. Roared out of nowhere like a demon from hell, crushed my foot and left me so that I couldn't stand like a man, couldn't walk like a man, looked like a deformed freak and lived with the memory of those crumbling bones day after day after day. And could I get a judgment against the state to repay me for the loss of my self? I could like hell. We have the noble old doctrine of governmental immunity in tort in this jurisdiction. The king can do no wrong. When the realization of the injustice of it all seeped into my bones, Loren, I remembered how you had argued with me back in law school about the infinite capacity of the law to be the enemy of fairness and decency. And I knew then that you were right, and I cursed and shook my fist and howled at the night until my voice was choked with my own tears.

"I wanted my own back, Loren. Not just from the society but from the uncontrollable powers of chance or fate or whatever you want to call it. I raged to be made whole. Day after day I hobbled to court and judged, and maybe the pain made me a better judge and maybe it didn't—I leave that to the scholars—but I bided my time. Silence and exile and cunning. Waiting for the occasion to come. And one day I began to consider the two hundred or so million dollars sitting in the Bennell trust fund, and I began to read all I could get my hands on about the family and the disease and the whole background. And I saw how I could carve a piece of that stupendous fortune for myself and give the back of my hand to the powers that be at the same time. I had to know that I was not a pawn in the hand of chance but a mover of events!" His voice climbed to a pitch of frenzy in the tiny cubicle, and Loren squinted to hold back his tears.

"The plan grew slowly," Dunphy went on. "It all turned on young John Philip Wood, the draft evader who'd gone underground, the ultimate taker of one-eighth of that trust. He'd been out of sight and sound for years. I needed a ringer, someone who could take Wood's place, bide his time in patience and wait for S. Gordon Bennell to pass away from this disgusting planet and then collect his share, half of which would be my share. There was a young man I defended the year before I gave up criminal practice and went to work for the law school. His name was Charles Eades, and he was the most hypnotically persuasive young con man I'd ever had the ill luck to be retained by. He could make you believe the law of gravity was a hoax. He could spin you the most fantastic yarn in the world, and you'd believe every word."

Loren thought back to all of the grandly complex contrivances in the labyrinth maker's scheme, like the two-step device for smuggling the shoebox into Ben's house, and the printed exterminator's bill, signed with an anagram of Eades' real name and sent to Iris after the phony inspection. "I know," he said.

"I put out a very discreet feeler," Dunphy continued, "and reeled him in, and without incriminating or committing myself in any way I put the proposal to him. It seemed to intoxicate him. He lived to ensnare people in his own fantasy worlds. I really think he was half mad. He began learning everything there was to know about the Bennells and all their works and pomps. He was a quick study; it took him only a few months.

"And then he slipped his leash. I swear to you, Loren, I never planned any violence, never. But after it was all over, I learned what Eades did. He went down to South America, spent months dogging the trail of the real John Philip Wood, who of course had gone through eight or nine false names by then. But Eades was a bloodhound. He hunted day and night and finally found him, working with the poor in one of the stinking suburbs outside Buenos Aires. He strangled Wood and buried the body so deep it hasn't been found yet. And then he came back to the States and quietly took up the identity of John Philip Wood in the confidence that the real Wood would never come back to call him a liar, and he sat back and spent my money and waited for S. Gordon Bennell to die."

"That's not all he did," Loren cut in. "He met Marisa Bennell and slipped his leash again. Learned all he could about politics in the Latin-American dictatorships and snared her in another one of those webs of his, planning to take over all of her share in the trust by simply marrying her after distribution time and then arranging a fatal accident."

"I didn't find out about all that till it was too late to stop him," Dunphy said. "I swear on my word of honor, Loren, I didn't want anyone to be hurt. Do you believe me?"

"I don't know and I don't care. What you did intend was disgusting enough. All right, you had your plan and Eades embellished it with his own, but S. Gordon Bennell gave the laugh to both of you by staying in the pink of health well up into his eighties, and he was too well guarded for Eades to try to kill him. So you worked out a legal gimmick. Pay the old man triple his annuity to sign away his rights; then bring a lawsuit to terminate the trust. And it worked like a charm all the way to the supreme court, until Ben Richmond cast the swing vote that dropped your plan dead in its tracks. Throwing you and Eades back to square one."

"I saved Ben's life, you know." Dunphy's voice quavered and he looked at Loren like a dying man begging for a sip of cool water. "Eades wanted to kill him when the decision came down. I talked him out of it, told him I'd find another way. I did care about Ben."

"Sure you did. And right after he died you set out to frame him as a corrupt judge. You and Eades dreamed up the plan to sneak the shoebox into the house. If Iris didn't find it soon enough on her own, you'd have seen to it that she did. And then there'd be an investigation and you'd make sure enough clues were dropped so that the investigator would conclude it was the Bennell case that had led to the bribe, and you could persuade your colleagues that in the interests of justice the case should be reopened.

"You picked me to be the investigator, and Eades began drawing me into the imaginary world he'd created for Marisa. You even used that cassette tape Ben hid in your file cabinet. You broke his confidence by playing it, and you saw how it could be interpreted as giving him a need for quick money and a motive to sell out. That's why you slipped the tape to me Tuesday night—so I'd reach that same conclusion." Loren broke off before he said any more. Since the tape had not named Ben's paramour, Dunphy couldn't know that she had been Corinne Kirk. If he had known, and leaked the affair to the media, the court might well have reopened the Bennell case on that ground alone, obviating the need for the elaborate shoebox frame. Loren made up his mind that Dunphy would never learn how simply he could have accomplished his purpose if only he had known the woman's identity.

"And then everything fell apart again," Loren continued, "when I proved from the serial numbers on that one run of shoebox bills that the money must have been planted after Ben's death. It was early Friday evening, Conor, when I explained to you how I'd cleared Ben. As soon as I hung up the phone, you got word to Eades. And he hit the panic button then, didn't he? He decided the only way to insure his safety was to destroy all the people who could tell the truth about the whole scam. He strangled Angella Carmer Friday evening and had his men half kill him just to throw suspicion off himself and give him an alibi, and to keep the illusion of his imaginary world running awhile longer. He paid off his goons and sent them packing. Those suitcases I saw in the

Humber Hotel tell me he was getting ready to pull out himself. The only link he had to sever yet was you."

"And I had to destroy him," Dunphy said. "When he told me about killing that black maid I'd seen so often at Ben's house, that was the last straw. I knew I'd created a monster, like the sorcerer's apprentice. I had to take control of events again, and undo what I'd done as far as I could. He sent for me, and I brought my gun. He would have killed me if he'd been faster. He was still weak from having himself garroted the night before. He went for me and I caught him in the pit of the stomach with Seamus here." He banged his shillelagh into the linoleum floor of the cubicle. "Then I waited for the next thunderclap, just in case there was a patrol car passing by outside, and I shot the dirty dog where he lay and made my exit. Just before you came on the scene."

Loren shook his head sadly, thinking of the long, involuted story, the webs within webs, the snares and corruptions that had festered for years before this night. The train clicked into a station again, and Loren swiveled to read the sign in the boarding area: AIRPORT PARKING LOT. He grasped Dunphy by the elbow as the compartment door opened. "Come on," he said. "We have to go to the police station. I'll carry your bag. Jeanette and Iris will be there waiting for us."

"Oh, my dear God," Dunphy whispered. "Ah, Loren, don't make me face them. If you've ever cared a damn for me please for God's sake don't make me face them."

Loren said nothing, stood with his shoulder wedged against the door frame, holding it open. Very slowly, his eyes misted with tears, Dunphy hoisted himself to his feet, head bent, and stumbled out of the cubicle and limped to the escalator and rode silently side by side with Loren. Up into the weeping night.

TWELVE

Loren was run ragged for the better part of a week, working with various officials to untangle the threads of the case. There were daily conferences with police and prosecutors, an anguished meeting with the other justices of the court, a session with the governor and the attorney general of the state on the propriety of indicting a sitting chief justice for murder. There were grueling interviews with the media, in which Loren kept as low a profile as possible. In the few free moments he could snatch he went to the hospital to see how Marisa was doing. She lay white and still and shrunken in the hospital bed, seeing nothing, hearing nothing; and Loren sat and held her hand for an hour. He called the Richmond home to see if Iris was all right, and Jeanette told him that Norm Abelson and his wife were looking after her. He called Val Tremaine's office several times but never seemed to catch her at her desk.

It was on the Thursday morning after he had brought a haggard Conor Dunphy to the police station that the phone in the midtown hotel room where he had hidden himself shrilled fiercely, jarring him out of uneasy sleep. He groped for the receiver in the darkness and muttered gibberish into the mouthpiece.

"If that's supposed to mean it's five A.M., I can tell time for myself." It was the deep rumble of Frank Bolish. "My God, but you've been elusive lately! Nice headlines you've been making."

"Frank, I'm not giving interviews." Loren tried to check his anger. "It's been a wretched week and I'm half dead, so—"

"I didn't call to interview you, dummy. I wanted to pass on some news about a mutual friend of ours." The journalist paused, cleared his throat importantly. "Bruno Ernesto Schreyach."

Loren jerked upright in bed, feeling as if someone had thrown lye in his face. "Schreyach!" he repeated. "What about him?"

"He's dead," Bolish grunted, and Loren detected a quiet satisfied pleasure in his voice. "Been dead more than two years now, in fact. And he died screaming in pain, which maybe proves there's still a little justice left in this miserable world. Want details?"

"What do *you* think?"

"Remember I told you about his nose being sliced off, and how the doctors sewed it back on, and about the little white scars at the base of his nose?"

"I couldn't forget a story like that," Loren said.

"Well, I had a long confidential phone conversation yesterday with the surgeon who performed the operation. He's in exile now but he wasn't talking for publication. The junta back home would send someone to take him out in two minutes if this ever leaked. But the doctor had had some good friends mutilated in Schreyach's prison and saw his chance to even the score. During the operation to graft Schreyach's nose back on, he infected the bastard with a slow-acting poison that would spread through his body like cancer and give him three or four weeks of the tortures of the damned before it killed him. It worked beautifully. His bosses had him buried secretly and clamped the lid on the story so no one else would get any bright ideas about knocking off secret-police officials. Outrageous violation of the Hippocratic oath. Makes you want to go whoopdedoo, doesn't it?"

"No comment," Loren said mechanically, but he felt a spasm of elation almost like sexual release, and wondered whether he shouldn't be ashamed of his delight. "Thanks for the tip, Frank. I appreciate knowing," he said finally.

"Give me a buzz when the heat's off," Bolish told him, and hung up.

For the few remaining hours of the night, Loren slept more serenely than he had all week.

One more long day and evening of meetings and conferences and, at least for a while, it was over. Dunphy had voluntarily resigned from the court, the governor had appointed Meyer Goldner as acting chief justice, and the grand jury would convene in two weeks to determine whether to indict Conor for murder and on other charges. The San Francisco police had picked up Moraga and Rojas, who turned out to be CIA-trained former members of an anti-Castro terrorist group turned private hit men. Loren snatched three hours of sleep, lurched awake at eight and showered and shaved and packed his two-suiter and checked out. While he was settling his bill, Val walked into the lobby. He waved to her, hefted his suitcase and followed her outside where her Pontiac was parked in a taxi zone. He tossed the bag into the rear and settled in the passenger seat beside her.

"It's been a bad week," he said. "I missed you."

"A rough one for me, too. You look beat."

He studied the circles under her eyes and the tautness around her mouth. "Likewise," he said. They drove in peaceful silence to the expressway and west along the superhighway to a county road at the edge of the inhabited area around the capital. Then she wound through a maze of back roads until the last houses were miles behind them and they were deep in wooded country. She turned onto a dirt track that curved around a lovely unspoiled hill and ended in front of a trim redwood-and-glass splitlevel tucked into the hillside out of sight of the world.

"So this is the famous house," he said. "How long did it take you to build?"

"Almost four years. Bit by bit. That was my therapy after Chris died. Come on, I'll give you the grand tour."

He followed her through long cool rooms, furnished for total comfort, the floors glistening with wax, the scent of freshly planed wood everywhere, mingling with the odor of the plants. Dozens and dozens of plants, potted and hanging from slings and from hooks on brass chains. She named each plant as they passed from room to room—sea grape and sweet olive and temple bells and baby tears, flamingo flowers and honey bells and jade plants and lantana. "My private paradise," she said. "Not many people get to see it."

"It's you all over," Loren said. "I wish I didn't have that noon plane home to catch."

She gestured toward the phone on a low mahogany table in front of the couch. "Cancel," she said. "Change your flight to Monday morning. Another two days of piled-up paperwork at the law school won't kill you."

He grinned slowly at her and felt a warmth spreading through him that did not come from the heat of the morning. "Will your agency run itself over the weekend?"

"It damn well better. I need a rest as badly as you."

"You twisted my arm," he said, and they shared a long eager kiss before he reached for the phone. When the change of reservation was completed, Val yanked the cord from the wall, her eyes bright, and began to unbutton her blouse.

That weekend was like nothing Loren had known before. They drove to a delicatessen in the tiny village six miles away and bought a whole pineapple and platters of cold roast beef and turkey and macaroni salad and slaw, loaves of fresh fragrant pumpernickel bread and half a dozen bottles of iced Sangria. Then they returned to the house and stowed the smorgasbord in the refrigerator. There would be no cooking over these holidays. Val threw open the sliding glass doors to the redwood deck that hung cantilevered over the hillside, and they dragged mattress pads out to the scorching center of the deck and toasted themselves, fingers intertwined, until the flower-patterned sun pads were drenched with their sweat and the heat had baked the accumulated anguish of the last ten days out of their bodies. Val screwed a garden hose into a wall nozzle and they stood in the shivery cold spray, squealing like children and splashing and clinging naked under the icy delight of the water. They patted each other dry and ran breathlessly to the cool dim bedroom and made long slow lazy love, and slept and ate pineapple and loved again. Living by their own clocks, in their own universe. They lay together in the scented dark and talked of their wants and needs and dreads, and woke before dawn to draw back the drapes over the eastern window and watch the unearthly beauty of the sun rising over the distant mountains. They opened to each other like flowers, and renewed each other.

And in the blue hour before Monday dawn, he caught himself looking at his watch for the first time since Friday, and knew that the spell was breaking. He lay on his side and gazed at her with a sadness rising in his throat that almost choked him, and bent to run his lips over her breasts one last time, until she stirred awake and sighed sleepily and smiled at him and they shared a final lovemaking in an infinitely slow sweet rhythm that Loren wished would go on till the end of the world.

Afterward they held each other close and listened to the dawn music of the birds. "You're a miracle," he told her softly. "You've made me remember something I came close to forgetting."

"What's that?" she asked him.

"How good life can be." He hesitated, groping for the right words, until she began to look questioningly at him. "I wish," he began, "I wish I could ask you to chuck the agency and everything else and come stay with me." It was one of the hardest things he had ever made himself say.

"Thanks for not asking," she said gravely, and smiled at him in a way that told him she knew how much he wanted her, and was grateful.

"You have your own life and your own world that you made for yourself. I don't see you giving all that up just for a man." In his thoughts he begged and pleaded with her to do just that.

"I need to keep my world," she said. "This house, my plants, my work, my freedom. We couldn't survive as a twosome. We'd be at each other's throats in a month if we lived together full time. Because you need your world, too. The way we'll do it will be so much better—believe me. Every time we're together will be special. I want us always to be special for each other."

"If only our worlds were the same," he whispered.

The alarm clock hidden behind a nest of plants on the dresser top buzzed wasplike in the pale dawn, and they rose with a leaden reluctance and made their quiet preparations to leave. As they left the house, Loren saw a brown cottontail staring at them for a moment from the dewy grass before it wheeled and bounded into the woods. Val spun the Pontiac into the dirt track that girded the hill and they began the all too brief drive to the airport. Loren flicked on the radio, adjusted the dial to the frequency of the state university's all-night FM station. The music was filled with a shivering loveliness, and he turned up the volume so it filled the car.

"It's so sad and beautiful," Val said. "Do you know what it is?"

"Schönberg," he answered. *"Transfigured Night."* He knew he would never hear it again without thinking of her, and they listened to its haunting strains in silence. Val turned off the two-lane blacktop onto the eastbound expressway. The last leg of the trip. Their last few minutes. *You'll never see her again*, a voice inside him whispered.

"You'll watch out for Marisa?" he asked.

"I'm stopping at the hospital right after I drop you off. She'll start to live again, and I'll help all I can. You know, I've sort of adopted her as my kid sister ever since that night we almost spent at the house."

"I hate myself for what I had to do to her," he said. "Will you ask her please not to hate me?"

"I will. I'm going to fly out to California with her when she goes for those annual tests."

"Will you call and let me know the results as soon as they're in?"

"Of course." She swerved onto the access road to the airport, and when she had negotiated the sharp curve she took her right hand from the wheel and held it out to him. "We'll pull her through," she smiled.

"And each other?" he asked.

The Pontiac braked in the traveler-discharge zone, outside the entrance to the Transstate ticket counters. Loren hauled his suitcase out of the backseat, set it on the curb, and leaned into the car. She inclined her head and their lips touched in a good-bye kiss.

"Take care of yourself," she murmured.

"See you soon," he said, and wondered if he would.

He slammed the door and watched her car merge into the stream of city-bound traffic until it was an indistinguishable steel dot among a thousand others. He felt drained and pensive and half convinced that the weekend had been nothing but the dream of a very lonely man. He turned out of the dazzling sunlight and trudged through the high-ceilinged emptiness of the airport to the plane that would lift him home.